DAVY HARWOOD IN TRANSITION

2

TIJAN

Copyright © 2014 Tijan

Cover Design by Eileen Carey

1

I felt stupid.

There was no other way around it; no way could I justify my emotions. I just felt stupid.

Emily had hounded me for the last two months. She wanted me to talk to Mr. Moser. Finally, after she'd held my cell phone hostage, I'd had to succumb. So this is how I found myself back in the infamous building where I used to volunteer with the hotline.

I suppressed a shudder. I really hated working at the hotline and it wasn't because of the last time I'd been in this building. Although that moment had changed my life, the real reason was because I hated talking on the phone. Only a select few got on my 'I'll talk to you on the phone' list.

"Davy Harwood," Mr. Moser boomed as he entered his own office. If he was trying for intimidation, it would've worked three weeks ago.

Mr. Moser did not qualify for my phone list.

I waited until he rounded his desk and sat. His leather chair squeaked underneath his weight, but his two beady green eyes weren't amused and didn't care. His orange tie had flapped over his shoulder and it stayed there, caught between the wrinkles of his green buttoned dress shirt. His khaki pants hadn't fared any better. I wasn't a wrinkle-noticing person, but I wouldn't have been surprised to find out they'd been rolled up and stuffed in the back of a drawer for the last two years.

He lifted an eyebrow. "Do you have anything to say to explain your actions three weeks ago?"

I was more concerned about how his tie still hadn't moved off his shoulder. He looked like an idiot. Was I supposed to tell him?

"My actions, sir?"

"You broke protocol."

Oh, that. The night that had changed my life. If only Mr. Moser actually knew I was supposed to go up to that roof.

"Oh," was all I said. I tried to sound apologetic. I folded my hands and when I looked down, I even fiddled my thumbs.

"I'm not buying it, Davy." Mr. Moser was very smart.

"Buying what, sir?"

"You answered the phones after we'd already closed. You broke protocol. You identified the caller's location; chose to intervene without any communication with your supervisors, and then you had the balls to resign by sneaking a letter under my door. I am not buying your act right now, young lady."

He said 'balls'. I loved that.

"Yes, but." I really had no defense. I'd claimed what had happened was too traumatic for me to continue working with the hotline. Things *had* been traumatic, but he was right. I'd chosen the coward's way out so that I wouldn't get in trouble.

I eyed Mr. Moser up and down. The beady eyes had a glaze of anger in them. "I had hoped better of you, Davy."

Wow. Guilt.

He sounded disappointed as he took a deep breath. "Emily is an outstanding Listener. She spoke highly of you, but perhaps she was biased since you are roommates. Still, even Adam seemed to have taken a liking to you. He respected you, Davy."

I had so many corrections to Mr. Moser's rose-colored

perspective. One, Emily was an awful listener. She might be a wonderful Listener at the hotline where she was fulfilling a requirement for a social work class, but she didn't listen to anyone in real life. And two, Adam had taken more than a liking to me. Adam had asked me out on one date. The date had failed miserably and I didn't think being kidnapped had been the problem.

"What are you thinking?"

"Well, under the circumstances I do not support your actions. You broke protocol and you should have the correct discipline. Then there's the item of your resignation. I know that you didn't really mean to resign and because of Miss Whistworth's death, the hotline is in need of any willing volunteers so I've decided to look past your actions."

What? Did he mean . . . ? There was no way.

Mr. Moser beamed. "You can start tonight. Adam needed a replacement since he's taken two weeks of vacation. You can take his desk."

I had no words. I couldn't even feel my toes and I felt everything, literally.

Mr. Moser was already up and out of his office before any thoughts could form in my brain. And when I realized I'd been duped, I groaned and dropped my forehead on the desk. Not only did I feel stupid, but I felt like a complete moron.

When my phone vibrated, I snapped it open. "Yeah?"

"What's wrong, slick?" Kates drawled. I heard music in the background and that meant one thing.

"Are you at the Shoilster?"

I'd been there twice and hated both times. Plus, it was a vampire bar. I wasn't the biggest fan of vampires.

"Hell no." Kates barked out a laugh. "Listen, I'm going to be out of town for awhile. I need to figure some stuff out."

My childhood friend had been camped out in my dorm room for two weeks. The news was met with varying shades of relief and concern. I knew if Emily was the type to shout for joy, my roommate would've been screaming at the top of her lungs. I was growing tired of the tension between the two. Of course, Emily had reason for her dislike. Kates had been the one to kidnap us, but Emily wasn't privy to the fact that Kates had tried to save me from her psychotic vampire boyfriend later that evening.

"Where are you going?" She might be a vampire slayer, but she'd find trouble. She always did.

"I'm not going to find Lucan."

I relaxed, just a little.

Kates added, "There's something I gotta do on my own. Trust me, slick. You can talk to Blue if you want. She agrees that I should go and do this thing."

"I don't know, Kates." I wasn't too concerned about what my Empath Sponsor had to say since I'd been avoiding her ever since I found out she was connected to my immortal enemy.

"What don't you know? You don't even know what I'm doing."

I opened my mouth.

Kates beat me to it. "I'm not telling you because you'll just worry. I've talked about it with Blue. She agrees that I should go and do this. And she thinks I shouldn't tell you so I'm not. Besides, you have enough to worry about. You're the freaking Immortal, Davy. I have no idea why you're still in college, much less going to see that idiot supervisor."

I was going because Emily made me, but I couldn't say that to Kates. "I'm living a normal life because I'm going to be living for a long time. Are you sure that you're not looking for him?"

Kates' boyfriend had been a psychotic vampire, but he was human now. So that made him a psychotic human with all this knowledge about vampires and how to become a vampire again.

Kates was silent for a couple beats. "I don't really have to, remember?"

I flushed and shut my mouth. The reminder was duly noted. If anyone was going to find Lucan, it'd be Lucas Roane, his twin.

"Have you heard from him?" Kates asked, gently.

I rolled my eyes. I didn't need kid gloves. "I haven't seen Roane since he took off."

That had been ten days ago. And since he was hunting Lucan, I had no idea how long it would take. Lucan was human, but he thought as a vampire. Roane was not only a vampire, but a hunter. I was surprised he was still gone actually. Hunters had the skill and jurisdiction to hunt and kill any vampire that broke the decree that stated no humans were to be bitten or harmed by vampires. They were the elite of their race and Roane was one of the best.

Lucan didn't stand a chance.

"Your roommate has been buzzing around the room like she's on meth. You sure she's a sober saint? She ain't acting like it."

"Did you say something?" I was so thankful to Kates' attention deficit. No more questions about Roane.

"What? I've been perfect."

"Kates, no," I groaned.

"The chit needs to toughen up, seriously. I've gotta go, Davy. I'll be in touch. Don't worry about me. I love you. I'll be fine." And my childhood friend hung up.

I sighed and dropped my forehead on the desk. What else could I do?

"Okay, Miss Harwood, we've got you back in the program!" Mr. Moser broadcasted as he strode back into his office.

Yes, my life could get weirder. I lifted my forehead from the desk. "Mr. Moser, I hate phones. I'm not good on the phone. I'm not good at this work."

"Nonsense! You're perfect."

Meaning, he was desperate. Adam's two weeks to mourn his girlfriend of one day must've put the hotline in a dire spot.

"When is Adam coming back? Maybe I could fill in until he gets back?"

Mr. Moser squashed that idea as he slapped a file on his desk. "We'll figure that out when the time comes."

I winced from the slap and resigned myself to my fate. I had an entire six hour shift answering a phone in my future. You'd think I would've seen this coming since I was the Immortal and empathic, but I was lame.

2

"**N**o, Anne, you shouldn't let your roommate eat your peanut butter. If it bothers you, you could ask her not to eat your food. And don't feel foolish calling the hotline about this issue. Sometimes the smallest arguments stand for the bigger problems."

I was bored. Five hours and fifty-eight minutes had passed and my eyes gleamed in excited anticipation. Two more minutes and I could hang up the phone. No after hour calls would lure me back. I'd gone that route and see where I was—in the exact same spot! Never again. And I fought back a yawn.

"Davy."

I glanced over and saw Holly Brightner waving. She leaned across our desks and tapped my Dialogue Reassurances sheet.

I rolled my eyes and shooed her away. Still, I recited like a sympathetic moron, "Anne, the peanut butter probably stands for something more. What does the peanut butter really stand for?"

Shoot me, one more minute.

Holly gave me a smile in approval and I resisted the urge to kick her underneath our desks. Her pasty white skin and round brown eyes were enlarged underneath her glasses. When she blinked, I swear that her lips formed a small oval and the image of an owl flashed in my mind. And her brown hair was pulled back into a tight bun. If Holly had a spirit animal, it would've been an owl.

Thirty seconds and I no longer cared what Anne had to say. I'd used my empathic stuff on her and felt the normal jealousy and insecurities that so many girls suffered. The girl wasn't homicidal or suicidal. That was all I cared about.

Five seconds, four, three, two, one . . . I hung up and grabbed my bag.

Holly stopped me. "Davy, you didn't cite the proper farewell greeting. It's very important to the callers. You never know what they're going to do after they end their call with us."

"It was peanut butter, Holly. Peanut Butter."

"We have the guidelines for reasons. I know you've been away for a few weeks, but—"

My phone cut her off, which was a mixed blessing. I was ready to eviscerate Holly.

The phone rang again and I looked at the clock. My shift was over.

Rang a third time.

Holly's mouth fell open.

The fourth ring seemed demanding. I knew what I should do, but my shift was over and Mr. Moser had said no calls after hours. When Holly saw that I had no intention of answering the phone, she reached over and did it for me. She listened for a moment and then held the phone away from her ear. "They hung up."

I wouldn't have wanted to talk to Holly either.

My bladder was screaming for attention so I made a trip to the bathroom before heading home. When I popped back in for my bag, I saw that Holly had left. I'd never been so happy in my life.

Then my phone rang again.

Doom and gloom settled on my chest. I knew who was on the other side. Consider it my empathic curse.

It rang again. And again. And again.

I knew it wasn't going to stop.

I dropped my bag, plopped down in my chair, and picked up the phone.

"You're right. That other girl has the attitude of an owl. I don't blame you for being irritated."

Welcome to my world of craziness and the supernatural.

"So you're not in my head anymore, you're on the phone now?" For being my next Immortal guide, I wasn't sure I liked this new route of communication.

"I'm on the roof. Be there in five."

When I heard the dial tone, I stared in disbelief. Not only was I going to meet my next guide in person, she hung up on me. I hoped that she meant five minutes, not five seconds. Who could get up there in five seconds. That's right, me. I squared my shoulders, nervously smoothed out my jeans and pressed my yellow tee shirt tighter around me. I shouldn't be nervous. Whatever I looked like didn't matter. The Immortal was already inside of me, it's not like the guide was going to take one look at me and yank it out because I wasn't pretty.

Still. I wished that I had used my anti-frizzy curl gel when Emily had chucked it across the room at Kates. Kates had laughed. I had laughed. Emily had stormed off and my gel had been left underneath my bed.

I trekked out of the office and headed towards the roof door. As I started up the sparse stairs, I heard my footsteps echo all the way down to the basement. Each echo made my heart pound. By the time I got to the top, I felt like I was going to explode, like a bomb was ticking underneath my skin.

Then the door was open and I stepped onto the roof.

For a second, just a briefest of moments, I saw Talia on the edge again with her hair waving in the air and her white dress billowing from the wind. The same sad acceptance railed against me.

But I blinked and the image was gone. Instead, a different girl was there and this one was a doozy. Red eyes, black and blue sleek hair that fell past her waist, and ivory skin that any vampire would've marveled at. She stood at my height, a little slim with her hipbones sticking out, and a mark that covered the entire left side of her face.

I gulped and froze. There was no way I was getting closer.

She snorted, rolled her eyes, and her disgust blasted me.

I was safer where I was.

And then in a flash, she was in front of me.

Oh man, those red eyes looked like they were on fire. That mark was an intricate symbol of weaving lines. I wondered if it meant something and then cursed my foolishness. Of course, it meant something. Everything meant something in my insane world.

"You're right. It does mean something, but it's nothing for you to know. Not yet." She was smug as she leaned closer.

I gulped again. The red in her eyes that looked like fire was fire. An actual flame was in her eyes. It moved in perfect rhythm with the wind that swirled around us on the roof.

"What are you?"

She laughed. "I'm not a vampire."

"Are you a werewolf?"

"I'm not a werewolf either. And no, I'm not anything that your precious vampire is going to know either. I'm beyond his knowledge. I'm beyond a lot of people's knowledge."

"Are you a witch?"

The flame glowed brighter for a moment and then settled back down. "Very good, Davy, but as I said I'm not anything that your lover knows. He knows witches."

There was a riddle there, but I retorted, "He's not my lover."

"He was. He will be again. And he's much more than that." As she spoke, her head tilted to the side and smoke swirled in her eyes to cover up the flame.

"You're a fortune teller witch. You see the future, don't you?" I hated fortune tellers. And, even though I've never met a witch, I was pretty sure I didn't like them either.

She laughed again and the smoke vanished with a swift pop. Her fire was back. "I come from a witch, but I'm no longer a witch, Davy. I'm much, much more and I'm here to help you."

"Help me with what? The last one who told me that needed me to accept the Immortal inside of me. What's your agenda with me?" They always had agendas.

"The other one annoyed you, yes?"

She already knew the answer to that.

She had a smug smile on her face. "I'm here to piss you off."

I barked out a laugh. "It's not hard to do that—"

"No." she stepped closer. The fire tripled. Her jaw was so strong, so poignant, and it told me that she meant every word she uttered. "Stepianhas annoyed you. She was sent to you to help you accept who you were, but I know her methods. She used riddles. I will not use riddles. I will tell you bluntly and directly. And I will piss you off. I will not annoy you. I will make you angry. I will make you furious and if so be it, all the better."

Okay.

One, Stepianhas? Two, what did she mean by making me furious? And three, I was already pissed off.

"You're already doing a good job. Who the hell is Stepianhas?"

"My name is Saren. Stepianhas was your last messenger. I will not talk further about my sister. My job is to challenge you and help you learn your powers."

Stretching. Learning. Powers. All I could hear was a name. "There was a name to the annoying voice in my head? That was a person? That wasn't me?"

"She was sent to you as I have been sent to you. We are not of your world, but we will help guide you among this world."

"I thought you said no riddles." Dumbass.

She paused, thought, and then smiled sheepishly. "It seems that my attempt at directness has different meaning in your world than mine. I apologize. I believe that I should've said that I am not my sister. I am the one to teach you of your consequences."

"You suck at this job." I was tired of all this Immortal stuff. "Why now? It's been two weeks."

"Uh—" Her mouth gaped open for a second and I saw the thoughts fly through her head. Literally.

I watched them for a moment before it hit me what I was doing. The last one said something about *'She's the Immortal, she will know. She mustn't know. If she shall ever find out, it will be catastrophe. Remember the vampire. It's about the vampire.'*

It was like reading words on a page. "What do you mean when you say that it's about the vampire?"

Saren's eyes widened as she saw me inch closer, but she didn't say anything for a moment. "He is important."

"Why?" I wanted to intrude on her personal space. It worked on me, it should work on her.

She grinned and lifted a palm in the air. I felt the air being sucked into her hand and knew she was going to use it against me to shoot me away from her. To a normal person, this would've happened in an instant. To me, I felt the air swirl around me and halted the speed. When I saw her slam the force at me, I lifted my own hand and waved it. It bounced off me and shoved her backwards.

She hadn't fallen down, but it pushed her to the edge of the building. She lifted her head in shock. "You are better than I expected."

I lifted my chin. "You can't bully me. I'm the Immortal." As I said it, I knew I shouldn't have. Saren straightened upright and her eyes changed from a flame to a bonfire. The outline disappeared around her eyes. Flames leapt from outside of her eyes and smoldered the air. I smelled the burning in the air. Then she lifted a hand and flames shot at me.

"No!" I held up my hand. Something charged out of my body and met the flames full force. Instead of coming at me, they shot in the air. The entire sky lit up in flame. I looked up and thought three things. It looked pretty, there was no way that was inconspicuous, and holy crap! Sirens sounded in the distance and I looked over. Saren was gone.

What a surprise.

I turned towards the exit and wished I knew how to transport myself by snapping my fingers. Some Immortal perks still needed to be learned. When I got to the street, I ducked into an alley as the fire truck braked in front.

I cut across the middle of the campus and was almost to my dorm when I felt the air change. The hairs on my back stood up. There was a shift in the atmosphere. It was like if I'd been walking with a blanket on me and someone ripped it off me. I knew someone was there and I was out in the open. When I heard a slight growl, I reacted without thinking and twisted my body around. I bent backwards.

Bennett leapt at me. His eyes were shocked as he went over me. His dirty blonde locks had grown longer since I'd seen him last, but he was dressed in a black leather vest and jeans. His boots clipped my chin and I fell to the ground.

"Ouch!" I snapped up and held my chin. I felt blood against my fingers. "What'd you do that for?"

His eye gleamed with a purple shine. His chest heaved up and down and his hands fisted together as he stood there. "You turned him." Then he charged and caught me. With my back against his chest, he lowered his head to my neck and growled. "Turn him back."

"Bennett, stop that!"

He clamped me tighter against him and his teeth touched my skin. They didn't break the skin or draw blood, but he wanted me to know he could. I was starting to wonder how demented he'd become. Didn't he remember the last time a vampire drank from me? "Bennett, you will become a human if you drink from me."

"You're the Immortal. You can turn him back."

"Turn who?" Then it clicked in place. "You want me to turn Lucan? Are you crazy? I don't even know where he is or if I can do that."

"You're the Immortal. You can do anything."

A part of me puffed up in pride. I was the Immortal. Of course, I could do anything. Then reality set in. "Bennett, I turned into the Immortal two weeks ago. I wouldn't know how to do it."

"Think it and it happens!" he growled and lifted me in the air.

"Oh—" Not good. My feet dangled for a second before he slammed me back down. This time I fell all the way to the ground and laid there. Bennett was on top as he whispered in my ear, "You will change him or I will hurt you."

Then the air changed again. Something was coming and they were coming fast. Before I could look, Bennett was off me. I scrambled up in time to see Roane throw Bennett into the building across the yard. The brick cracked from the force. Before Bennett could fall to the ground, he caught himself and jumped from the building at him.

I sat there with my mouth open as I watched Roane stand in place with his shoulders ready. His knees didn't look like they moved when he caught Bennett, twisted, and slammed him on the ground. Instead of catching his throat to hold him in place as I expected, he impaled him to the ground and flicked a lighter on him. Bennett's eyes got wide and he gasped. He started to kick, trying to scramble away, but whatever Roane had impaled him with kept him in place. Before the lighter hit his chest, Roane swept a hand around me and lifted me in the air. I felt myself being carried away, but I tried to watch Bennett. Roane tucked my head into his shoulder. He wouldn't let me look. When he moved past a building, I saw the air light up.

"Block him. Block him now."

I hadn't realized that I'd been trying to feel him when I closed my eyes and did it. Not a second later, Bennett's screams filled the air. I clasped onto Roane tighter and wound my legs around his waist. No matter the circumstances, it was good to feel him again, maybe too good.

3

Roane carried me to the roof of a building. When he set me back on my feet, he went to the edge and looked down. A red glow lit the sky from where Bennett had been and I grabbed his hand to help steady myself. My knees were shaking so loudly, I was surprised Roane didn't hush them.

"I want to see who comes." Roane gripped my hand.

Instead of Bennett, a fire burned in his place. "His body's gone?" There was a citrus smell in the air that mixed with the fire. Both odors made my stomach churn.

A small smile flashed over his face, but it was gone quickly. His face contrasted in a myriad of shadows from the glow. The tops of his cheekbones and nose were highlighted, but everything else was dark. It gave him a supernatural look, but then again, he was a vampire.

"It burned faster than normal. He drank from someone who'd overdosed on heroin. It speeds everything up."

"That explains the purple eyes." I was about to ask more when Roane touched my shoulder and nodded at the quad below. I didn't see anything, but he spoke in my head, *Let the Immortal see.*

Everything switched.

The fire felt like it was all around me and Roane's inner tension lashed at me like a whip. I could taste the heroin from the human's blood in Bennett. That was the citrusy feel in the air. Wrinkling my nose, I started to share how weird that was, but closed my mouth as I sensed movement from all corners of the quad. They were vampires. They moved at a slow synchronized pace and made sure no one could see them. With my human eye, I wouldn't have. But as the Immortal, I knew what they thought and knew their arrogance. As I closed my eyes, I felt into them. They were used to doing what they wanted. They thought they were above everyone else, including other vampires.

"*Who are they?*"

Roane gripped my hand and shook his head.

And below us, they froze as one entity. Their black forms, masked from the shadows, melted backwards. They were gone in the next instant.

He expelled a deep breath.

I knew I messed up, but I had no idea how.

"You twitched when you asked me that. Your hand twitched."

"They could see that?"

"They felt it." He sounded disappointed.

"They felt my hand twitch, but they didn't know we were here? How's that possible?"

"They didn't know we were here because as they move in, they blanket their surroundings."

"We're above them."

"Doesn't matter." Roane sat on the edge. He dropped his head in his hands. "They have sonar that sends pulses all around them. They map the ground. One disturbance or change in their 'map' and they go away. It could be as little as a bird or a rock that fell. One movement, a hand twitch, and they leave."

Talk about anal. "They're scared of a bird?"

"They aren't scared. They're powerful, stronger than the hunters' bloodline."

"They're vampires." No one was stronger than the hunters.

"They're more. They're a different species of vampires."

"You guys have species?!"

Roane chuckled and found my hand with his. "Each vampire is born from the bloodline of the vamp that turned him or her, but those guys are different. They were born as vampires. There's magic in their blood that lets them reproduce. They give birth just like humans."

"Baby vamps." Holy crap.

"Baby vampires." He nodded.

"How do they do their sonar stuff?"

"No one knows. They stick to their own. We don't even know if they follow the decree. We know about them only because Lucan found a baby girl one time. He had a thing for anything unusual. My brother was obsessed with anything more powerful than us. It's why we found Talia when she was so little."

Every hair on my body stood upright. I shuddered. "How did you know they'd be here tonight?"

"I didn't. I knew Bennett was obsessed with having you change Lucan."

"You think Bennett knew where Lucan is?"

He shook his head. "I know he didn't, but he knew where you were. I think Lucan found that girl and her line has taken him in. If I were him, I'd have them find you. You're an unknown to him now. He thought he knew everything about the Immortal, but he now knows that he doesn't. He didn't take your power. You made him human instead. That's never been in the lore. You're going to become his new obsession now."

And that was alarming on a whole other level. "They were following him to find me?"

He nodded and clenched his jaw.

My eyes got wide. "That's why you killed Bennett, isn't it?"

"As much as I'd love to follow them back, I won't risk you."

"How would you be able to follow them? It sounds like they're living ghosts to the vampire community."

Roane looked at me and tilted my head up. His hand cupped the side of my face and his thumb caressed my cheek. "I'd follow you, not them."

There went my heart. It stopped its pitter pattering.

"I could follow you anywhere."

Now it took off like a horse race.

His hand dropped and he stood up. "I drank from you before you fully became the Immortal. I can smell you from a continent away."

My shoulders slumped down. The pitter patter race ground to a halt. "You know just what to say to a girl."

"It's the aroma. Your blood overwhelms me at times."

My nose wrinkled. "So I'm smelly?"

He looked out over the quad and murmured, "Yes. Exactly." Then he abruptly looked down. "No, not in a bad way. It's a good way. We were lovers. It's an intimate aroma, like perfume."

"Were?"

Roane laughed and took my hand. He pulled me to my feet and then hugged me tightly. "We will be again. I'm hoping." His eyes held mine captive and the Derby race started once more.

"I'd like that too."

He rested his forehead against mine. "Bennett is dead."

"Yeah. And the fire is gone already." The burning smell and glow had both vanished.

"Don't you want to check on your roommate?"

"What? Why?" Talk about curveballs.

"He nipped from her. That means she was under his spell. Now he's dead—"

"I can't believe I didn't think of that already. She's going to be flipping out. She thought she was in love with him." I surged upright and then stopped to glower. I used to hate vampires.

Roane and a few others had redeemed them in my eyes, but now I remembered why I hated them so much. Their stupid little spells they could put on humans. "I have to get home right now. The abrupt break will be sending her off the deep end."

Roane nodded and kissed my forehead. "I'll be at the Alexander tonight."

"Okay. I'll come by after she's calmed down."

Roane walked me back to my dorm and left with one last kiss to my forehead. I watched him leave and sighed. I was glowing. How could I not? I just hoped my roommate wouldn't notice.

When I walked into my room, Emily took one look and threw a book at me. I ducked, but the second one hit my chin. "Ouch!"

"What? Did you just see Adam? You're happy!" Her chest heaved up and down. She was seething. Then she twisted her hands in her hair and pulled at it. "I'm going crazy, Davy! I don't know what's wrong with me."

I did, but I wasn't going to tell her. "Do you have your period?"

"I just had it."

"There's a full moon tonight. That makes people go crazy."

She stopped pulling her hair and her hands dropped against her legs. "Really?"

I shrugged in my head. "Sure. Unless you really are going crazy."

"No, no. It must be the full moon. It has to be. It came out of nowhere."

"What does it feel like?"

"Like my reason for living just died. I have no purpose anymore. I should kill myself."

She answered so quickly, my eyes popped out. "Okay. You shouldn't work at the hotline until this is gone."

"Why?" she asked with a blank face.

"Because." You're crazy. "Trust me. It's the full moon effect. You're not normal right now."

"Will this go away?" Desperation flashed over her face and her hands started to go for her hair again.

I rushed forward and caught her hands. "It will go away. Promise."

"How long does the full moon last?" Her voice hitched on a hysterical note.

"There's the pre moon stage and the post moon stage. Plus, you have the half moon and partial moon. I'm sure all of that makes it go longer."

"Oh." She sounded dejected as she sat on the couch. "What am I supposed to do? I felt like I lost my husband, like he was brutally murdered and slowly ripped to pieces."

"Uh." I saw some wine coolers in the corner and grabbed them. "Drink."

She pushed it away. "That won't help. It'll make it worse."

"Okay." Then I sat beside her. "What can I do to help you?"

"I don't know. Take my pain away."

Oh no. I swallowed tightly. I knew Emily wasn't serious. She didn't know I was empathic and her request was an actual possibility, but I didn't know if I wanted that madness in me. "How about a sleeping pill? You'll sleep right through it and wake up refreshed for a month?"

I settled for a second best option.

"I don't feel like that's a healthy thing to do. I feel like I should go through this. I should feel this torment."

"You're crazy. Why would you want to do that? This isn't your fault. You're feeling this because of—" I clamped my mouth shut. "Because of the moon."

"Yeah."

I watched Emily and saw she was determined to feel this thing through. Sometimes she amazed me and other times she made my head spin around. Who would want to feel this type of madness? Emily would.

She hugged a blanket around her. Tears coursed down her

cheeks and she sneezed a few times. I handed over a tissue box. "You're determined to stay awake for this?"

"Yes." She sounded determined, but I heard a waver in her voice.

It was all the permission I needed. "I'll get you some juice."

She looked at me with grateful tears in those eyes. "I'd appreciate it so much. Thank you, Davy."

I grabbed one of the cups from our dirty bin and went to the door to wash it. Emily didn't spare me a look as she huddled into the couch and I grabbed my purse. When I went to the bathroom, I cleaned the cup and pulled out some sleeping pills Kates gave me awhile ago.

I dumped three in Emily's drink and stirred it so the powder dissolved. And when I handed over the juice to her trusting hands, I felt no guilt. I was drugging my roommate out of love. If I left her alone with the madness that came when a love bite was broken, she would have tried to commit suicide. I'd seen it before and I wasn't going to let Emily do something stupid like that. "Drink all of it. Your body needs those vitamins."

She guzzled it down and wiped at her chin. "Thanks, Davy. You're the best roommate."

The jury's out on that one. I popped in a movie, grabbed my blanket, and settled beside her. Emily's eyes kept watering through the movie until I reached over and grabbed her hand. She would quiet right away and I allowed myself to pull some of that pain out of her. I felt the madness trying to get through my barrier, lashing at me, snarling, but I kept it at bay. Emily's pain was pushed underneath the craziness and it streamed into me like a calm river. If I hadn't been the Immortal, I couldn't have separated the threads. An hour later, I opened my eyes and saw that she'd fallen asleep with both hands clenched on mine. There was a feel of desperation in her body.

When my eyelids started to feel heavy and drop, I realized some of the sleeping pills must've gotten into my system too.

Roane was at the Alexander and I wanted to see him, but my eyelids refused to stay open. After five minutes, I gave up the fight and moved to my bed. It wasn't long until I found myself dreaming of vampires with rabid purple eyes. And then a voice screamed in my head, "Davy! Wake up!"

I shot upright and banged my head on Emily's bunk. I rubbed my head, expecting to see someone in my room. There was no one and I started to lie back down.

"Get up! Get up! You're needed at the Alexander NOW!"

Alexander. Roane. Crap.

4

When I got to the Alexander, I wasn't surprised to find it filled to the maximum. It had always been the hotspot for the showy and shallow. And those were just the humans. The basement was filled as well, but with vampires.

"Davina."

I turned and saw Gregory. He stood by the bar with a drink in hand. His face was stiff and his thick square-like jaw seemed cemented in place.

"Hi, Gregory." I held a hand out and the blond Viking vampire took it for a handshake. He had never warmed up to me, but as one of Roane's loyal followers he was forced to be nice. He smiled thinly and offered his drink. "Lucas is in his office. I'll take you there."

As I followed him into a narrow back hallway, I was startled to hear Roane's given name. I'd grown so comfortable thinking of him as his bloodline's name that I'd forgotten it wasn't his first name. As we continued through a few more hallways, I was surprised how Gregory fit through them. Then, at the end of one, he knocked on a black door. I would've walked past it and not known it was there, but it opened to Roane's office. He sat behind

a massive mahogany desk. While the entrance was plain, everything inside the office was not. The desk was large enough for a
king to lie on. Leather couches and chairs sat beside it while a
painting was mounted on the wall. I watched the smiling woman
in the painting and half expected her to speak to me. She looked
too life-like.

Roane lifted his head and his coal eyes flickered when he
stood. "Davy. You came. Thank you, Gregory."

"Lucas."

Roane gestured towards a chair when the blonde giant left. "I
need a few minutes to finish some paperwork."

"So I better get comfortable, huh?" I looked at the door as I
sat down. "For being Hulk Hogan, he's quiet like a ghost. It's
scary."

"He's a vampire."

"Again. Scary."

Roane shifted some papers and piled them on a corner of his
desk. "Vampires can't hurt you anymore. You can get that chip off
your shoulder you have against us."

I shuddered in my chair. "And yet, they keep coming
after me."

"Because some of us are dumb." Then he smirked. "We're like
humans in that way."

"Was that a joke?" I arched an eyebrow. "Where's this new
Roane come from? I thought everything was serious, the world is
ending, and the Immortal needs to be protected."

"Maybe this is the real me? Maybe I'm a funny vampire
underneath everything?" His hands paused as they shifted some
papers into a folder. Then they continued and a smile flittered
over his face. It was gone in the next instant.

I narrowed my eyes as I watched him. He might be joking
about being funny, but I'd felt inside of him. He was all resolve,
determination, and death bended beneath him. Then I smiled.
"You've missed me."

His hands paused again and gripped the folder before he closed it and lifted his head. His eyes sparkled.

I was across the desk in an instant and in his arms. He gripped me tight as I settled on his lap, straddling him in the leather chair. I clasped behind his back and breathed him in. His neck trembled slightly and then I pressed a kiss against it. He groaned and stood up with his hands underneath my legs. He held me tight against him and lifted to carry me to a nearby couch. As he laid me down, he held himself above me and studied me. His eyes were intense. Something shifted in them when he traced my face with a finger, down my cheek, around my lips, and back up the other cheek to brush some hair from my forehead. It was a loving touch and my eyes started to water as I felt the tenderness.

"What's wrong?" he asked in a gentle voice.

I tugged him down on top of me and hugged him with all my might.

"You missed me too." His voice was muffled against my neck. It teased my skin and shivers broke out over my body. I felt him smile as he added, "A lot."

It was more than that. Something in me would always yearn for Roane. When I saw him again, that something woke up. It was as if I'd been asleep till he got back and now he was back, everything else woke up too. Did he feel the same? The old question burned in the back of my head, or did he feel it for Talia?

Roane pulled away and sat up. "What's wrong?"

"Talia." I didn't hesitate. I didn't see why I should.

Roane shut down. His eyes had been open and alive. "What about her?"

"You loved her. She held the Immortal thread before me. I can't help but feel that there's a part of her inside of me and that's who you want." Most girls wouldn't have managed the first words, but I was more now.

Roane stood and crossed to a bar. After he poured himself a

drink, he offered me one. I shook my head, suddenly cold. Roane moved back to lean against his desk as he regarded me. His eyes were dark. "I loved Talia. I won't deny that."

There it was. I didn't flinch.

Roane added, "I've never lied about that. I did love Talia, but I don't love her anymore."

My eyes shot to his.

"I don't know what you're really asking me, but I can guess. It's not the right time for that, but what I can tell you is that what's between us is between us. You may think Talia is a part of you, but she's not. There's nothing in you from her. She held the Immortal thread inside of her and gave it to you. You've taken the thread and you've become the Immortal. If anything, it should've been that Talia held something of you inside her when I loved her." He studied me when he was finished and then sipped his drink. His throat swallowed in a slow motion.

I gulped. When those eyes were focused on me and intense, when he said words like that, I had to grip the couch to keep myself from launching at him. I wanted to beg him to take me then and there, but I didn't. Then I fought to calm my trembling voice. "Okay."

Roane flashed a smile. "Okay? That's it?"

Someone knocked on the door at that moment. Roane turned his back to me when it opened and I expelled a ragged breath. I tried moving off the couch, but my legs were jelly.

Then Gregory spoke from the doorway, "We have an impending."

Roane didn't move at all, but everything changed; danger emanated from him. An alarm bell went off in my stomach and my jelly legs were suddenly sturdy as stone. I stood, but stayed by the couch. I wanted to go to his side, but Roane wasn't a vampire who enjoyed the comforting damsel. When he nodded with his jaw clenched, Gregory looked at me and then closed the door behind him. He said it all in that one glance. Something was wrong and Roane wasn't telling me any of it.

"What's going on?"

He took my arm and led me to the door. "It's time for you to go."

Hello, I thought we were going to have sex. Now I was really alarmed. "What was that about? Gregory looked at me before he left. He felt bad about something. What is it?"

I dug in my heels and looked directly at him. He had his shields up, he always had them up, but I went through them like vapor. His manner had been a show. He'd been flirting and forcing himself to feel relaxed, but it was the opposite. He had lied about Talia. He still loved her, but there was more. Something had gone wrong with the Roane Council and his insides were on edge, murderous edge, because of it. I slipped out and saw he hadn't a clue that I'd been there.

"You never told me about the council meeting. What happened there?"

His eyes flared in anger. "You stay out of me."

"Then tell me the truth. Tell me what's going on."

"You need to leave." He pushed me towards the door, but stopped to grab two daggers and a 9mm. He strapped a sword over his back and when he turned back to me, I didn't recognize the hunter who stood there. I'd seen him in fighting mode, but this was different. There was no emotion, just business. That business was killing.

When he took my arm again, my head snapped back and I felt the Immortal rush through me. She coursed through my arms, toes, veins, and into my eyes. I knew Roane saw my white eyes when he cursed.

"Do you know?" he asked.

I closed my eyes and lifted into the air. The room swirled around me. Everything moved around me as if I was in the eye of a tornado and then I looked out and saw who approached.

They were a group of vampires. All were heavily armed with weapons, similar swords as the one Roane wore. Wren was with them, but two large Goliath vampires held her arms. Her wrists were bound in greenery. Her eyes were strained and teeth clenched against the pain. I didn't know what was going on, but I knew what side I stood with. Before the thought entered my mind, I was already behind Wren and the two giant guards.

Everyone was in a time warp so no one saw me when I took a knife from one of the guards and cut through Wren's bandages. Her shoulders lifted up as if refreshed. The pain left her and she sprang into action. I pulled back from the group, watching her take the sword from one of them and plunging it into their heart. As they fell, she whirled around and decapitated both of them in one movement. Then she landed on her feet, primed for attack as the rest of the group turned in shock. Only a few reacted. The rest paused a second to wonder how she got free. They paused too long.

Roane was already on them. Wren saw him fighting and a crooked smirk flashed over her face before she began fighting with renewed energy. She fought freely without pausing as she sliced and diced through the vampires. Roane killed the same way. He cut down every vampire in his trail, but gave no feeling or thought to any of them. When they were both done, each stood in the middle of the wreckage and looked at the other. Wren smiled shakily as her body trembled in excitement. Her coral eyes looked wild, hyper. Roane felt nothing. There was no emotion in his eyes. Then he turned towards me and I vanished.

I was waiting in his office when they arrived a few minutes later. Wren burst through the door and her adrenalin blasted against me. She was on a high, but when her eyes caught sight of me all that energy faded. It left her depleted and she snarled, "You."

"Me."

She looked the same. I hadn't noticed when she'd been held

captive, but now her attention was focused on me. It was intimidating, or should've been, as I studied her in turn. She wore the same leather corset with silver snappings and leather boots. Her eyes snapped in disgust when she felt my appraisal and she flipped those long auburn curls over her shoulders to purse her lips together. "Like what you see?"

"You still look like a hooker." Disdain oozed from my pores.

She drew to her full height and took a menacing step towards me. That's when Roane passed around her to his desk and murmured underneath his breath, "She can make you human."

She stopped, snarled again, and swept out of the room. The door slammed shut with enough force to shatter glass.

Then I looked up and met Roane's gaze. Any smart comment I might've made about Wren's departure died in my throat.

His eyes snapped at me. "You want to tell me what you were doing out there when we're still trying to keep your identity a secret?!"

5

"What are you talking about?"
"The Elders know that the Immortal is alive, but they don't know your name. Anyone who knows it's you is either loyal to me or dead."

"Except Lucan and Kates."

"Yeah," he sighed. "Except those two, but Lucan won't say anything. He'll want to keep that information to himself. And Kates is loyal to you, right? She is, right?"

"Yeah." I gulped. "She's loyal to me." And now she'd left for some reason that she wouldn't tell me. He didn't need to know that bit.

"You need to stay away from me."

"What?" I cried out. "You told me to come here tonight. You told me that you wanted to see me and now you're telling me to stay away?!"

Roane looked resigned. "I have to protect you and one way I can do that is if you have no connection to me. They might know the Immortal is here—"

"Who?!"

"Vampires, Davy! All the vampires." He sat now as if surrendering. "The secret's out. Everyone knows the Immortal exists and she's here. I tried to tell the Elders that you left, but they must not have bought it. They know you're here. They might not know who you are, but they know the Immortal is here."

"What does this mean for me?"

He shrugged. "I have no idea, but it's not good for you. My guess is that they'll try to kill you first. When they realize that won't work, they'll capture you and they'll figure something else out. They aren't friendly, Davy. They're scared of you and vampires don't handle fear very well. Everything else is supposed to be afraid of us, not the other way around."

"They can't kill me. Can they?"

"I don't know. Do you even know?"

"No." I looked away. Saren hadn't been helpful with any information. Riddles. Everything was riddles. "So I go and do the normal thing that you wanted me to do before?"

"I don't see any other way right now." Roane's hand rested on the desk and then he clenched it into a fist. "It'd be good if you go. I'm sorry."

With a knot in my throat, I nodded. "When will I see you again?" He looked up and sorrow flashed for a moment before it was replaced with regret. Guilt came next. I knew he wasn't going to answer me so I said, "I know you still love Talia. I saw that inside of you."

He tried to smile, but failed. "I hate that I can't keep a secret from you."

"Trust me. I wished I didn't know half the stuff I do." Then I turned and started to leave. As I reached the door, Roane stopped me.

"Davy."

I turned and my heart jumped.

He smiled, but it was haunted. "Gregory can drive you back. After that you need to stay away from me."

My heart fell back in place. "Okay."

The Viking vampire was silent as he took me to my dorm. Roane had sent me away. He didn't want to see me anymore. I knew the reason behind it, but it stung. A part of me, the little girl inside of me wanted to fall into his arms and live happily ever after. The rest of me knew better.

"We're here," Gregory said as he put the car into park.

As I was about to get out of the car, I reached over and grabbed his arm. Gregory didn't react. He made no movement, but I knew he was guarded against me. That's when I realized the sound of his little girl's laugh had been tickling my empathic abilities since I'd gotten in the car. I just hadn't noticed it till then.

The laugh came from his unconscious and my empathic sense had reached for it. I met his gaze. "I will turn your daughter back. She can be yours again."

Something shifted inside of him and he jerked his head in a nod. "Thank you."

I nodded back and climbed out.

"Davy," he called after me. I looked over my shoulder. "Please don't make a promise like that unless you can fulfill it."

"I have no doubt that no matter what Roane promises, there's going to be another war. I'll be at the center of it and I will meet your daughter. I will turn her human again."

He smiled, shaken.

Then reality clicked with me. "Don't tell Roane I said any of that."

He shook his head. "He'd advise me not to believe you. For some reason, I do."

I wasn't sure how old Gregory was, but he looked old for a vampire. And when he smiled, I wondered when he had last smiled. His face looked cracked until the smile disappeared. Then all the cracks fell back in place and it was smooth again.

"Okay." I waved goodbye before I headed back inside. When I got to my floor, I saw a girl standing outside my room with her nose pressed against the door.

And I thought I was coming back into the world of normal. "Hey, what are you doing?"

She turned with wide eyes. She was a petite girl with reddish hair that was separated into two braids. They hung over her shoulders and touched the suspenders of her blue jumpsuit.

"Who are you?"

"Um." She bit her lip and looked back at the door. Then she looked at me again. Panic filled her eyes and she bolted. A door slammed shut down the hallway almost as soon as I blinked.

"I don't see that every day either." I took a deep breath and opened my door. The vision of Emily tangled in a ball of blankets on the floor greeted me. She snored happily and some drool trailed to the floor. I checked the clock and realized that I'd need to put another dose of sleeping pills in her juice.

As I went to the bathroom to mix the concoction in the glass, I heard someone behind me.

"What's wrong with her?"

The weirdo stood in the bathroom doorway. She blocked me from the hallway." I can tell something's wrong with her. What is it?"

I stared at her and then started giggling. When I couldn't stop, I realized something was making me laugh and I looked at her with tears in my eyes. "It's you. You're doing this to me."

"Doing what?" She frowned.

"You're tickling me! What are you? You're a werewolf!" It was their constant sniffing. They sniffed out everything in the air, even if they didn't know they were doing it. It was as natural to them as breathing.

Her eyes bulged out. "I smell vampire on you, but you're not. What are you?"

I bent over, giggling.

"What can I do? This has never happened before." She looked panicked as more giggles erupted from me.

"It's because—" I couldn't even talk.

"Should I leave?"

Still giggling, I nodded with tears running down my face. The door slammed shut and almost immediately the laughing fit lessened so I was able to stand upright. I breathed out and wiped the tears from my eyes.

"Are you better now?" she called from the hallway.

"Yeah," I called back. "How far down the hallway are you?"

"A few doors away. I'm sorry?"

"That's okay. It's not really your fault."

"I feel ridiculous talking like this. What's your phone number?" Her voice trembled.

My phone? I felt in my pockets and tried to remember the last time I had used my cell phone. "My phone's in my room. Leave your number on my board. I'll call you when I can. I have to check on Emily first."

"Okay. I'll do that."

When my eyes stopped tearing up, I finished mixing the sleeping pills with some orange juice and headed back to my room. There was no werewolf lingering in the hallway and when I got inside, I woke Emily enough until she drank the juice. As soon as she was done, she groaned and rolled over. Snores came from her soon after.

I heard a knock on my door and a piece of paper slid underneath. *'My name is Pippa. The number is 555—. Call me!'*

I didn't recognize the area code. I frowned at the paper.

"Are you going to call me?" she asked through the door.

"My roommate's fine. I don't have to explain anything to you."

"What? Something's wrong with her. I need to know."

"No, you don't. I'm not hurting her. I'm helping her. She'll be as good as new in two days. You can ask her yourself then."

Good luck getting a real answer.

"What? Come on. Please! I need to know." Her voice hitched on a note, like she was about to cry.

An empath could only deal with so much. I sighed and

crossed to the door. I pressed against it and whispered, "I am not trying to be mean. I just can't do this right now. Leave, please?"

She whimpered on the other side. "I have to know."

"If you don't leave, I will have this building streaming with vampires. I know your kind doesn't like them." As far as threats went, I thought it was a solid one.

She was silent for awhile. "I have to know what's wrong with your roommate. If she doesn't get better in two days, I'll call my pack."

I had no doubt she would. "This isn't your business."

Again, she was quiet for a little bit. "My inner wolf is telling me otherwise."

Oh—ugh! I was tired of everything supernatural. "Whatever. Just go away."

I felt her leave. I didn't feel the slight tickling anymore, but I knew she'd be back. Anything supernatural always came back. They were always ominous. Then I watched Emily snore into the floor.

Nope. Nothing supernatural with her.

She wouldn't wake again for a long time, so I fell into my bed. At last.

Halfway through my first dream, a bloodcurdling scream woke me up. I bolted upright in bed and saw Emily in the middle of the room. She was pulling at her hair. Her hands had formed fists and were entangled in her hair. "AHHHHH!"

"Hey, hey!" I tried to soothe her. "It's okay."

"It's not okay! What's wrong with me?" Tears cascaded down her face and she looked at me. The pain was so powerful, it staggered me back. "What's wrong with me, Davy? I am going crazy, aren't I?"

"No, no you aren't." I hugged her close and made soothing sounds. I rocked her back and forth.

"Do something. Make this stop. I can't handle it anymore," she sobbed into my chest.

I closed my eyes and held her tighter. Then I took a deep breath because I already knew what I was going to do. God help me, I went inside of her. I didn't control it like I had before. I didn't have the time. I went all in and choked on the emotions. It felt as if a bucket of vipers had been let loose. They were everywhere. Slithering. Biting. Angry.

Once I managed to stand my ground in the midst of the madness, I reached out and grabbed one of the emotions. It was hopeless. I gathered it to me and reached for another. I kept going until I had enough clasped to me that she could calm down. I wasn't sure how long this had taken, but then I enveloped the emotions into me. They passed the barrier of our bodies and I took them into me.

As they bounced around inside of me, I opened my eyes and saw that Emily had calmed. I managed out, strained, "Go to the bathroom and come back to bed."

Emily nodded, still trembling. I'd taken what I could, but there was still Bennett's madness inside of her. When the door opened, I wasn't shocked to see Pippa there with concerned eyes. She looked from Emily to me and her eyes widened. She knew what I'd done.

They had never met, but Pippa extended an arm to Emily and she went to her. The two walked together.

I knew it wouldn't be long until they came back and I tried to hurry and get another potion of sleeping pills ready for Emily. My hands were shaking, but I only spilled a little bit before the door opened. Emily came in. She was calmer than when she had left.

I looked at Pippa and saw she must've done the same thing I did. I had no idea wolves could do that, but it didn't matter at that moment. I held out the glass to Emily. "Drink!"

She did and it wasn't long before her eyelids started to droop. When she curled into her bed, I looked at Pippa who had remained in the hallway. She watched me in sympathy.

"What are you?" she asked.

I jerked a shoulder up. It looked more like a twitch. "Does it matter? How'd you help her?"

"I did what you did. Wolves can go inside of other wolves. We can take their pain too."

I frowned as I still twitched. "Emily's not a wolf."

"Her soul is entwined with one."

"What does that mean?"

She gave me a sad smile. "You'll see."

Then she left and I closed the door. As I slumped on my bed, I shook my head. That was weird, even for me.

6

The next few days were the same. I went to class, the hotline, and checked on Emily as I could. At first I'd been reluctant, but Pippa won me over. Her wolf's sniffing didn't tickle me as much and she wanted to help with Emily. She made a good argument. There was something unnatural about Emily's willingness to go to Pippa that night. I wasn't sure what to believe about the wolf thing, but I couldn't sense any bad intentions from Pippa. So Emily found herself with one more friend when she finally sat up three days later, weaned from Bennett's love spell.

"Who is she?" Emily asked an hour later after Pippa had come with coffee and left again. "She lives on our floor? I've never noticed her before and I notice everything."

Well, not everything.

I shrugged and reached for a coffee. "I don't know. She likes you."

Emily went still at my words. "What do you mean?"

I frowned at her. "I don't mean that!"

"Oh." She relaxed in her seat.

"I just meant, I don't know. She likes you. I think she needs friends and can tell you're one of the good ones." I hurried towards the door since I was late for the stupid empath meeting that Blue kept making me promise to go to.

"Davy." Emily halted me when my hand reached for the handle. I glanced back and she smiled. "You're one of those too."

Awkward. "Sure. Have fun with your new girlfriend!"

"She's not my girlfriend," Emily shouted after me as I rushed down the hallway.

I couldn't stop my grin, but it vanished as Pippa came out of the bathroom. Judging by the look on her face, she'd heard Emily's comment. "Girlfriend?"

I slammed on my brakes, right in front of her, and spoke in my mind, *'If you hurt her, I will hurt you and trust me, I can. If you tell her anything about this, I will come after you and your whole pack. I don't need a slew of vampires. I can do a whole lotta damage by myself.'*

Pippa's eyes widened when she heard my voice. *'You don't know what you just did. The Mother Wolf knows about you now.'* Then she spoke, "How can you do that? What are you?"

A part of me regretted my impulse, but I covered it up and gave her a smug smile. "I think you should be asking 'who am I?' Don't say anything to Emily."

Pippa turned and watched when I started to inch towards the hallway's door. "It's not for me to say anything. She's linked to another wolf. It's his place to say it."

I paused in the doorway. "Good then." Was it? As I turned and left, I knew I needed to learn as much as I could about werewolves. I knew they repressed their emotions, but they were different from vampires, a lot different.

I'd gotten as far as my car before my skin started to tingle. Talk about annoying and then everything rushed at me. I'd been about to open my car door when the Immortal took over. Everything flew around me and I was lifted into the air. My eyes narrowed as I looked out and saw another approaching vampire group. There was no captured Wren with them and these vampires didn't seem bent on war. I hoped not. Then I closed my eyes and found myself in Roane's office. Everything still circled around me, but I saw him and Wren at his desk. Their voices were muffled when I heard her say, "—for her. Why can't we let that happen?"

Roane straightened. "If you're loyal to me, you're loyal to my decisions. Are you not, Wren?"

She stepped away from the desk and sighed with her head bent. "You know I am. You know what I gave up."

Roane narrowed his eyes. "Then trust me."

Gregory swept through the door in that moment. "They're here."

Wren's eyes widened and Roane shut down. He clipped out, "Let's get ready."

Gregory and Wren left the room, but Roane stayed behind for a moment and scanned the room. His eyes were narrowed and lingered where I stood, but then he left with a guarded look over his face.

When his door shut, I was back at my car. I gasped and bent over to rest my forehead on my car. What had just happened?

"You're transitioning."

Saren materialized on the other side of my car. Her eyes were still the same smoldering flames, but she was dressed as a normal college student in a white sweatshirt and jeans. The black hair was swept up in a simple braid.

"You look normal except for those things." I pointed at her eyes.

They burst into flame, but quickly sizzled as if someone had thrown a blanket over the fire. "I'm not here to play with your mind. I'm here to help you."

"What's the catch?" I eyed her in suspicion.

She held up her hands in surrender. "I'm here to help. What did you just see?"

"Really?" There was no catch?

"I'm to help you."

"What'd you mean when you said that I'm transitioning?"

"Your powers. When you accepted the Immortal before, it was only the start. Everything molded to your body, but you don't know your full power. You don't know an eighth of your powers and you have to learn them one at a time. You can't learn it all at once. It's too much. Your mind would be overwhelmed. I'm here to help and explain things to you."

"So what was that just now? Any time that I've been around Roane, even when I slowed time, he always knew I was there." And why did she seem so much nicer than the last time?

Saren smiled. The flames lit again, but they were small embers. "I'm not nicer. I'm here to do my job and that's to tell you what's going on. When I need to make you angry, I won't hold back. You need gentle guidance and answers right now."

I still didn't like her. "About what just happened?"

"The Immortal sensed something that you needed to know. It/you sent yourself there."

"Why didn't he know I was there?"

"He's powerful, too powerful, but if you don't want him to know you're there, he won't. That was you, not the Immortal. You didn't want him to know you were there. What did you see?"

"A group of vampires are coming to town. Roane is going to meet them."

She nodded. "What does that mean to you?"

"They're coming for me. I'm guessing that they'll try to kill me."

"Try."

"Try." I nodded.

Saren nodded too. "Who were the vampires?"

"I don't know—" I started to say, but Saren shook her head. She stepped close. "You know who they are. Who are they?"

I didn't even consider it. I just answered. "They were Roane vampires. They were sent by his Elders."

"And?"

I had no idea how I knew it, but I did. "They're here to usurp Roane from his position as their hunter."

"Are they going to succeed?"

"No." I spoke so quickly, my eyes widened in surprise. I hadn't known that I knew any of that.

"Why not?" Saren knew. She measured every thought I had. "Why not, Davy?"

"Because he's powerful," I blurted out. The knowledge simmered beyond my reach. Now I grabbed it. "He's powerful because his blood is in me. He's connected to me."

Saren smiled and stepped back. "You're doing well. You might not need my help."

I frowned. I wasn't sure how I felt about that.

"He's more powerful than all the hunters." She still watched me.

I nodded. I hadn't known that, but it made sense.

"You don't like that?"

"Like what? That he's connected to me?"

She took a stalking step towards me. "That bothers you. You don't like that he's connected to you, do you? You *really* don't like it."

I looked away, but I couldn't ignore what she'd said. Did I like it? No. I'll be honest. Everything was too much. I wasn't ready for this, much less ready for my abilities to help someone else. Roane was something personal, too personal to me. I didn't enjoy that I helped him become more powerful. At least, I didn't enjoy that I hadn't made that decision. It was taken from me.

"He doesn't know how powerful he is." Saren glided close behind me. "He knew you were the Immortal, but he didn't know your power would go to him. That's not why he wanted you to take his blood."

"Then why?" I turned back around. "No riddles. I need to know."

"Because he was answering something inside of him. Something in him beckons to him just like I beckon to you. It doesn't make sense, but it will. Someday. And as for what you heard just now, you needed to know they were here. You're the Immortal. You'll start to know everything that happens, whether you want to know or not. Right now, I'd be less worried about the Roane Elders and more worried about that Mother Wolf. She's a bitch."

And I needed more on my plate. "I'm supposed to go to an empath meeting. My sponsor is making me go."

Saren laughed. "I'm your sponsor, Davy. Don't go. You'll overwhelm them. They'll feel inside of you and most won't make it to the hospital. Trust me. And dump Blue as your sponsor. She doesn't mean well in the end."

My eyes snapped to her. "What do you mean by that? She's like a mother to me."

Saren smirked and stepped back. I felt her absence before it happened so I reached out and grabbed her arm. "Don't go."

She glared at my hand. I felt like it had been scorched and I let go. I didn't have another second to react. Saren was gone. I almost expected a puff of smoke to linger where she'd been, but there was nothing. Just air. Now I was really frustrated.

"Davy?" Emily called out behind me. "I thought you were leaving for something? Where do you go all the time?"

My roommate was such the inquisitive one. I wasn't too worried. She'd forget about it in two seconds, but I was relieved to see that her normal coloring had come back to her cheeks. In the broad sunlight, she almost looked like nothing had happened. She had changed to a similar outfit that Saren had worn, but her hair was pulled back in a ponytail. Pippa was dressed in something that made her look like a hippie, complete with the same two braids as before. The shirt was full of flowers and her pants were brown suede?

"Davy," Emily spoke again.

"Oh. Right. I'm not going anymore. I changed my mind."

"Oh. Well, we're going to get some breakfast. Did you want to come with?"

Pippa shifted behind my roommate, but the movement was so small. I wouldn't have noticed it four weeks ago. When she refused to meet my gaze, I shook my head. "I'm going to head to the library instead. There's something I need to look up."

Emily frowned. "You're going to do homework?"

"Yeah."

"By yourself?"

"Who else would I go with?"

"I'm the one who usually forces you to do homework. With me. And you're going alone?" My roommate looked too speculative for my taste. "Are you sick?"

"Ha ha. That's funny. See you." Then I hurried away. I didn't like that Emily was with Pippa, but I knew the wolf would keep her safe and I needed information on werewolves. I couldn't ask Roane. I didn't think to ask Saren. I was advised against seeing Blue. Kates was gone. So that left the library. Fun times.

7

I wasn't sure the library would have literature on werewolves. I expected cartoons, teen romance novels, maybe some articles, but I was surprised they had an entire selection of older books. When I looked for where they were, I wasn't surprised. They were on the sixth and creepiest floor.

The book was gone when I got there. So I hoofed it back to the main floor and requested to check it out whenever it was due back. The guy looked like I had three heads when he informed me that the book was not allowed to be checked out. I gave him a blank look in return. Then he sniffled up his nose, lifted his arms like he was a tyrannosaurus rex, and proceeded to walk me back up six flights of stairs. As soon as we got there, he looked dumbfounded when he saw the book was gone. I enjoyed that.

"Well," he sputtered. "I have no idea. That book isn't allowed to be checked out. No one knows where it is. No one cares about where it is unless . . . ." He gave me a meaningful look. "Why are you looking for it?"

I gave him a blank face. "I'd like to be a werewolf. You?"

He rolled his eyes and dismissed me with a hand. "I thought you were looking for a class. Perhaps one of your classmates has it, but I can see that I'm wrong. Hmmm?" Then he threw both hands in the air. "It'll show up."

"You're not very helpful."

He shrugged. "It's my last week. Do your worst."

As he left, I glowered at his back. When it didn't burst into flame, I gave up. I must not have really wanted to hurt him. Then I turned for the bathroom and as I walked past an aisle, I caught sight of someone bent over a table with a very large, very old, book in front of her.

I approached with caution at first, but the girl was oblivious to anything around her. Her nose was pressed into that book and I wondered how she could handle the dust from it.

I drew closer to her table and checked the book. It was the one I wanted. "How long are you going to be reading that?"

She shrieked and fell from her chair.

"I'm sorry."

She pulled herself back up and studied me. "Who are you?"

"Who are you?" I narrowed my eyes. The girl had long brown hair that fell to her waist. She had a heart shaped face and glasses that covered dark eyes. Though she was dressed in a baggy sweater and jeans, I knew she was stick thin. Her feet peeked out from underneath her jeans in red ballet shoes. "I like your shoes."

She blushed. "Thanks. My sister didn't want them so I got them. I was over the moon when my mom sent—wait—Why do you want to read this book?"

"Werewolves."

She blinked and pushed up her glasses. "I didn't expect that answer."

"Why are you reading it?"

"Not for the werewolves." She laughed and turned back to her page. "This book has one of the best chapters on witches from Caduna. Do you know where that's at?"

I didn't.

"It's a secret place the Quakers first settled, but there was an abolition of witches so they moved and decided no one should know of the place."

"How do you know of it?"

"My family. One of the witches was my great-great-great-great-well, one of the founding witches was in my family. The secret was passed down."

"So you know all about that place?"

She frowned and scratched behind her ear.

"What's wrong? The secret didn't go to you?"

Tears welled up in her eyes as she shook her head. "It's always passed to the oldest daughter and I'm not the oldest. Tabitha doesn't care about this stuff, but she got everything. The stone. The books. The pendant. I got nothing." She sighed heavily. "I'm the witch of the family. I can do magic. The most magic she can do is with guys. She can get any of them. Not me. What's your name again?"

I extended my hand. "My name's Davy. What's yours?"

She placed her hand in mine. "I'm Sarah, but you can call me Brown. I prefer that name. I feel like I'm part of the earth and that's the natural color of the earth. Brown."

"It's blue. The oceans cover most of the planet."

Something sparked in her and shot through me. "I know, but my connection is to the land, not the water. Maybe Tabitha has that connection."

I heard her voice, but it came from a distance. When that something sparked through her, I was bombarded with images. One was the ocean as if someone was riding over it to us. The other was of a girl in a field. She was watching me. Slim. Long brown hair. Blue eyes. Another image was at night. Brown was standing in front of me and she held her hand out to me. She was trying to warn me about something.

"Davy?"

Brown stared at me. "Are you okay? Wait! Are you a witch too?"

"No." My voice came out hoarse. "How long have you been one?"

She sighed in disgust. "I've felt like I've been one all my life, but I didn't start doing spells until now. I was forbidden to talk about it or do anything with magic in high school. Tabitha's the chosen one in my family and that's only if she chooses to become a witch. All the family powers will go to her. Not me."

"Is your mom a witch?"

"No. She chose to pass on her powers. You can do that in my family. You can get all the powers from our ancestors."

"And if you don't? What then?"

She shrugged. "You just live a normal life."

"And if you choose the powers?"

Her voice trembled. "Then you have the responsibilities of all the other witches in my family."

"What are those?"

"I don't know. You don't know until the powers pass onto you."

"What if your sister decides she wants to be normal?" I flushed as I realized I was jealous. The girl had a choice.

"Then the powers will go to the next oldest daughter, hers or mine, or Kendra's. Not me."

Her eyes looked like she was seeing something far away, remembering something painful. She bit her lip for a moment and more tears welled up in her eyes. When she brushed one away, I realized that she'd forgotten about my existence.

I felt magic in her and she was just beginning, but the power in her was enormous. I felt it. It reached out to me. It was why she told me any of this. And I knew her magic would grow the more she trained and reached for it.

A wave of sadness swept over me and I knew it was hers. My empathic abilities had gone inside of her. I wanted to heal her. When she didn't react, I knew she couldn't sense my powers. I decided to push a little further inside of her.

When I found the thread of her magic, I followed it deeper

inside. It stopped and I felt it was boxed in. That's when I realized that though she was blocked from her own magic, it still seeped out slowly. She was pulling it out the more she learned and she was determined to get it all.

"You really want your powers, don't you?"

Brown jerked her eyes to mine. "What? Oh, yeah. Is it that obvious?"

"I can feel it from you." I frowned. "What happens if your sister gets the powers and you do too? Can there be two?"

"There never has been before so I'm not sure. Why?" Then her eyes popped out again. "I can't believe I've told you all this. I'm usually—I never talk to people. What is it about you? Do you have a special power over me? That's the only thing that would make sense." As she spoke, she shot to her feet and started stuffing papers in her bag. When she shoved the book in too, I opened my mouth to remind her it wasn't supposed to be taken home, but she rushed away before I could say anything. It wasn't long before I heard the door alarms sound.

Then I sat back down. I knew I should've been curious about her powers as a witch, but anything magical or supernatural didn't surprise me anymore.

"Your thoughts are transmitting so loud, I could've heard them on a radio."

Roane glided out from one of the book shelves and sat where Brown had left.

"I thought we weren't supposed to see each other?" I frowned when my voice came out raspy, but I couldn't help it. There was something about Brown that made me sad. I didn't think it came from her anymore because I still felt it and then Roane showed up.

It was me. I was sad.

'Were you in my office before? I felt you, but I couldn't place you.'

'I know about the Roane Elders, about the other vampires.'

'What do you know?'

'They want to take away your huntership and they want to kill me.'

'What else?'

'That they can't. You're too powerful because your blood is in me.'

He looked away and swallowed. Roane kept his emotions in check, but I felt his fear for a second before it was taken away the next moment. He didn't want me to feel what he felt. I chose not to comment how that hurt, but was it my place to know those things? He loved her, not me.

He thought, 'The Elders sent a sorcerer. He felt your presence, but he can't narrow it down to where you are in town. I shouldn't be here. They might be tracking me—'

'They're not. You know they aren't. You're better than them.'

Roane frowned for a moment. "I wanted to ask if I had been imagining things or not. I should be going now."

I wasn't going to say good-bye. I didn't want to do that anymore, but I watched him. He didn't move. Then he looked around, and still didn't move. "Was that a witch you were talking to?"

I nodded. "She's powerful, but something's blocking her. She has a weird family thing. She was telling me about it."

"She's a Bright. I've heard of their line, but I've never met one before."

"You know of them?"

He nodded. "Lucan was lovers with one of them when we first became vampires. She stirred a lot of his thirst for the unknown. The Bright women are powerful witches, but most of them don't use their power. No one knows why."

"It only goes to the eldest daughter."

He shrugged. "Regardless, they all have the ability, but they don't want their power or they don't use it. The Vampire nation would be more curious about them if they did. I'm glad they don't. We have enough problems with witches and sorcerers. Your friend doesn't have power? I thought I felt some from her."

"She has power, but it's blocked to her. She can't access it. A curse was put on their bloodline. I could remove what's blocking her, but I don't know if I should. I'm afraid what might happen."

"Don't. It'll draw more attention to you. You need to stay hidden. Do normal things." Roane stood up again and looked around. A flash of emotions crossed his face. "Are you doing okay? It's been a few days. How's Emily?"

"She's normal again. Bennett's love spell was nasty. I went in her a few times and removed some of that madness. Horrible. I hate vampires." I cringed and then realized what I had said. "I'm sorry! That's not what I meant."

Roane smiled gently. "It's fine. I'm not too fond of my race right now either."

Oh right. "Is it bad for you? What are they going to do to you?"

"They tried to kill me. It didn't work. They left and they'll send hunters this time."

"You'll be going against what you are?" But he was better. He was more powerful because of me. He'd be fine. Right?

His eyes sought mine and held them. "I'll be fine. Gregory, Wren, and others are loyal to me. They'll help me, but yes, I am more powerful than them."

I was relieved to hear that. I knew it, but it seemed more real when he said it.

"Davy, why didn't you let me see you today? I felt you. I wanted to see you," Roane spoke in a soft voice.

"It wasn't really me. It was what I am. It didn't want you to know I was there. I was confused too." That was when I realized that I'd never told him about Saren. Then I realized that I didn't have any intention of telling him. I trusted Roane, but something held me back from telling him. I wasn't sure why and that bothered me. I didn't want to always feel alone.

"You're transitioning into your powers. You don't know them, not fully."

Saren had said the same thing.

Roane looked towards where he had come from. He still didn't move so I asked, "Is there something else? Is something bothering you?" Was it her? Was he thinking of Talia?

His eyes whirled back to mine. I saw her in them. He *had* been thinking of her and that hurt more than I ever wanted to admit. "Do you miss her?"

Everything in him shut down. "I'll check with you every now and then. I don't want you to worry about me. I'll be fine and if something happens, Gregory and Wren will come for you. You'll be protected by one of us if you should need it."

He left abruptly and I couldn't help but think more should've been spoken between us, but she changed everything. The memory of Talia would always come between us and I had to accept it. He loved her, not me. A part of me wanted that to change. That same part of me clung to the idea that it would, that he'd turn his love to me, but I wasn't so sure now.

8

I tried to be normal after that day. Blue called me a few times, but I never answered. I knew she called because I skipped that meeting and the next two, but I couldn't tell her why. Saren told me not to speak to Blue anymore and for some reason, that didn't bother me. It should've, but it didn't. Maybe I had sensed what she was trying to warn me about my sponsor?

"Hiya, roommate!" Pippa called out when she came through the door. My actual roommate followed behind carrying a shopping bag.

"Hey guys." I tried to sound cheerful, as much as Pippa, but I didn't have the heart. And I didn't think her greeting was that funny. She had become like a roommate since she and Emily had become best bosom buddies. "You guys look happy. Why?"

Emily frowned. "What's wrong with you?"

What was wrong with me? What was wrong with her? More and more my roommate had started to transform into someone who was direct and dare I say it? She met problems head-on? Was this possible?

I narrowed my eyes. "You're changing. Why?"

Pippa's eyes widened and she grew silent. I felt her melt into the background.

Emily dropped her bags. "Excuse me if I'm changing. I don't feel right, if you really want to know. And who are you to talk? You've changed too, Davy. It's like you're moping. You ignore calls from that purple lady and you don't go anywhere except for class." Then her eyes got wide. "Is this about Kates? Did you guys have a fight and I didn't know? Am I being a bad friend?"

Pippa glanced at Emily. Her nostrils flared and I felt the wolf sniffing the air. It felt like she was trying to sniff her way into me. When I felt the tickling, the giggle rose up and I stood from the desk. "This has nothing to do with Kates. This is about you. You were going crazy and now you seem off. I don't know why, but it's different."

"Bad different?" I heard the caution in Emily's voice.

"No." The tickling hadn't stopped. "It's a good different. I don't feel like I've been a part of it and that makes me a little sad, I guess." Then I laughed.

Emily frowned.

I laughed harder and glared at Pippa.

"What?" My roommate looked between us two. "Davy, do you think this is funny?"

"Not at all." I couldn't stop giggling.

"You're laughing. That's not polite."

She sounded so offended, which only made me giggle harder. Pippa was sniffing like crazy. It felt like her nose was pressed into my butt.

"I'm sorry." I bit down on my lip, trying to silence the laughter. Then I snapped at Pippa, "Stop it!"

She squeaked and rushed out of the room.

"What?" Emily's mouth hung open. "What is wrong with you? She wasn't doing anything."

She was, but I couldn't tell that to Emily so I shrugged. "I'm jealous of her. She's your new best friend. You two are always together and it's like you're attached at the hip. I'm sorry. I'm human. I felt left out."

I was going to hell. A very bad, dungeons-with-fire type of hell.

Emily melted. "Oh, I'm so sorry, Davy. I didn't think you cared. You seem so aloof sometimes, like there are things bothering you, but you never tell me. I had no idea it was me." She put her hand on her chest. "I'm touched, I really am."

I saw that she was genuine and my self-loathing kicked up a notch. Emily was a good person. She was human. She was a bystander and she'd already taken a few hits from the life I lived. Vampires. Being kidnapped. Now a werewolf was her best friend.

"Oh. Don't feel bad. Really."

"But I do." Then she threw her arms around me and hugged me tight. "We will hang out. You. Me. Pippa. All three of us. I want the two of you to become friends. It'll be great."

This was the last thing I wanted, but she was right about one thing. I had been moping. I had no real life. I was pathetic so I plastered on a bright fake smile. "Okay! Let's do it. Us three. We should go drinking."

Emily's smile disappeared. "What? Drinking? Nooo."

"It won't be like the last time. I promise." There was no Kates this time. We'd be fine.

"I was hungover for three days and I don't even remember drinking." Emily shook her head. "I don't think that's a good idea."

"Oh, come on. It'll be fun."

Emily still didn't look convinced.

"You need a pick-me-up, right?" I clasped her shoulders and smiled again. I even showed my teeth. I blinded her. "Let me give that to you. You need something to help jump-start your life."

"Not really," Emily murmured. "I thought that was you?"

"You. Me. What's the difference? Let's go out, have an adventure, and laugh about it over coffee tomorrow."

"I don't want to be hungover," she mumbled.

I shoved her towards the closet. "Pick out a hot outfit. I'll go tell the dog and then we'll head out. It'll be fun. Trust me."

"Dog?"

But I was already out the door. By the time I knocked on Pippa's door, I had another fake smile on. "Hiya, neighbor!" I even waved cheerfully.

Pippa stepped back. "Hey."

"Emily and I are going out for a drink. Come with."

"I don't know." She glanced up and down the hallway. "I might stay in."

"You're coming with us. No debate. We'll have a grand time."

Pippa tried to grin, but it faltered. "Are you sure?" Then she drew me into the room and shut the door. "What about, you know, me being a werewolf and whatever you are. I still haven't figured it out. You're not a witch, are you?"

Images of Brown flashed through my brain. "No. I'm not a witch."

"Oh." She visibly relaxed.

"You don't like witches?"

"No. Not at all. They don't like us."

I couldn't imagine why. My smile went up a notch. "So are you coming?"

She bit her lip and twisted her hands together in front of her. "Can you tell me what you are? It's really been bothering me."

I fought against the urge to roll my eyes. "I'm empathic."

"What?" There was confusion first and then understanding dawned. "Oh, I get it. Vampires go crazy about empaths. No wonder you smell like them so much. Or, used to. You don't smell like vampires much lately. Are they leaving you alone?"

A part of me felt like she bought that half-truth too easily, but the other part condemned me to hell again. "Are you ever going to tell Emily about you?"

Then Pippa shrugged. "It's not my place to tell her what I am. Her mate will tell her. It's his place."

Mate. I didn't like the sound of that. "Who is this guy?"

Pippa smiled again and tugged at the ends of her two braids. "I have no idea, but she'll meet him. I feel it in my blood. So does she. She feels the promise of him through me. It calms her when she's near me."

I'd seen it in Emily. If Pippa went away, the old Emily would be back within a week. I wasn't sure how I felt about that. The new Emily seemed stronger, but if I had learned anything through my ordeal with the vampires it was that if something was being kept hidden, it wasn't a good thing.

I wasn't a good thing.

Ugh. The guilt flared inside of me again. Lies and secrecy. Both words weren't good and my life was all about them now.

"You know what? Nevermind. We can go for a milkshake instead."

Pippa frowned. "Are you sure?"

"Yeah. That'd be better." I was kicking myself as I went back to my room.

Emily had already changed for the night out. She was dressed in a shimmering white shirt over gray slacks. She looked good, very good. She smiled and waved towards my desk chair. "You didn't tell me about Brown. She should come with us."

My eyes popped wide when I saw the witch at my desk with a book in her hands. She smiled politely and stood. "Hi, Davy. Remember me from the library? I've thought a lot about that day and decided that you'd been sent to me for some answers. I can give you those answers." Then she extended the book to me. "You can read as much about werewolves as you want. It's not my place to stand in your way."

What?!

Emily gushed, "She's a witch! Can you imagine that? We know our own witch."

Oh. Not good.

Then my roommate murmured, "I didn't know you liked werewolves?"

"What?!" Pippa squeaked from the open doorway.

"Pippa, this is Davy's friend, Brown. She's a witch."

Brown smiled and lifted the book again. "And I brought this for Davy. She wanted to learn about werewolves."

"She did?" Then Pippa seemed to regroup. "You're a witch?"

Brown lifted her shoulders and preened. "I'm a new witch. I don't have much power, but I can feel it. It runs in my family and I know, I just do, that someday I'm going to be a great witch. I know it."

"Oh."

While the wolf was at a loss for words, I stepped in. "That's wonderful, Brown. You'll be a great wol—witch. You'll be a great witch."

"I'm going to be sick," Pippa whimpered behind me.

Brown's chest puffed up and her cheeks got red. "Thanks, Davy. That means a lot and you barely know me too, not like that vampire that was watching us until I left. I saw him, you know. I felt him, I should say. He was a hottie. I didn't know you knew any vampires."

"Oh my—" Pippa crashed to the floor behind me.

"Vampire?" Emily questioned.

I checked behind me and Pippa gave me a weak wave. One of her shoulders was propped against the wall. "I'm okay."

"Did you say vampires?"

Brown turned to Emily and nodded. "You couldn't guess how many go to this college. They're everywhere. Well, they were everywhere, but I didn't notice them much for awhile. Now they seem to be everywhere again. I don't know what's going on. My family doesn't practice witchcraft enough to be considered a threat or an asset by the vampire world. I think that's a good thing. How about you? Do you know any vampires?"

Emily bristled. "There are no such things as vampires."

Brown laughed. "Next you're going to tell me that you don't really think I'm a witch, right?"

"No. I believe in Wiccans. I had a friend who became a Wiccan in high school, but there are no vampires, except in movies."

Brown stood tall and straightened her shoulders. She seemed miffed. "Excuse me? I am not a Wiccan. There is a big difference between a Wiccan and a witch. Wiccan is a way of life for normal humans. It's a religion, but they're not born with magic. Witches are. I was. There's a difference."

Emily fought back a grin and glanced sideways to me. "I'm sure you are."

The air instantly sizzled around us and Brown lifted a hand. "You don't think I'm a witch?"

"What?" Emily was at a loss for words. "Davy?"

I jerked a shoulder up. "So what if she's a witch?"

Pippa melted to the floor and Brown perked up. "That's right." The air lost its sizzle. The witch had been appeased. And then something came over me. I picked the sizzle back up, but it was louder.

Emily glanced around. "What's going on?"

Pippa stood up and looked around me.

Brown glowed as she looked around.

My body hummed. I felt it all over and remembered when I had changed Lucan back to being human. My body hummed at that time too. I had snapped my fingers then, but this time I merely narrowed my eyes and the microwave exploded. Sparks flew from it and Emily jumped back, screaming.

Brown clamped both hands to her cheeks. "Oh my gosh. I don't even know how I'm doing that."

Emily swung horrified eyes to her, but I grinned. "What were you saying about the difference between Wiccans and witches?"

Then I glanced at Pippa from the corner of my eye and stopped cold. She wasn't amused. My stomach dropped. She knew I was more than empathic.

9

I made a quick dash for the shower. A half hour later, I found our room sparkling with cleanliness. I sighed internally as I dropped my shower caboodle. Emily only cleaned when she was nervous.

"Did the witch leave?"

Emily's eyes shot to mine. "Do you believe in that stuff?"

I shrugged as I pulled a shirt on. "Our microwave is kapoot. I think we better." It was meant as a joke, but when her eyes widened and she paled, I thought better of it. So I sighed again, pulled on some jeans, and quickly combed my hair. "Come on, let's go out."

"What?"

"Let's go out. I know somewhere we can get some drinks, maybe even free drinks."

Slowly, she stood. "We're going for a drink?"

"Yeah. We went before."

"That was with Kates. I met Bennett that night." Something flashed over her face and Emily crumbled in front of me. Her face fell. Her shoulders slumped and she dropped like a stone on my bed.

My mouth dropped with her. "Hey. Come on. It'll be good for you."

"I haven't seen him since that horrible night, when we were kidnapped. I know the police said there was nothing we could do about it and that he skipped town. I know you said that Kates was working undercover and went after him, but I still feel like I lost him. I constantly have this sense of being cheated. It's like he died and I felt it." She stopped and a few tears came to her eyes.

One, he had died. Two, you're better off. Three, Kates hadn't been working undercover. None of that was going to make her feel better, so I patted her shoulder instead.

"I feel like I'm grieving for him." She turned and started to sob in my shoulder.

Awkward.

I kept patting her shoulder and then switched to brushing her hair from her forehead. That was always soothing.

"I still think we should go out." I tried to sound cheerful. The wolf would've been handy in this moment.

"Why am I like this?" She kept crying and pulled away to stare at her hands. She held them up with her fingers spread out, and stared down at her palms. "I feel so dirty. I feel like I'm going crazy. I know you said it had something to do with the full moon, but I still don't feel right. I keep up a good front in front of Pippa, but I'm a basket case."

"Oh come now." I shook her shoulder. "You're normal. The guy did a number on you and you have to go through what every other girl does. They're called crushes for a reason, Em. This is the time you jump back up and keep going. Hell, let's invite Pippa. Maybe the witch too? We have friends. We should celebrate."

Her eyes popped out. "Not the witch. Do you believe in that? Really? I couldn't believe it, but then there's the microwave. She's loony."

"Ah. She's harmless."

Emily dropped her voice to a whisper, "I think she's actually a witch. She seemed sure of it and I don't think she's crazy. She said there are vampires. Do you believe in them? Maybe she's delusional. I don't believe in that stuff, but then I never believed in witches." She shuddered.

I laughed on a forced note. "Vampires? Next thing you're going to say that werewolves exist, maybe even were-cats."

"Davy." Emily stood and stared down at me. She was too serious. "I think she does have magical powers. Our microwave is destroyed. We have to get a new one because of her."

I stood and patted her hand. "It'll be okay. Promise. Witches can't hurt humans."

"Really?"

"Really." I smiled at my lie and toed on some sandals. "Are you going like that?"

"We're really going out?"

"Why not? Neither of us have early classes. Let's go. Did you want to invite Pippa too?"

"Really?" Emily stood uncertainly in the middle of the room. Then she gasped and dove for her closet. When she pulled out a red shirt, she stopped, and glanced at me. She looked at my simple white tee shirt and took out a green one of hers. Then she reached for her khaki capris, but veered to her jeans instead. We now looked like twins. Super.

"I'm going to see if Pippa wants to come." Emily darted out the door.

I took a deep breath, but it wasn't long before I heard a knock at our door. Pippa popped her head around the door. "Emily said we're still going out? Is it okay if I come?"

"Why wouldn't it be?"

She glanced over her shoulder. "Emily went to the bathroom. I wanted to make sure it's okay with you if I come. I don't really think you and I get along?"

"Which is funny because we're both lying to the same person.

You'd think we'd be best friends." I tried not to sound so bitchy, but I failed.

Pippa cringed.

"Sorry. That was unfair. I don't like lying to her, but I have to. I'm taking my stuff out on you. I know you said that her kindred will tell her, maybe then neither of us will have to lie to her."

Pippa narrowed her eyes. "I don't really know what powers you have or what you are, but I know you're more than empathic. If she finds out about me, why would that mean you're caught too?"

I opened my mouth and then shut it. The wolf had a point, which was irksome. Emily might not ever find out about me. That should be good news, but it was then that I realized I wanted my roommate to know about me. I didn't want to lie anymore. I didn't want to hide anymore.

So I closed my mouth. 'Well. Fuck me.'

Pippa kept winding a finger around one of her braids. "Where are we going? She mentioned Buds before? That's a vampire bar. I don't want to go there."

I cringed. "You're not the only one. I want to stay as far away from vampires as much as you."

She flashed a relieved smile. "Oh good. I didn't know. I mean, I assumed, but you smelled like vampires so much before. Never-mind. That sounds good to me."

Then Emily came in, excited and scared at the same time. I knew Pippa sensed it too because her nostrils flared and she shot me a look.

"Looking good, roomie." She flushed, but she was happy. That was all I cared about. "Ready to go?"

"Yes, I am. You guys?"

Pippa nodded, dressed in her overalls and a pink shirt this time. I was starting to wonder if she ever changed her outfit or her hair. She still had the same two braids that hung over her shoulders as she had the first time I met her.

"My pick?" I took my car keys and purse. I started for the door.

"I was wondering if we could go to the Shoilster? Some girls on our floor told me it's supposed to be awesome."

Pippa and I both froze.

"Please?"

The wolf and I shared a shaky look. "Sure."

"I call shotgun!" Emily bounced out the door and we followed at a sedate pace. This night was definitely going to be interesting.

The drive over was tense. Emily fully welcomed the idea of going out so she couldn't sit still in her seat. Pippa and I were much less excited. As we got out of the car and headed towards the bar, I saw Gregory at the door in all black with sunglasses over his eyes.

"They have bouncers?" Pippa looked at me.

I shrugged and burst ahead of the girls. Gregory saw me and froze. I felt suspicion and caution come over him as I slapped a hand on his huge bicep. It twitched under my hand and my hand shot away. I felt scolded somehow and let out a nervous giggle. "Hi! So, I'm Davy. I had a friend that used to come here all the time. Kates? Do you know her? She said we'd be welcome to get in. This is my roommate, Emily, and her friend, Pippa."

They drew beside me as Gregory's gaze slid over both girls and then back to me. He sniffed the air as Pippa was trying not to and turned back to me. I felt his meaningful look. Oh yes. He was aware I had a werewolf in my company. So my fake smile spread wider. "Can we get in? We go to school here and want a fun night out. My *roommate* heard a lot about this place." My smile slipped.

There was no reaction from the giant vampire, but his mouth flattened into a small frown. "You girls need to stay on the main floor. No one goes into the basement."

Emily was gleeful and skipped through. "Thanks!" Pippa hung her head and dragged her feet behind. Once they were out of hearing distance, I murmured, "Please don't kill me."

He harrumphed. "You wait till Roane hears about this."

"Davy! Come on. What are you doing?" Emily called from inside and I hurried ahead. A sense of doom washed over me.

As we went in, waves of vampires rushed over me. They were everywhere. Before they'd always stayed to the basement, but this time they were in each corridor, in every booth, and on the dance floor. And these weren't normal vampires that went to our university. I glanced around and my eyes went wide. I didn't know what type of vampires they were, but they weren't the normal kind. If they were at the Shoilster and Gregory let us in, they must've been loyal to Roane.

Two vampire males strolled by and eyed us up and down. I scowled at them as Emily gushed. "This place is amazing. The bright lights. Is that smoke on the floor? And what kind of music is that? Is that techno? Don't they listen to that in Europe? Where did all these gorgeous guys come from?"

"It's not smoke, Em. It's dry ice."

It was supposed to make the club more mysterious and it worked. I kept eyeing all the nooks and crannies. I wondered what was happening in those shadows that no one could see. She was right about the guys too. Most vampires were good looking, but these seemed to be the crème de la crème. Some of them were tall and lean while others were a little stockier, built like Gregory. The females resembled Wren, complete with the hooker outfits. They wore lace corsets and leather. A few of them narrowed their eyes at us, and watched us with something that resembled hatred.

Pippa shifted beside me. Her hand touched mine. *'I can't be here. A werewolf can't be here.'*

'You're with two humans. They won't say anything.'

'I can't risk it. I'm sorry, Davy. I have to leave. Make up an excuse for me, please?'

'But—'

But she was already gone.

Then Emily looked around, wide eyed. "This was the best idea you've had, Davy. Wait. Where'd Pippa go?"

"Her cousin was sick." It wasn't my best lie.

"Really?" But then Emily was back to basking in the glow of the vampires.

"Excuse me, misses. I have a table ready for you." A server appeared with a black buttoned down shirt tucked in black slacks with two menus in his hand. His hair was slicked back in gel, giving a smooth Casanova look to him.

A smirk appeared on his face as his eyes shifted from Emily to me. At first he looked at my roommate in anticipation, but then he saw me and read my eyes. *'Back off, buddy.'*

He looked away as he led us through the crowd. We kept going upwards, which was surprising. I knew the Shoilster. Customers didn't get preferred seating unless they called ahead for reservations. It was the type of club where VIPs got private boxes, but we went past even those. He took us to a back corner where the music could barely be heard, but we were tucked at an angle where we could still see most of the activity and dance floor.

As we sat, Emily took the offered menu and leaned across the table. "This place is so pretty and we got a great table. It's everything the girls were saying. Oh, thank you so much."

The server took our order and left quietly.

Emily whispered after he'd gone a few steps, "He's cute."

"He's off limits," I growled and opened my own menu.

I hated the Shoilster. The food was made to look pretty on the plate, but the quality wasn't taste-worthy. However, what do you expect from a club/bar/restaurant that's geared towards the vampire customers. They didn't care about the food. As long as it looked pretty, appeased the humans they brought with them, and allowed a lot of drinks to come in dark colored glass, they were satisfied. They could consume their blood in front of any stupid human.

Emily gaped. "What? Why? He's cute."

"You're fragile right now. You need to go out a few more times before dating again. Bennett did a number on you."

"But," she sputtered. "Didn't you say the best thing was to go out and get over him?"

I closed my menu. "No. I said going out, but not going with a guy. It is okay to go out, let yourself soak up the fun, maybe even some attention from some guys, but that's it. Guys are dangerous. You need to get your head on straight in order to handle them."

My roommate made a disgusted face. "You make them sound like they're predators."

If the shoe fits.

Then she added, "What happened to you? You were crazy about Adam before and he wasn't a good guy."

"Adam was a cheater and a douchebag."

"Oh." She fell silent because we both knew she agreed with my sentiments about him. She'd been the first to tell me. Eyeing my roommate, I saw the confusion in her eyes. Maybe if she knew about vampires, about what they could do? Maybe if I told her?

Just then someone appeared at our table and Emily gasped, "Luke?"

My stomach fell and I looked up. Sure enough. There he was, glowering down at me. Emily just smiled at him. I realized she still had her crush for him from before.

"Um, hi."

"Emily, right? You're in one of my classes?" Roane put on a polished façade and seemed happy to see her as he pushed into my side of the booth, shoving me over. As his arm touched mine and I felt how tense he was, I knew he was pissed.

When he continued to chat with my roommate, I tried to sense inside of him. I hadn't gone far before he lashed at me, *'Get out! You shouldn't be here.'*

Oh yes. He was pissed.

I hung my head for a moment because he was right. I

shouldn't have been there, but I couldn't even deny it. I had wanted to see him. I wanted to go there to maybe see him. When Emily suggested the Shoilster, I hadn't argued, at all. Then I looked back up. My eyes skimmed over his chiseled features that seemed more mysterious from the shadows dancing over his face and I caught a glimpse of Gregory in the background. He'd taken point behind a post with a drink in hand. His eyes met mine for a second before he shifted and looked away. I knew he agreed with Roane, I had been stupid to go there.

I also knew he was our bodyguard for the rest of the night.

It was then that I felt Roane's hand grip mine underneath the booth and he squeezed tight. I didn't know if it was to convey how angry he was with me or if he was trying to warn me about something. Either way, I was fearful of sharing thoughts with him. Other vampires were too close, they might hear them. So I was forced to sit there as Luke talked with Emily because I knew what he was doing. He was making her feel like she was the focal point of his arrival so she wouldn't suspect a thing. I saw how her eyes lit up. She was eating it up and lavishing in it.

I was in hell.

10

Roane never spoke to me as he sat with us. And once he left, Emily gave me a dreamy smile and sighed. "He's a great guy. Doesn't seem to like you much, but he's nice."

I cleared my throat and sat up straight, but she stopped me with a wave. "Don't worry. I'm not going to chase Luke Roane. He's way out of my league. I'm not completely stupid. Besides, he's probably already devoted to some beautiful creature."

"What do you mean by that?" What did she know?

Emily shrugged. "That's the fourth time he's ever talked to me, but he never once flirted with me. He's always been nice, polite, and stand-offish. Trust me; he's one of the good ones."

"Right." I breathed easier. I wasn't sure what I was going to say, but our food came at that moment. Roane had been there when our orders were taken so the server was the epitome of professional now. I caught him glancing over his shoulder at Gregory too.

I ordered a salad. Emily ordered chicken. Then our drinks started coming.

Emily's face lit up again. "What is this?"

"They're on the house." And he placed two fruity cocktails in front of us, followed by our own pitchers of the same liquid.

Roane had done this. He sat us where we were and he was paying for everything.

Then the server slipped me a note. I slid it on my lap and opened it to read. *'If you're going out, stay here where I can protect you. Enjoy. Don't come back here again. Why are you keeping company with a werewolf?'*

Talk about being blunt and hurtful at the same time. I ripped it to shreds and dropped the pieces in our candle throughout the rest of the evening. Anybody with magic could've put them back together, but I made sure each piece was destroyed when Emily went to the bathroom.

A few hours later, I learned that alcohol had no effect on me and that Emily was the same drunk as before.

Still giggling, she slapped a hand on the table. "Thank you for this. It means a lot. I don't have a lot of friends. My close friends are all home, but then I met you. You're a close friend now too, Davy. You were right. I needed to get out. I needed this."

"You did."

"You're right. I feel like a new woman. I feel like I can go to all my classes alone now. Maybe I'll even tackle this feeling of grief I have. I know—" She snapped her fingers. "I'll go to a grief counseling group. That's what I'll do. It'll help me get Bennett out of my system."

I froze with my straw in my mouth.

"What do you think?"

What did I think? She'd have a place to talk and an outlet for her emotions. A smile spread on my face. "I think that's a great idea."

"It's decided. Tomorrow I'm looking for one on campus." She bent over, giggling. "How in the world are we going to get home? I can barely sit up."

"Ladies." Gregory materialized at our table. "There is a car ready for you downstairs. We will give you a ride home."

"Oh!" Emily was taken aback. "That's so nice of you. Is there money you need? I mean, do we pay? How much is it? I'm sorry. I'm a little drunk." Then she giggled a bit more, blushing behind a hand over her mouth.

Gregory swept his detached eyes over us both. "It's free of charge. It's part of the service."

"That's wonderful." She clapped and then frowned. "This isn't normal? We're getting such great service. Why? Davy, do you know?"

I smiled and patted her hand. "The owner is a friend of Kates. I dropped her name before."

"Oh!" Then her eyes narrowed and disgust flared over her face. "I think I'm going to throw up." And then she scrambled out of the booth and to the bathroom.

Gregory's face twitched and then cleared again. He sat in her seat. "I don't think she'll be coming back soon. Her levels of intoxication are massive for a human."

I sighed and threw the last piece of Roane's note in the candle. Gregory studied me as I watched it go up in smoke and a small smile appeared on his face. He looked softer for a second. "You came to see him."

My heart sank and I shook my head. "Emily suggested this place. I couldn't say no. This night was about her."

"His office overlooks this table."

My head shot up. "What?"

He nodded and gestured upwards. "You can't see through the glass, but he hasn't moved from that spot all night since you'd been here."

Hope flared in me for a moment, but I shook my head and turned it off. I couldn't get excited at the idea he might have feelings for me. Talia still remained in his heart. He was just confused.

I looked where he had pointed and saw glass mirrors. At one section of the wall, they jetted out and around, framing an office above the entire club. I could tell Roane stood on the other side of them. Able to make out his silhouette, I pushed through and it opened up to my eyes. Gregory was wrong; I was able to see through them. My eyes met Roane's, his narrowed as he mouthed the word, "Stop."

I narrowed mine in defiance and sensed into him. It was so easy to slip in him now and I was met by his same boiling anger. He snarled at me in his head, 'What are you doing? You're not supposed to use your powers.'

'I'm in your head, your head only. No one can hear our thoughts here.'

'My shields are too hard. You're right. No one can read my mind, except you.' And I felt how he hated that.

I sparked back at him, 'Sucks, doesn't it? When someone might be more powerful than you.'

'Shut up. Return to your table. Gregory is annoyed that you're ignoring him.'

'He'll get over it.'

'He's grown a soft spot for you. He wanted to be the one to take you home tonight.'

'I like Gregory. He's nicer than Wren.'

Roane bit back a laugh. 'Go, Davy. Emily is returning to the table.'

I looked and saw her approaching. 'I'm sorry for bringing her here. I wanted to see you. I'm sorry again.' Then I slipped out of him and saw that Gregory had a perturbed look on his face. I was afraid to ask what that meant, but Emily had arrived.

She was pale with a green tinge and held a hand to her stomach. "I just threw up eight times. I don't ever want to drink again. Davy, don't let me drink again."

I stood and held a hand to her back. "You can still drink, just not that much next time."

Gregory led the way out of the club. As we followed behind, Emily groaned and clutched her stomach. I saw how the other customers turned and stared as we passed. Some of them were interested because we were humans. They knew Gregory protected us. A few others smelled Emily's nausea and turned away in disgust. Still others watched and their eyes lingered on the right hand of Lucas Roane.

As we climbed into the backseat of a car, I caught sight of my own car parked not far away. I could've driven, but Emily thought I was drunk. I had as much as her. I should've been affected. If I told her the truth, that I was stone cold sober, she would've wondered why. So I burrowed into my seat and waited as Gregory drove us back home. When we got to the dorm, she stumbled out first and headed in without a second look.

I remained in the car and looked out my window.

Gregory got out, closed Emily's door and returned to his seat behind the steering wheel. He tilted the rearview mirror, but then turned in his seat.

A wave of sadness swept over me. "I finally realized and accepted tonight that I am completely alone. I've been fighting it, but I have to accept it now."

I didn't see his reaction, but I felt his acceptance. It was okay to speak to him about this.

I stared out the window, but I wasn't seeing anything. Saren told me to stay away from Blue, so I did. Roane told me to stay away and I tried. My roommate thought I was something I wasn't. The witch was too alarming and Pippa couldn't ever know.

I was supposed to be normal, do normal things, and that's what I had wanted in the first place.

"I feel like I'm in a prison. Every lie I tell is another door that I've shut around me. I can't talk to anybody about this."

Gregory didn't say anything for a moment. "Roane is building an army. All those vampires have declared their loyalty to him. He is going against the Roane Family line."

"What?"

"The Roane Elders are coming with their Family of vampires. They know the Immortal is here and they're going to fight their way in. Roane has declared war against them. He is no longer a part of the Roane Family. He is doing this to protect you."

"I'm the Immortal. No one can hurt me."

Wariness flashed in his eyes. "Yes, they can. They can torture you. They can imprison you with magic. No one knows how powerful you are, even us, but there's always a way to contain something. Roane fears that Lucan is with the Mori, that he is studying their ways to find a way to take the thread from you."

"Who are the Mori?"

"The ancient vampires. They have magic in them. Roane said you had an encounter with them earlier. He thinks his brother is with them."

"The ones who can have baby vamps? That's not good."

I didn't know how magic could affect me, if I was immune, or if there was something that could be used against me. I knew that the Immortal thread no longer existed. It had dissembled when my body molded to the Immortal.

"Why are you telling me this? Why didn't Roane?" And could I still call him Roane if he wasn't with that Family anymore?

Gregory smiled. "You talk out loud sometimes. You should not do that so much."

Oh, yeah. My smile felt a bit foolish. "Why did you tell me this?"

"Because you should know. Roane chose not to because he is trying to let you live as normal a life as possible. If he needs to take you away from this place, you would never be able to be a normal human again. You would be on the run for the rest of your life."

And that would be forever. I shuddered.

Then he continued, "You can always call him Roane. His given name is Lucas, but he prefers his Family name even if he is no longer associated with them. He has their standards in his blood. It is why he is making this stand against them."

I felt his trust and belief in Roane again. It was so powerful; it was almost stifling to me, but I could sympathize. Roane had a way of pulling that loyalty out of everyone, human or not.

"Okay." I nodded and reached for my door. "I know what to do. Be normal. Right?"

"It's what he wants for you."

"Then I will do that." And I needed to put a cork in my self-pity talk. Seriously. People had worse problems than mine, like Brown. Everyone would think she was crazy.

As I got out of the car and walked around, Gregory wound down his window. "If you really need to talk to someone, here's a number you can reach me. I warn you that Roane will be told every detail that we discuss, but I can be a sounding board for you."

I took the piece of paper he offered and tucked it away. "Thanks, Gregory. And tell him thanks too. I know he said you could do this."

He jerked his head in a nod, a sign of respect from him. "He cares more for you than you might think."

When I finally went inside, I was a mass of emotions. I'd been rejuvenated, but when I heard Emily in the bathroom, guilt flared in me too. Pippa rushed out of the bathroom. "What's wrong with her? She won't stop puking."

"She had too much to drink. I should've stopped her." But I'd been distracted.

Pippa rolled her eyes. "She's actually green from vomiting so much, but she still says she had fun tonight. What did you guys do?"

"Nothing. We stayed there and drank. That was it."

"I can smell vampires all over both of you. It's disgusting." She wrinkled her nose and then went around me. "I'm going to grab some medication for her."

When she left, I went into the bathroom and found Emily in a back stall. She was bent over the toilet and gave me a weak grin. "I feel horrible."

"I'm sorry, Em." I patted her back as I sat beside her. I drew my knees against my chest.

As she felt another spell coming on and bent forward over the toilet again, I closed my eyes and drew some of her illness into me. It was there—ugly, slimy, and icky stuff. Along with it remained some of her love spell from Bennett. It still hadn't fully left her system. As it flowed into me, I felt Pippa's presence and then I felt her surprise. She knew what I was doing and I could sense that Emily was starting to feel better. After a few more minutes of drawing the illness into me, Emily was able to sit up straight and she sighed.

"I feel much better." She panted and gave us a stupid grin. Sweat soaked her hair. Some of it clung to her forehead in clumps and she brushed it back. "Much better."

I smiled and squeezed her hand before I stood up.

Pippa helped me up and met my gaze for a brief second. She studied me hard. Then she murmured, "You're not even affected."

I turned away from Pippa. It wasn't any of her business. "Emily, you want to watch a movie to end the night?"

"Pippa, you want to watch too?"

The wolf stood with a dazed look. Her mouth opened and closed. "I . . . uh . . ."

"Grab your blanket. We'll crawl in our beds and fall asleep. You can have the couch." I made sure there was a welcoming tone in my voice, but my eyes sent their own message. She knew not to say anything.

Then she closed her mouth and nodded in surrender. "I'll get my stuff. I have a stuffed animal."

"You do?" Emily mumbled as she cleaned her mouth.

"Let me guess? A little wolf?"

Pippa grinned before she went out the door.

"How'd you know that?" Emily asked, but she didn't care. Now that I'd taken the illness away, the exhaustion was evident in her. She was going to be asleep before her head hit her pillow. And as I put the movie in and she crawled into her top bunk, she was snoring before I even curled up in my own blankets. Pippa came through the door and stood in the doorway with her hand on the doorknob. "She's already asleep?"

"Yeah."

She fidgeted with the door handle. "Should I go?"

Emily's snores roared through the room.

I gestured to the couch. "I already put the movie in. If she wakes up and doesn't see you on the couch, she'll wonder why you didn't come. She's going to swear that she never fell asleep and watched the whole time."

Pippa grinned. "I guess I can stay a little bit."

Then I pressed play and nestled back.

Twenty minutes into the movie, she asked. "What are you?"

I'd been tired, but I jerked awake now.

She hesitated. "I mean, you're not just empathic."

"I can't tell you and if you ever find out, you can't say a word to anyone."

Pippa didn't comment for a while. "The wolves know you exist. They know there's something different about you. I'm sorry. We don't have an open channel for our thoughts with each other, but we're highly in tune with the other wolves. The matriarch knew about you. She sensed my unease."

At her words, everything froze inside of me. I knew about the mother wolf, but I hadn't given her enough thought. First Brown had distracted me, then Roane came, and then Saren.

"Are they going to do anything?" My heart stopped.

She shook her head. "No. They're just waiting and watching right now. If you do something against us, then they'll act. They're protective of Emily, you know. Her kindred is important to the pack. They consider her one of us."

I grinned at that thought. "Can you imagine when Emily finds all that out?" I whistled under my breath. "I'd like to be a fly on the wall that day."

She giggled. "I think everyone in the pack will feel her kindred's emotions. I'll tell you how it goes."

I shook my head. Emily's world was going to split wide open. She was still uneasy about the possibility of witches. I had quieted her questions about vampires, but all the folklore was going to become real to her soon. Except me. I wasn't in the folklore.

I settled back and tried to watch the movie.

———

WREN PAUSED in his doorway and saw Roane with his back to the desk. He gazed over the club below him. She couldn't see from below, but she knew he'd be there and he was.

Gregory had passed the message that Davy was there. The ones who knew what she meant to Roane felt her presence immediately. They understood why a sudden intensity swept around the club and most of them waited. They watched warily to see what might happen next. Wren knew that her master wouldn't be leaving this spot for the rest of the night.

"Are you going to stand there and watch the whole night?"

Roane didn't turn around. He'd known she was there before she opened the door.

When he didn't answer, she took a seat on one of his leather couches and swung a leg over the armrest. "So what's the plan? Are you going to kick her out? She's here with her roommate and a wolf. She's here under her cover. Sneaky little bitch."

He tossed his drink back. "Gregory is going to watch her."

Wren snorted. "I bet he loved that assignment. Let's all watch the Imm—"

Roane was in her face before she finished. He grabbed her

jaw in one hand and lifted her in the air. "You do not say that word. Ever."

Wren's eyes flashed in anger, but she managed a tight nod. She couldn't speak.

Roane placed her on her feet, but he didn't let go. "I get that you don't like her. I don't care. You will treat her with respect or you will be sent away. Let's not forget the last time you tangled with one of them. Talia wasn't as forgiving, was she?"

She shrugged off his touch. "That wasn't about you. Let's not forget that either or what I lost to be loyal to you."

He rolled his eyes and moved to refill his drink. "If that's how you think of this, you can leave. You made your choice long ago."

She growled, but didn't move. Her hands remained against her sides as she clenched and unclenched them into fists. With fevered eyes and a tight jaw, she struggled not to lash out and then gave up the fight. She burst out, "Tracey's coming here! She's marching with the new Roane hunter. I found out from some soldiers who defected to Gavin's Family. What are you going to do when they get here? We aren't ready for an entire army."

Roane glanced back. "Am I supposed to be surprised by this? We've known they would send an army. We've always known. They *already* captured you with a small clan, but Davy released your bonds. Did you know that?"

She froze for a second, and then shrugged. "So what?"

He turned back to the window and found Davy below; laughing with the girl who'd had a crush on him. Then he murmured as he sipped his drink, "I'm sorry that Tracey is coming here. I truly am. I know what she meant to you."

With those words, her anger was gone. She groaned. "Why do you do that? You make me so mad and then, nothing. It's all gone. You're a dick sometimes."

Roane grinned, but didn't look back. "We will deal with the army. Look around, Wren. Everybody here has come to join us. We're not powerless."

"She should be testing her powers. She should be figuring them out so she can control and use them. We will need her in the end. We won't win without her."

His jaw hardened. "She's living a normal life. That was the deal. We stay and hold this off as long as possible and she can be normal. It's what she's always wanted."

"We should be running."

He whirled back to her and pinned her against the wall. His face was inches from hers. "You didn't want to run before. You wanted to fight. Wish granted. This is what we're doing. Now you're going to bolt? Are you going to go to Tracey when she gets here?" He waited a beat. "Are you going to betray me, Wren?"

"NO—I—" She closed her mouth and looked away. "I don't think we'll win, Lucas."

His eyes softened and he let her go. "Trust me?"

With a sigh, she closed her eyes and hung her head. "I always have."

"Then please continue."

It broke her and she lifted her eyes back up. A renewed determination was in them. "Until I die."

Roane didn't respond, but clenched his jaw. It meant more than he had expressed to her, but he knew that Wren was terrified. She wanted to fight, even when the odds were against them. For her to come and request for them to run meant others were scared as well. Fear was dangerous. It was intoxicating and maddening. And he knew he'd have to do something to diffuse it.

"For the record, the reason why I don't like her isn't because she took Talia's place." Wren moved to the door.

He lifted piercing eyes to her and waited.

She finished, "Because you don't think clearly when it comes to her. And for god's sake, if you want to see her, just go! Make up some excuse."

Roane didn't tell her that he already had.

As Wren shoved through the door, it swung open and

revealed an athletic looking vampire with golden curls. His blue eyes smirked in amusement. "You don't have to knock me unconscious, Wren. I'm yours for the taking."

She brushed past and growled, "Get lost!"

Gavin chuckled as he walked inside and helped himself to a drink. He cast a cursory glance over the vampire at the window. "Hope you don't mind, Lukey dear. I was a bit parched. I haven't fed in a long while with how fast we were urged to get here. Really, Luke. It was breakneck speed. I think I should earn some points for being the bestie I am to you. How many other complete armies have gotten here? What's that? Oh, right. One. Me. No welcoming hug? No hello? No, 'what's up mate?' Nothing? I'm hurt."

A grin teased the corners of Roane's mouth. "You can have Wren for the night."

Gavin burst out laughing. "Oh yeah. I can imagine her reaction at that order. Even if you did try to enforce it, I wouldn't make it through the night alive or with my balls intact."

"You're interested," Roane shot back.

The blonde vampire shrugged and poured a second drink. "Who wouldn't be? She's hot under all that black leather. Has no one told her the vampire cliché look is outdated? Look at me; most humans think I'm a professional athlete. I get more pussy looking like this than I ever would wearing leather chaps. No vampire magic needed."

"You did wear leather chaps. Assless."

"Still." Gavin shuddered and crossed to stand beside Roane. He looked out the window. "What are we looking at? Is that her down there?" He gestured with his drink and Roane glanced down.

His eyes fell on Davy, who was laughing with a hand over her mouth. Her mate had been telling a story with hand gestures that grew bigger with each drink she had. By the look in Davy's eyes, she knew her roommate was properly drunk, but she didn't mind.

Roane knew that had been Davy's intention, to make her friend forget her troubles. And he wondered if she had wanted to do the same thing.

Gavin watched the two in the booth and then watched his best friend of five hundred years. When Roane's eyes shifted and darkness replaced the shimmer of emotion that had been too brief to be caught, he already knew what the real story behind this war was.

He decided to change the subject. Further investigation would need to be had. "Tracey's coming, you know. What are you going to do about that?"

"She's the enemy."

Gavin choked on his drink. "The enemy? Are you dense? Tracey's not the enemy. She's Talia's sister. Oh no no no. She is not the enemy. She'll *never* be the enemy."

"She defected to the new Roane hunter. She's coming with their army."

Gavin rolled his eyes. "And you have Wren. She's the ace up your sleeve. Use her to get Tracey back with us. They were bosom buddies for years. Best friends, right?"

"I won't use Wren that way." Roane's voice was hard. "If she chooses to pursue a relationship with Tracey, then so be it. If she wants to bring her to us, then that is her choice."

"Oh hell, buddy." Gavin sat down his glass and grabbed the bottle. "You still have that stick up your ass, huh?"

A smile flashed over Roane's face. "I've named it. It's called Gavin."

"And your humor is piss poor. You know what your problem is? You're too noble. You need to not be so damn noble. Screw up once in awhile. Make a mistake on purpose."

"I did make a mistake."

"Not that, you didn't. You had to leave. You were ordered to leave." Gavin sighed as he saw how Roane's eyes hardened. There was no getting through to his best friend now. "Leaving Talia wasn't a mistake."

"She died because of it."

"There was more to it and you know it." He swung his eyes and watched the girl below. She had an aura around her. Gavin understood why Luke was captivated. "No one really knows what happened to bring that about, do we? It probably would've happened even if you had been there and you might've died because of it."

"Or I might've saved her life."

"Lucan found this one, didn't he? He would've found Talia. He would've bit her and he would've gotten her powers. This one stopped it. She was supposed to get the thread when she did."

"Maybe." Roane tossed the rest of his drink down his throat. Gavin handed him the bottle and soon the two were going back and forth, sharing drink for drink. When Luke excused himself, not long after the two girls left, Gavin resolved to meet this new Immortal. She had too much power over his best friend, more than he was comfortable with.

11

Over the next weeks, Pippa and I became friends. Emily started attending a grief counseling group and I persuaded her into taking over my hours at the hotline. Heaven forbid. I shuddered at the thought of spending more time in that building. Everything seemed normal until Emily left Pippa and me at the library.

"Hi, guys!" Brown drew next to our table. She panted and brushed a chunk of her sweaty hair off her face. She wore a bohemian dress that clung to her, all the way to her little toes that were in brown leather sandals. "Man, it's hot. Are you guys as hot as me?"

Pippa looked at me for a second. "I'm actually a little cold."

Brown laughed. "You're so funny. Werewolves aren't ever cold. At least, I didn't think they were."

We both sat up straight at that statement. "You know what she is?"

"Of course." Then she looked alarmed. "Wait, you didn't know? Oh my gosh. I am so sorry." She looked at Pippa and bit her lip. "You aren't going to eat me, are you?"

The wolf's mouth hung open. Not only did Brown know who

she was, but she just blabbed it like it was the weather. Then she slammed her with a stereotype right after.

I laughed.

"I can't do this." Pippa gathered up her books and left. Her back and shoulders were rigid at she went to the door.

Brown took her seat. "I did something wrong, didn't I? I have this problem. I speak without thinking sometimes."

"Really?" I tried to hold back my sarcasm.

She nodded. "I do and sometimes I overstep boundaries that I should know are there. I had no idea you didn't know. I'm sorry to you too. You're handling it really well. Do you know what that means, that she's a werewolf? They exist. Trust me."

"Brown." I leaned across the table. I wanted to make sure she heard me. "You need to stop talking about being a witch, or about werewolves, or about vampires. Ninety percent of the population doesn't believe in that stuff and the ones who do are going to be uncomfortable around you. You're going to get a reputation as being crazy and no one will talk to you or someone is going to hurt you." I leaned back. "So shut up."

Her eyes went wide. "Really? They'd think I was crazy?"

"I'm surprised it already hasn't happened."

"But it's just the truth. I lived in a community where witches and all that stuff were common. Everyone knew about it. People really don't know about it here?"

I shook my head. The girl was going to be an outcast.

"Oh my gosh. I have to tell you this. I haven't seen you since that last time I was at your room and by the way, here's the book I meant to take to you that day. Everything got so chaotic with my powers that day; I was in such a rush that I forgot to leave it for you."

"You brought that book to me?"

Then she produced it from her bag and it fell with a thud on the table. "Here it is! And don't worry. I did a little spell so you can walk through the door. The alarms won't go off. Promise. I've been in and out with this book many times since then." She caressed the tan dusty book in a loving gesture. "It has so many interesting tidbits in here. But you wanted it to learn about wolves, right? Probably because of the one that was just here, right?"

I shifted in my seat. Even I was uncomfortable. "You did a spell, huh?"

"Yeah." She tucked some of her curls behind her ears. "I know it's supposed to stay here, but that clerk really made me mad that day. I decided to take it with me and if he gets in trouble, he deserves it. Plus, I took it to my mom's business and made copies of it. I have three copies, just to be safe." She giggled. I could see she was proud.

"How illegal of you." I grinned and reached for the book. The cover had a velvety feel to it, but she was right." Thank you for the book. I have to head home now, though. Thanks a lot, Brown. Really." As I stood up and grabbed my bag, Brown stood in front of me. She looked uncertain and there was something swimming inside her. I could feel it. It wanted to come out at me, but I didn't know what it was.

Then she folded her hands in front of her. "Do you think you'd like to hang out sometime?" She laughed and her voice hitched higher. "You were right. I don't have any friends. I think it's because of what you said before. I talk too much, about things that I shouldn't. You're the only one who hasn't shunned me."

Oh goodness. She needed a friend.

"I thought, maybe, we could go for ice cream or something? Maybe coffee?" She gave me a tight smile. "I'll pay."

I closed my eyes. I couldn't believe I was going to do this, but there was something about her that I liked, even if she pushed the boundaries. "Okay. Maybe. I don't know. Tomorrow?"

She perked up. "Tomorrow would be great. Awesome! Thanks. I can't wait."

What had I gotten myself into? She flashed a radiant smile

and grabbed her bag, which was filled to the brim with books. Then she waved over her shoulder as she ran out of the library. "Thanks, Davy! I'll see you tomorrow." A clerk appeared in front of her, but Brown turned and as she did, her bag bounced on her back and decked the clerk in the face.

She hurried away and he held a hand to his face.

I shook my head and strolled past him with the book in my own bag. No matter what kind of a person she was, Brown was a witch. And she was right. Once that box inside of her that anchored all her magic was unlocked, she'd be a very powerful witch. Until then, I was glad it only let her do a little. She'd be lethal and out of control if it wasn't the case.

As I was walking to my dorm, a sudden wave of urgency washed over me. I stopped in the middle of the sidewalk and gasped. I bent over until my head touched the tops of my knees. I gasped again and felt like I was drowning. Wave after wave crashed over me and I heard a small voice in the distance, "Tell him, please. Tell him."

I gasped against the onslaught of waves. "Tell who? Tell him what?"

Another set of waves rocked my body. The sense of drowning increased. As I closed my eyes, I felt as if I was in the ocean and something held me down. It kept me from getting to the surface. Then, in the break of the waves, I heard the same voice. It was weaker than before. "Roane. Tell him about my daughter."

"What? What daughter?" He had a daughter?

As sudden as it had come upon me, it was gone. I stood there, gasping, and blinked away tears as I felt the campus around me. The air was calm, too calm. There was no ocean. There was only the sidewalk, a few buildings, and green lawn all around me. Then I looked to the side and saw Irene watching me. The angel statue hadn't aged a day since I'd sat beside it. She gave me the same expression she had that day.

I flicked her off. She made me feel crazy and it wasn't any of her business.

When I got in my room, I had closed the door when a voice murmured behind me, "Would you like to tell me why my best friend has declared war against the very Family he has only declared his loyalty to for the last five hundred years?"

My mouth fell open and I saw a vampire dressed in gym clothes. He had blonde hair that was cut short with tight curls. His blue eyes warned of depths and ominous promises and he was graced with a lean build that professional athletes had. Something told me this guy wasn't a professional athlete.

"Who are you?" I shut my door with a bang. "Your element of surprise doesn't work with me. Nor do you scare me. If your best friend is Luke Roane, we both know he has no idea you're here because he wouldn't be okay with that. And the fact that I know that means that anything else you might try to scare out of me is useless."

He snapped his mouth shut and clenched his jaw. It was a very manly looking jaw, rigid, tight, but his blue eyes had taken on a lethal look.

Craig had instilled a loathing for all vampires in me. Some of them, like Roane, promised me they weren't all the same. This vampire was like Craig. He wanted to scare me. He wanted to make me quake in my pants. Hell no. I was not going back to that person.

I felt the room shake as my rage built.

He glanced around, but he still seemed nonplussed.

"Get out." My eyes snapped their own warning.

He watched me and studied me intently for a moment, and then something shifted in his eyes. "You're the reason why he's doing this. It's not because you're the Immortal, it's because he cares about you."

The room stopped shaking, but then I heard footsteps in the

hallway. People were running. This guy didn't seem alarmed. He looked resigned.

"Who are you?" I clipped out and my eyes flashed. I knew he saw the Immortal's whites.

He scratched his forehead and shook his head. "You're not anything like her. I like that. That's okay with me." Then he held out his hand. "I go by Gavin. I'm Lucas' best friend. How are you?"

I stared at his hand like it was an alien limb that he extended. I had no plans to touch it. Since he knew who I was and didn't seem to be bothered with it, I smiled. "Wanna have a drink?" We both knew I didn't mean a normal beverage.

He drew his hand back in a heartbeat. "Ah no. I enjoy living how I am. That was a good one. Good trick." He bent forward as if tipping his hat to me. "You're a sneaky one. You've gotta be sneaky in this life. You'll do just fine."

The room started to shake again. This guy was pissing me off. He treated me like I was some newbie. But then I stopped. I was a newbie.

Then the door burst open and Brown panted, "I had a premonition. Sorry, I can't breathe." She bent over and took deep breaths. Once she had, she looked back up and smiled. "Why do you have a vampire in here?"

His eyes shifted again and he drew back. "You're a witch."

"Really?" I was dumbfounded. "You're scared of *her*?"

Brown hissed and then frowned at me. "Why shouldn't he be?"

Gavin withdrew to the window. "You won't hurt me whereas she could. Plus, I don't like witches."

"Only because you loved one once," Brown snorted and then clamped a hand over her mouth. "How did I know that? It must've been my powers."

All of this was annoying. I rolled my eyes and flicked a finger so the windows locked. I didn't want Gavin to escape so easily. Then I turned to her. "What was your premonition?"

"That you were drowning. But you look fine? Did you take a shower?"

"No."

Gavin's eyes darted from her to me. "You know her?"

I nodded.

Then he turned to her. "You know what she is?"

Her eyes leapt. "What? What is she?"

The room shook again, but he smirked back at me. Brown bounced around in a circle. Her eyes were wide as she looked around.

"She's dating my best friend." He smiled. "Luke Roane. Do you know who he is?"

"No." But she frowned. "Should I? I should, shouldn't I? You said it like I should've."

"Ah. No." I was starting to believe I lived in the insane asylum.

"You're dating Luke Roane?" Emily asked from the doorway. She looked as if she'd seen a ghost.

Oh, shit.

12

Emily stumbled forward, but grabbed Brown as if she were about to fall. "You know Luke?"

I closed my mouth and glanced at Gavin, who winked at me. *'Bastard vampire.'*

"Ooh, I heard that!" Brown squeaked.

Gavin looked at her, surprised. So did I, oh hell. If she could hear thoughts, this wasn't good.

"I just heard a thought! Someone thought, 'Bitch?' Is that right? Who would—" Then she jumped and looked at Emily, whose hand was now fisted into her sleeve. "Oh. Nevermind!" She sent us an impish grin. "My bad."

"What's going on?" Pippa stood in the doorway. Her hand stayed on the frame as if she was going to bolt any moment.

Emily turned to her. "Davy is a liar and a cheat. And a backstabber."

Pippa looked at me. Her mouth fell open and the questions flew over her mind. 'What happened? What is Davy lying about? I didn't know she was dating anybody—wait—she's not dating Emily, is she? That wouldn't be good. Oh no. Davy's looking at me! I forgot she can hear my thoughts. Davy, don't listen to me!'

I heard Gavin chuckle behind me and glared at him. I couldn't do anything to Emily or the other girls, but I could hurt him and before I realized what I was doing, a surge of power burst through me. My eyes shifted to the Immortal's whites.

'Get out!' I roared in my head.

The window flung open behind him, the screen disappeared and his body flew backwards, through it. It happened so fast, no one gasped before the screen had reappeared and the window was closed again.

A beat of silence filled the room. Then a thud was heard behind me. I whirled to find Emily on the floor.

Pippa screamed and dropped to her knees. "She fainted! Oh my goodness." Then she glared at me. "This is your fault."

Brown bounced up and down where she stood. "Did you see that?! That was amazing. I'm way more powerful than I thought!"

Pippa's mouth fell open and then closed it with a snap. "I cannot believe any of this."

"Is she okay?" I asked. I hesitated before I crossed the room and knelt beside my roommate.

"She fainted. She's not dead," Pippa snapped at me and stroked Emily's cheek. Then she went still and gasped again.

"What? What?" I reached out and clamped a hand on the wolf's arm. Instantly, I heard her thoughts and was in the swirl of her emotions. They were memories intermixed with images. I saw Pippa as a little girl with the same two braids and overalls. Then I saw her as a puppy. She had a coat of tawny-colored fur. She was running around, stumbling from paws that were too big for her. Then there was another image of a young man. His face was round in shape with brown hair that looked messily rumpled. His eyes stared straight at me, as if he could see me.

I ripped out of her, but not before I heard her shock, *'She's already met him. It's Pete!'*

As I sat back on my heels, I knew Pippa was hurt that she

hadn't been told this. Something in her had assumed she would've known right away.

She looked at me, dazed. "He saw you. He knows who you are. And he's going to tell her."

My throat had a knot in it. "Who is he? Who is Pete to you?"

"He's no one. He's another wolf. That's all." She jerked upright and grabbed our dresser for balance.

'Like hell he was no one to her.'

I stood, slower, and watched the wolf. A myriad of emotions were flashing across her face, one after another. I knew Brown saw it too and she came to stand beside me. Then Pippa shook her head again and muttered, "I can't handle this."

She rushed from the room. The door remained open behind her and a second later, hers slammed shut.

Brown jumped from the sound. "Oh wow. Geez." She looked at me. "Are all wolves like that? She's jumpy for how quiet she seems. They repress too much for their well-being."

"Werewolves repress a lot. They're very secretive."

"I know. It's not healthy. Humans have a better balance of their primal and logical side. Vampires are all about the primal and werewolves are all about the logical. It's not right. There should be something that fixes it and everyone can be happy. Hmmm. Maybe I could do a spell?"

I shuddered at the thought before I started to lift Emily to the couch. Brown picked up her legs and we placed her gently down. After I covered her with a blanket, I sat at my desk with no idea how to repair anything. There had been too much damage done.

Brown sat the edge of my bed. I felt her presence trying to comfort me. "Who is Luke Roane?"

What did I even say about him? "He's complicated."

"Are you two dating like that guy said?"

Hell. Were we? "No. We're not dating."

"But you want to?"

I glanced up and felt strangely vulnerable.

She smiled to reassure me. "It's okay if you said you want to. You wouldn't be the first girl to fall for a guy they couldn't have. It's common." Her eyes saddened.

Then I stopped thinking. I let it out. "It's not how Emily thinks. I didn't meet him through her. We met because, it's complicated, but it has to do with something that happened to me, something that no one knows about. He's been helping me with it or he did help me with it until recently. Things happened. We crossed the line, did things, but we haven't since—" I took a deep breath. "Since I found out that he's in love with someone else who is dead and who died because of—he still loves her and she's still dead. Then he has this other friend who hates me. Roane's come to see me a few times, but it's never just to see me. It's always to check on me. He wants to make sure I'm okay. He feels like it's his duty that I'm okay. And Emily knew him from a class. I knew she liked him, but I didn't realize how strong her feelings were until now."

"Who's Pete?"

I shrugged. "I have no idea. She hasn't told me about him."

"Do you blame me?" Emily asked. She sat up, looking pale. "I fainted, didn't I?"

Brown and I nodded.

Emily rolled her eyes. "That's so embarrassing."

"It happens to me all the time, especially when I try a powerful spell." She shrugged. "Or when I do any spell."

My roommate caught my gaze. "Is that true? Everything you just said?"

I nodded. I couldn't shake that vulnerable feeling.

She groaned and fell backwards. "How am I supposed to be mad at you now? You sound like you're in love with him and can't be with him. I hate this. I hate it."

Brown sighed, "I think it's romantic. She loves him, but he loves someone else. He still wants to make sure she's okay."

"Shut up," Emily said at the same time I did.

We glanced at each other and both grinned. Then I cleared my throat. "I'm sorry about Luke. I really am."

Emily dismissed me. "Don't worry about it. I'm not even that upset. I'm hurt. I feel like you went behind my back, but it's not like you're the only one keeping secrets. You know about Pete?" She blinked then. "How do you know about Pete?"

Uh, hell. "Pippa knows him and she figured it out. Don't ask me how. I have no idea." I gestured towards the door. "She took off. I think she's pretty hurt you didn't tell her about him."

"Why would I? I wanted to keep him to myself for a little bit. I hadn't even told you and I would've told you first. You're my closest friend here."

Warmth spread through me when I heard that. I felt so touched, honored. I realized then Emily had become one of my best friends. She might not know as much about me as Kates did, but she defended me at times. "Thanks, Em."

"I want friends like you." Brown blinked back tears. "You guys are so awesome to each other. You both are so understanding. It's so much. This is so great."

Emily sat back. "Do you do drugs?"

"See. Like that! You're so honest with each other, with me too." Brown laughed to herself. "And I don't do drugs, but I can see why you might think that."

Emily asked me, "Was she hurt that I hadn't said anything? I didn't know she knew Pete."

"I think," I chose my words very carefully. "I think she feels like she's closer to you than you think you are to her and yes, it looked to me that she knew Pete. It looked like there was some history between her and him."

"Who is Pete?" Brown plopped down between us. Emily looked down at her hands. Then Brown added, "Don't be shy now. We all know. You heard about Davy and this Roane character. Your turn."

Emily looked back up and glared. Then she gave up the fight.

"I met him at the grief group I've been going to. It's so amazing. He's so amazing. He's funny and smart and nice and just wonderful." She smiled to herself with a dreamy look on her face. "He's there because he lost someone close to him and needed to talk to people who understood. He said no one understood. When I went in and sat down at the first meeting it was love at first sight." She sighed. "I love him, Davy. He's so amazing. I feel like a part of me is home now. It's like I'm complete with him."

I smiled. "That's wonderful, Emily. It really is." I kept the sharp retort that she'd felt the same with Bennett in the back of my mind.

Brown's head swiveled between us. "If you're in love with this Pete, why were you mad at Davy about this other guy?

The dreamy look vanished.

I sighed. It was now awkward again.

Emily stood up. "I wasn't mad about the guy. I was mad because she lied to me."

"What did she lie about? I mean, she just didn't tell you, did you?"

"It's different." I placed a hand on Brown's arm.

"It's not different. She's falling in love with some guy and never said a word to you, but she's mad at you. You never told her about this guy you fell in love with even though he's with someone else? So you're not even with him. You met him separately from her."

I gave a small shrug. "There were different circumstances, but Emily feels I betrayed her because she knew him and I never told her that I did."

"But you didn't because it was too painful to say anything. Who wants to tell someone that you like a guy she knows too, but he's with someone else? What's the point then? That's humiliating. I'd keep that to myself too. I don't think you did anything wrong."

Emily stood in front of her closet. Her head was bent. Her door was still closed and she didn't move.

Brown looked at me. "You didn't do anything wrong. If Emily can fall in love with someone and not tell you, she wouldn't say a thing if she liked someone who loved someone else. She wouldn't want to be embarrassed in front of you and she would be because you're more—"

I clamped a hand over Brown's mouth. Whatever she was about to say did not need to be said. After she quieted and sat back on the couch, I let go and watched my roommate. What was she thinking and why was I so hesitant to read her thoughts?

Then I closed my eyes. I had to go in there. I had to violate my roommate. And I heard, *'Pete said she wouldn't understand. No one would. He said that she couldn't know. Am I wrong in not telling her? I didn't lie because—yes I did. Who am I lying to? Myself? That stupid girl is right. I wouldn't have told Davy if Pete hadn't felt the same as me. What do I do now? Pete, come help me.'*

Suddenly the whole room shook again. The ferocity of it shocked even me and I stood. This wasn't me. This wasn't Brown. What was coming?

Brown gasped, excited and scared at the same time.

Emily looked around, but there was a waiting look in her. That's when I realized that she knew what he was. She had asked for him to come and she thought it was him coming.

Pippa ran to our door and braced herself. "What's going on?"

Brown screamed, "Something's happening!"

Then it stopped and the air felt eerie. I had a moment to wonder what stood outside our door before three bursts of light exploded from the hallway. Pippa fell to the ground. Emily crumbled. And Brown dropped. All of them were unconscious.

"What?" I gaped at them.

Saren stood in the doorway, in blue leather this time. The fire in her eyes was blazing and it smoldered in the air. A burning smell filled the room. "We have to go. Now."

"What did you just do?" I couldn't look away from their fallen bodies.

"They aren't dead, but they will be soon if I don't get you out of here."

"But—"

She grabbed my hand and both of us teleported. The room wrapped around us and we were on our feet in an alley somewhere.

I threw down Saren's hand. "What just happened?!"

She ignored me and scanned our surroundings. "We're safe. For now."

"Saren!" I clipped out. "Fill me in on what's going on or I'm going back. I'll figure it out for myself."

A burst of fire exploded from her eyes. It zapped and burned me before she retracted it. "Don't threaten me. I am still your superior and you need me if you're going to survive the near future."

"What?!" My mouth hung open. Again. "What are you talking about?"

She stopped and turned to me. "Do you know what kind of wolf your roommate is mixed up with?"

"Like Pippa? She's harmless."

"The girl is. He's not. Pete Young is the next leader of the werewolf nation. He's at your school to unite the werewolves for an uprising against the vampires."

"They're going to war with them?"

"The werewolves have laid low for thousands of years, but they're strong. Their power is ancient, more ancient that the vampires and it's rising again. Pete Young is meant to bring them together. They don't want to replace vampires, but they want to usurp them. And this guy is the equivalent of your vampire to their species."

A part of me was proud of Emily. "But what does that have to do with me?"

"She called him. He was going to her, fast. The second he got there he would've felt your power and tried to drain you from it. He wouldn't have been able to stop himself."

"Vampires can't sense my power. Why could he?" Pippa hadn't sensed my powers.

Saren sighed in frustration and paced up and down the alley. She was tense, ready for a fight. "We should be moving and not talking. He probably sensed your trail and could be coming after us."

"Stop!" I held onto her shoulders. "He's just a werewolf, right? Right?"

Saren shook her head. "He's not *just* a werewolf. He's got power, magic in him. He was created using the essence of the Immortal thread from a dead Immortal."

"Talia?"

"Her mother. The wolves took her mother after Lucan and Lucas left her. They took the essence of the thread that was still in her body with magic."

I had no idea how to figure this all out. "What? Huh?"

She rolled her eyes and sighed in disgust. "It's like a boat that makes waves in the water. They caught the waves that remained after the boat had left. Does that make sense to your human brain?"

"Hey! Back off, fiery witch from hell! You think I like this? You think I like running from magical beings?" I snapped at her and then ran a hand through my hair. "You said that my friends would've died if we hadn't left. Why? What would've happened?"

"When he tried to drain you, you would've defended yourself. You still don't know your powers. Your reaction would have been stronger than you wanted and would have killed him. You would've killed your friends too. I stopped it from happening. I stopped him from figuring out who you are, at least until we can figure out how to blanket your powers to him."

"Oh! So I can go back?" At her dark look, I added, "Sometime?"

Saren rolled her eyes. They looked like sparklers waving in the air. Then she stalked off with her leather-clad legs rubbing against each other.

I took in the sight of her black hair flowing behind her, sleek and shiny with her blue leather outfit. "You look like a superhero right now. Did you go for that on purpose?"

She sighed in disgust. The blue leather transformed into a black-colored outfit. The fabric was loose and flowed behind her, billowing in the wind. She kept going.

"Can I do that? Can you show me how to do that?"

She barked over her shoulder, "We have work to do."

"Where are we?"

13

"Not to be a nag, but where are we going?" I followed behind Saren as we walked down another set of streets. We'd been walking in circles for the last hour. I wasn't sure if she was aware of the attention she was attracting dressed like a rich person in the back streets that accumulated the back street type of person. A few homeless. A few drunks. More than a few illegal activities were going on around us.

Saren kept trudging around and cursed underneath her breath.

She whipped back to me now. "What do you think I'm doing? I'm mixing your scent with all these other things. He's good. He's going to be able to pick your scent out of all these places, but I want him confused."

"I get that, but where are we going? Shouldn't we go?"

She rolled her eyes. "You are so human, it annoys me." Then she grabbed my hand and we were whisked into another teleport. When we stopped, I looked around and saw only cement floors. There were no windows, just open areas in brick walls. A tree had grown in the corner of our room with vines that climbed up the wall and onto the ceiling. A few flowers intermingled among the vines.

"Where are we? Is this some magical place?"

"It's an abandoned castle, used by a coven that was killed off in the early 1800s." Saren left for another room.

I followed, wide eyed. "Castle? Are you serious? I didn't think we had castles in America."

She stopped and glanced over her shoulder. "We're not in America anymore."

My eyes went even wider. "What?"

Then she kept going, down some steps that looked like they had been put together with brick and cement by hand.

"Where are we?"

"It doesn't matter." She strode through another opening and then paused before an altar. A moment later, she lit candles on it. A banner hung from it with a sign that looked like a hand surrounded with weaving loops of rope. A tiny blade of grass grew out of the middle of the hand.

"What does that mean?"

Saren stopped and looked where I pointed. The hand seemed to turn till it was pointed at me. It looked like it was stretched for my own to take it in a hold. Her voice was quiet. "It's the sign of the Immortal."

"The sign of me?"

"No. It's the sign of its creator, the true essence of the Immortal, what created it from the thread."

I swallowed. "You told me before not to talk to Blue. Then before that, I was told that Jacith wasn't the real creator. The vampires all think he is. They think he's some super powerful sorcerer. I don't know, but Roane told me before that Jacith created the Immortal. What's the real story?"

Saren watched me for a moment and then the air circled around her. It picked up speed and her eyes gleamed. Dust rose up from her feet and moved upwards. It covered her entire body until I couldn't see her through it. Then it stopped and everything fell back in place.

Saren didn't look like Saren anymore. The black hair was gone. The fire eyes had been replaced with soft almond ones. The black outfit was now a white robe wrapped around her body. Her hair was a golden wheat color, braided in crowns on top of her head. She smiled and I knew then this was not Saren.

"My name is Sireenia. I am a sister to Saren and Stepianhas, your last guide."

"Are you my new guide?" I wasn't sure I'd miss Saren.

She smiled again. It was a tender look. "No, but I will help you along the way. Saren is your guide for a reason. She will fight when you are unable to. No one will harm you and many will try. She is here to help you embrace your powers because you are very powerful, but you need to become your powers."

"Who is Jacith? How is my old sponsor involved?"

"You are ready for some answers. We can tell that you know more than you think." She gestured to the side where a chair carved in rock appeared. Another was beside it and we both sat in them. Sireenia folded her hands in her lap. All her movements were graceful. "Your empathic sponsor was assigned to you for a reason. She came from a long line of witches that worshiped their original sorcerer Jacith. Her attributes matched yours. You needed someone who was motherly, but aloof. She was that, but she also had a sense of purpose that you respected. She had humor that met yours. She was picked for you and her assignment was to bring you to Jacith when the thread went into you."

My eyes were wide and my soul felt like it had a hole in it. It was gaping open. Everything she said was true.

Sireenia had been watching me and then took my hand. I felt her calm enter me and the peace soothed over everything, all my agitation, panic, and it even seemed to lick other wounds inside of me.

"You're very beautiful." She held my eyes. "They've told me of your will, your spirit, but they haven't shared your looks. Do you know how beautiful you are?"

I looked away. Then she squeezed my hand and I looked back. "You're not normally bashful. Why are you now? You know you're attractive."

I had no idea. "You're so direct. No one's told me like that." I knew I wasn't ugly, but I never thought about my looks. I wasn't known for them. I was the carefree, funny one.

"Oh. Maybe they should've." Then she winked and sat back. "But you're right. We're not here about your looks. I'm here because you wanted to learn about Jacith and Saren didn't want to be the one to tell you. She wanted me to explain it to you so here we go."

My fingers dug into the armrests of my chair and I braced for what I was about to hear.

Sireenia looked at me warmly. "Jacith used to be Jacob Withering. It's an old name with old roots and he wanted a new one. He didn't want ties to where he came from so he changed it to Jacith when he became a vampire. He lived and ruled under the normal hierarchy that each vampire does, with their Family that might be allied with other Families and so forth. This was all fine until Jacith met a witch one day. He fed from her and she turned him human. Jacith was fascinated by this. He loved the power it gave him and he had her turn him back into a vampire.

This began his long fall into sorcery and dark magic, but he kept his darkness from his vampire Family. They thought he used his magic for good, but he didn't. Even then his Family strove to protect the humans; they felt it would restore their own humanity so they wouldn't forget their true beginnings. They knew if they did forget it would only be a matter of time before all was lost. Madness and chaos would ensue. The slayers were created for this reason and then the decree occurred and hunters now hunt their own. Jacith wanted to win favor with the ruling Queen. He wanted to use her power for himself. He could use it for more magic so he created the Immortal prophecy.

He had hoped the legend of the Immortal, which would balance all powers in the universe, would make her happy. It did. She fell in love with him and he's slowly been draining her of all her power. He only created the thread of the Immortal, which vampires could get power from. He thought this was the Immortal."

There was so much I didn't understand, but I asked the one question that burned in my mind. "Is he still alive?"

She smiled, saddened. "He is and he is protected still by the Romah Family, the most powerful of all vampire Families. The Roane family is second to them, but they protect the Romah Family. They are their guardians. It's an alliance that has never been broken. Your vampire is hoping to destroy that alliance, but it'll create a divide instead. The Romah and Roane Family will bind together against him and they'll never see reason. They believe to this day that Jacith is a good sorcerer. They believe he created the Immortal for balance and equality."

"Why does the thread only go from human to human?"

"The Romah Family felt humans were sacred so Jacith made the thread to remain solely in humans. If a vampire did take on the thread inside of them, it would jump to the first human they encountered. He didn't inform the Queen that once the vampire fed from an Immortal, that vampire would have enormous power. They found this out after the first human and then protected the Immortal from that day forward. Of course, Jacith said that he hadn't known it would do that. After a hundred thousand years, they entrusted the Immortal to be defended by the Roane Family, which is why Lucas, their best hunter, became Talia's protector."

But I was the Immortal. I didn't have the thread. Jacith didn't intend for a true Immortal to ever come. The first guide had told me that.

She held my hand and squeezed it. "Jacith thought that a human with the mere thread of the Immortal would be the Immortal. He never realized the thread would take a life of its own and become an actual entity. That is what you are. You have been infused with the essence of life; this is why you make the undead alive. You take away their death."

I shook my head. There was so much information. I couldn't understand all of it. Then Sireenia whispered, "You will in time. You will know all. You will understand all."

"Why are you telling me this now?"

Her hand cupped my cheek. "You are so beautiful. You need to know this because Jacith is going to be your enemy. He is going to try and take the Immortal out of you. He will try to destroy it all."

"Why?" I felt gutted.

"Because you are not what he created. He cannot control you. He cannot control us. And he will fear you once the Romah and Roane Elders realize what you really are. "

"What do I do then?"

"You will fight him. You were created to destroy him. We were created to help you. He is too powerful for the world to have. He is the unbalance, not you."

When she put it like that, I wanted to crap my pants. "I'm not ready for that! I'm not ready for him! What if he comes tomorrow? What if he already knows? What am I going to do?"

My heart started to race and everything swirled around me. I tried concentrating on Sireenia, but she looked as if she were swimming around me. She flailed her arms at me. When I asked what was happening to me, my voice sounded in the distance and a baritone tone had taken root in my throat. Then my body felt like it was falling backwards.

I heard Saren in the distance, "Snap her out of it, Sire. We need her with us, not in the Orca."

"If she goes, then Stepianhas will calm her down."

A burst of energy zapped me. I felt like my insides had exploded, but I jerked upright from the chair, gasping and pounding my chest. My heart had stopped. When I didn't hear the constant beat again, I looked up, terrified. "What—what—what just happened?" I fell off my chair and scrambled to my feet. I pounded on my chest. "My heart stopped. My heart isn't beating. I don't—"

They stood before me. Sireenia had her hands folded in front of her. Saren had her hands on her hips. Then she snapped, "You're immortal. You're not going to die. Ever. Your heart is the least of your problems right now."

"Wha—but—my heart!" I gasped with each word. They didn't understand. They weren't human anymore. "I need to be normal. I need my heart to beat!"

They glanced at each other and a look was shared between them.

"Stop that! Stop looking at each other about me. Do something. You're all magical things. Make my heart beat again. Please." I nearly sobbed the last word. It felt like my world had changed. It was irreversible. Everything shifted in that moment and I didn't want it to happen. I didn't want to fight this guy. I didn't want to have to deal with the fact that my heart didn't beat like Emily's, Brown's, or Pippa's.

Then Saren stepped forward. She spoke with authority, "You're doing this to yourself. You stopped your heart. Only you can make it start again. Calm down. CALM!"

Everything stopped.

I stopped and I felt my body jerk upright. I stood at my highest height.

She took my shoulders then in her hands and looked me straight in the eyes. Her fire was mesmerizing. "You stopped it. You can make it start." Then she kept repeating that until I found myself mouthing the words with her. After a few minutes, I felt my heart start again.

Thump, thump, thump

"It's okay!" I exclaimed. "I'm okay. I'm going to be okay." But I wasn't. I had so much more to do and I wanted to cry. I wanted to bury my head in a pillow and make everything go away.

"I think that's enough for sharing time." Saren released my shoulders and sat in my vacant chair. She threw a blue-leathered leg over the side and pursed her lips.

"Hey, you changed your outfit back."

She shrugged. "It's my favorite. I don't care what you think."

"Oh."

Sireenia watched me during our exchange and glided forward now. "Are you okay, Davy?"

I jerked my shoulders in a casual shrug. I could be casual about this. They were. I could be one of them. Then I broke. "No! No, I'm not!"

She sighed.

Saren waved her away. "She'll be fine. She's a fighter. Besides, I have to work with her now."

"Are you sure that's a good idea? She seems fragile right now." Sireenia bit her lip as she watched me.

"She's fine. Go. Brood up something so we can disguise her power to that wolf. The sooner we can get her back, the better."

"Okay." But Sireenia glanced at me over her shoulder as she left.

"Catch!" Saren called out to me as I looked back at her. Something slammed into me and I flew against the wall.

I glared at her. "What was that about?"

She smirked and gestured at me. "Look at yourself."

I did. I was flat against the wall in mid-air. My mouth fell open. "Are you doing that?"

"You caught yourself. I bet you didn't dent the wall."

I let my body glide downwards. I asked as my feet touched the floor, "Was I supposed to?"

"Someone normal would've gone through three buildings.

You barely touched the first wall. You're good, better than you think." Then she reared back to throw her power again. This time I saw it coming.

The power radiated from her toes and rose through her body. It built in power until she released it at me.

14

"Do my eyes deceive me or is that your missing girlfriend's roommate down there? And is she sitting with a wolf?" Gavin glanced over his shoulder where Roane was sitting at his desk. Then he looked back down at the booth below.

Roane glanced up from his paperwork and stood beside his best friend. The view was massive, writhing bodies below, flashing lights everywhere, but he saw where Gavin had his eyes trained and there she was, Emily. She looked different, serious and gaunt, but there was a glow about her too. The guy next to her had a lean build with a round baby face, but his eyes weren't babyish at all. They had seen too much. He was scanning the nightclub, on the prowl with an intelligence that told Roane he wasn't there by accident.

Gavin grunted. "He's got balls being in your establishment."

Roane narrowed his eyes and watched how the wolf leaned over and placed a kiss on Emily's jaw. He lingered there, sending a possessive claim to the rest of the club. "He knows that he's being watched right now."

"Of course he's being watched. He's a wolf in enemy territory."

Roane walked back to his desk and grabbed a small dagger that he tucked into his pocket. "Come on. Let's get this over with." As they walked to the door, Roane held it open and then murmured in Gavin's ear as he passed by, "You know he's the Alpha, right?"

Gavin halted and wheeled around. "What? Why didn't you say something before?"

Roane shook his head with a small grin. He kept going and made his best friend follow at a slower pace. "He's here trying to get her scent. And I'm guessing that he knows who I am too."

"The roommate knows about you and Davy. I spilled the beans the last time I was there."

"You told me." And he had, followed by an apology every day since Davy had gone missing. It'd been three months and no one had a lead where she'd gone to. Gavin had included a detailed account of what had happened, but promised that she'd been fine when she shoved him out of her window. The roommate and a witch had been there with her, but no one could figure out what happened. Roane had listened to all the testimonies they gave to the police. Emily and the witch, along with another wolf, had been knocked unconscious. None of them could explain how Davy had gone. No vampire caught her scent. No wolf could either, but Roane had a very strong hunch that the Alpha had been persuaded to try again. If the Alpha wolf was in his club, he was at the end of the rope.

"You think he's here for a brawl?" Gavin asked in his ear, treading close behind him as they both weaved around vampires and drunken humans. Some were laughing. Some were drinking. Others were doing more.

"He might be the Alpha, but he's not stupid. He's outnumbered five hundred to one. Emily's desperate to find Davy." Then they turned one last time and the Alpha sensed them immediately.

He could smell Talia's blood, or the blood of her mother on

him. It clung to the wolf like a third skin and it made his own stomach churn.

As they drew near the booth, Roane waited till Emily looked up. As soon as she did, she gasped and shrunk back in her seat. Gavin smiled brightly and slid in next to her. Roane sat beside him. They pushed the couple to the far end of the circular booth till the Alpha was directly across from Roane. Both of their gazes were locked on each other.

Emily glanced between them. She was nervous. Roane could smell it. He also felt her desperation. Her hand fell to the Alpha's lap and was gripped by his. He held it in a comforting hold and Roane grinned. "Should I give congratulations to the happy couple?"

Emily flushed and skirted further underneath the table.

He broke eye contact with the wolf and locked onto Emily who wanted to look anywhere, but at him. It was then, seeing a blush on her cheeks, that he knew she still had feelings for him.

The wolf's nostrils flared, smelling her desire, but he didn't comment. Both Gavin and Roane smelled it.

"Emily," Roane said softly, but with a twinge of authority in his voice. She shouldn't avoid this and he wanted to remind her of that. When she looked up and held his gaze, he knew she registered his meaning. She even sat up straight and squared her shoulders back. Her hand still held onto the wolf's hand with a death grip. "You know about Davy and me."

She cleared her throat and took a deep breath. "Yes. Yes, I do."

Gavin looked between them and then at the wolf. He rolled his eyes. "This is boring and awkward. Someone start talking or I'm leaving."

"Uh." Emily seemed at a loss for words. She shook her head and shrunk back in the seat.

Roane was taken aback. He remembered an assertive nerd from his classes on campus. He knew she'd taken a liking to him, but he also remembered how she was never at a loss for words.

Davy had respect for her roommate, how she never feared tough situations or what to say, even if the truth was the hardest to deal with. This was not that girl. Then the Alpha held out his free hand and sat forward.

"My name is Pete Young."

Roane shook his hand, feeling strength and confidence. The Alpha was strong, the strongest he'd ever met in a wolf, but he was young. And he didn't know all the pieces, though he knew too much for Roane's liking.

"Lucas Roane. I own this nightclub."

"I know. We know. It's why we came here." Pete glanced around, a sense of unease teased at the edge of his surface. "I know that you and Emily know each other from college and that you were somewhat dating her roommate, Davy?" He looked to her for reassurance and she sighed and sat forward again.

"Do you know where Davy is?" Emily asked in a husky voice.

"I'm your last resort, aren't I?"

She jerked her head in a nod. "No one knows where she is. I can't get a hold of Kates. I don't know Davy's family and that blue lady can't find her either. She was freaking out the last time I talked to her. She said that no one could 'feel her on this world's aura' whatever that means."

"So you came to me." Roane nodded and caught Gavin's eye in the same movement.

'What are you thinking?' Gavin thought in his head.

Roane spoke to Emily, "And you've called the police?" He looked at Gavin. 'We need to get the Alpha out of here. He has the Immortal essence in him, Talia's mother. He can't know what we know about Davy.'

Gavin's eyelid twitched, but no other muscle moved on his face. 'Didn't the police report say that he showed up at their room the day Davy disappeared? Do you think he has something to do with it?'

Emily frowned, playing with a napkin on the table. "The police have no idea what happened. Davy was in the room with us and then it's like she just disappeared. Our dorm has video surveillance on all the exits and she's not in any of them."

Roane knew all of this. He read over every document, every witness testimony that the detectives had gotten from the event. None of it made sense to him except one item. It was tied to the Immortal. It was the only thing that made sense. If a vampire had been able to take her, he would've known by now. If another supernatural species had found out about her, he would've known too. He was linked to her and he agreed with the 'blue lady'. Davy wasn't nearby, maybe not even in the country or in their time line. The Immortal had infinite powers. She could be in another universe and he had no idea how to find her.

He smiled politely. "Unfortunately, I haven't heard from Davy for awhile before she went missing. We'd called things off because of, well for various reasons."

Emily ducked her head down and sucked in her breath. Pete glanced at her, but then understanding dawned. He jerked his eyes back up and stared at Roane. Lucas knew it was coming, felt the wolf sniffing through every layer of thought and emotion he had in him, but he steeled himself against the investigation. Yes, Pete knew there was history between Emily and Roane, but he was just now starting to guess the true nature of that history.

Then with a distant smile, Roane thrust Gavin from his head and met the Alpha full force. *'She didn't tell you the truth, did she?'*

Pete sat back, shocked and enraged. His lip started to quirk upwards in a growl. *'She told me you two were friends, nothing of what I'm getting from her now. Were you lovers? Did you throw her away once you were done as vampires always do? You discard people who care for you, treat them like garbage.'*

Roane's eyes narrowed. *'Emily had a crush on me. That was it. Your mate has never had any sort of relationship with me other than that of a classmate. That is all. We were not even friends. Search her mind. You'll find the truth.'*

'I don't go in her head unless she wants me to. I respect her privacy.'

A cruel smirk came over Roane and his eyes mocked. *'That's the biggest piece of bullshit I've ever heard a wolf tell me. You bulldoze your way through her head and heart, sniffing under every emotion she has, any memory from her past. You didn't find me because I'm telling you the truth. She had a school girl crush on me, still does apparently. And it means nothing to me.'*

Pete's eyes went feral and he surged to his feet.

Roane stood to meet him, calm as he smiled in his adversary's face. Gavin followed at a slower pace, but grinned in excited anticipation. He had a cocky glint to his eyes as he waited for the wolf to pounce. He thirsted for it even.

Emily sucked in her breath. The blood had drained from her face.

Gavin winked at her. "Don't worry, love. The two baddies need to figure out which is the alpha and who's the loser." Then his eyes found Pete's and he said with more promise, "Because there's always only one Alpha."

Pete drew back his thoughts and his fury was quickly gone. He forced a smile and looked down to grab Emily's hand. After he pulled her up and wrapped an arm around her shoulder, he laughed and forced a carefree note. "I can tell that Roane cared for Davy. If he knew where she was, he'd tell us. He misses her as much as you do." A sinister smile came over him as he thought, *'You're right about one thing. I can tell that Davy meant more to you than you want to admit. It's all over your thoughts. You're as desperate to find her as Emily is, but you're not as scared as her. You know more than you're telling. I intend to find out what that is.'*

Gavin narrowed his eyes. *'Go and pee somewhere else. This isn't your territory. It'd be a shame if a vampire decided to sneak a little taste from your lover. You know how powerful those spells can be, don't you? Or have you already tasted the last vampire that's been in her?'*

Pete snarled and showed his teeth.

"Pete!" Emily gasped as she clutched onto his arm.

Alerted by the sounds of a werewolf, the vampires

surrounding them dropped their conversations and turned. They squared off against the werewolf.

Gavin taunted, "Everyone here knows what you are. They stayed away because you seemed that you were under friendly terms. Those terms are gone and even a wolf as powerful as you can't take everyone here, not when there's a hunter in the room."

Emily squeaked and fell down. Pete caught her with one arm as he glared across the table at both vampires. "I could kill both of you in a heartbeat, then thirty more before any of them could touch me."

"They'd get her." Roane narrowed his eyes and watched as Emily seemed to swoon unsteadily on her feet. *'She doesn't know who we are. If you hope to protect her, you need to tell her everything.'*

The Alpha drew back. *'You talk now as if you care for her. Before, you were disrespectful to her.'*

"Not everything I do will make sense to you," Roane chose his words carefully. He wanted the wolf to feel unbalanced. He didn't want the Alpha to start connecting dots.

Pete stood at his fullest height. "I think we should leave. I've gotten the answer that we came for anyway." He watched the vampires around them cautiously as he edged out of the booth and then down the aisle.

Roane caught Gregory's gaze, who had been standing in a far corner. He nodded and then gestured towards the wolf. Gregory bent his head.

Gavin watched Gregory follow them and chuckled. "Let's hope the Viking can jump rooftops. That's the only way he's going to be able to follow that wolf."

"He can." Roane turned away and saw Wren in another corner. She was wrapped around another female vampire.

Both stopped and watched the display for a second and then Gregory burst out laughing. Wren looked up, but then bent back to her lover's neck, sucking on it. The other vampire seemed unaffected, unaware that Wren had ever stopped and clutched the back of her head. She moaned as she pressed closer against her.

As they went back to Roane's office, Gavin helped himself to a drink. "What do you think of the wolf? He's a powerful young pup."

Roane went to his tinted windows and watched below. "He is strong, stronger than the old Alpha, but he's young."

"Human age, he's what? 30s?"

"At least." Roane frowned as Wren grabbed another female vampire and included her in their embrace. All three were quickly caressing, kissing, licking, and gaining more attention than Roane wanted his second right-hand vampire to obtain. When a male pressed into the group, Roane saw that Wren grabbed his head and shoved it against her breast. He latched on and kneeled with one of the other women.

Gavin stood next to him and lifted his glass in a salute. "Here's to Wren getting an orgy. She knows how to fulfill that need, huh?"

"Most of these vampires have crossed the world, pledging their loyalty to me. They came because of my reputation of an honorable hunter. That's not honorable. That's primal. We're above that."

"Oh come on. Looks to me that Wren's just stressed. She's letting out some of her tension. When's Tracey supposed to arrive?"

"You mean with my sworn enemy?" Roane couldn't stop a smile as he regarded his best friend.

Gavin opened his mouth, but it hung there, suspended. Then he laughed and shut it. "I forgot about that little detail. Sorry, mate. You know what you're going to have to do, right?"

"What's that?"

"Just rip the new hunter's head off his body and take his army as yours. It was yours anyway. The Elders forced a new hunter, because they want to kill the Immortal and you want to protect her. Such a trivial little difference, you know? I think all those vampires will be thankful that you're making them follow you. You're a much better leader than they could ever get and you know it. They know it. Hell, even the new hunter knows it."

Roane grew somber, but then a hard glint appeared in his eyes. "They chose what side they were on, as all of these vampires here have. They've chosen my side."

"Because they believe in what you believe in." Gavin finished his drink and spoke with gravity. "There's a civil war brewing in the vampire nation. Every one of us knows it and the Immortal is the reason for it. Half of them don't even believe she exists. They're here because you stand for the new age, for a different standard of our living. That's why they're here. For you, not for Davy. They don't even know who she is or why you've stood your ground against the Roane Elders."

"Don't forget the Romah Elders."

"Forget those old bastards. They're so ancient; I could snap them in half. They've grown rusty, gotten too used to being protected by the Roane Family."

"Jacith is aligned with them."

Gavin narrowed his eyes at his best friend, who stared at the club below. "Maybe it's time for Jacith to end, huh?"

Roane smirked and now looked at Gavin. "And who's going to do that? Jacith is old. He's powerful as a vampire and he's powerful as a sorcerer. He'd snap you in half."

"I'm not saying that I have all the answers. I'm just telling you my opinion of them. I'm sure I'm not alone. If you were to declare war against the Romah Family, I'm sure you'd have more than my Family behind you, maybe even every vampire Family in the nation."

"Not the Mori Nation."

Gavin opened his mouth, but snapped it shut. "They don't count. They're freaks of nature."

Roane barked out a laugh, but stopped. "Are you serious? You know that's where Lucan is hiding. He might even be one of them by now."

"The birthing baby vampire magic circus? No. He's not one of them." Gavin's eyes grew dangerous. "No, no. He's not one of them. He's human. And he wants them to kidnap Davy and force the thread from her. Everyone knows the lore. It'll attach to the closest human. Oh no. Lucan will stay human because he wants to be the next Immortal."

Roane closed his eyes as he heard his worst nightmare. Davy would die. His brother would become the Immortal and he'd have too much power than any being should have in a lifetime. There was a reason why it chose the next holder of the thread, but according to Davy, she wasn't the thread. She was the Immortal, a prophecy no vampire had been foretold about. And that was one of the reasons why his former Family's Elders refused to believe what he had told them. There was no prophecy stating the thread would become an actual entity. The thread was just there. It jumped from human to human and they were always protected by it so no vampire could obtain that power.

"They're stupid. They refuse to listen to me," Roane bit out. "You're right. A new order has to come in power. They refuse to hear what I've told them and it'll be the death of them. She's not a thread. She is something we know nothing about."

Gavin's finger clenched around his glass and it shattered. He was unfazed by the broken shards of glass in his hands. "She might be missing right now, but she's coming back. And something tells me that she's coming back with a vengeance. Your girl will be okay, no matter how long she's away."

Roane closed his eyes. He wanted to believe what he heard. "Let's hope."

"No matter what we think, we have another problem on our hands. That Alpha has to be dealt with."

"He's a complication that I didn't foresee," Roane admitted as he remembered Emily's haunted eyes. No, he saw how she had trusted him. He'd been her last resort and she thought he could produce Davy, no matter how unrealistic that wish had been.

Gavin chuckled and turned for another drink. "Takes a strong man, wolf or human, to bring your lover to a place and ask for help from someone she's got her 'knight in shining armor' fantasy with. I'm surprised he took it that well."

"He didn't know." Roane felt his stomach twist. "She lied to him about her feelings and she kept them hidden from him. He thought I'd had a few classes with her. He didn't know about her feelings or how she'd handled the truth about Davy and me."

"Which she still hasn't." Gavin turned back and looked out the window with Roane. They stood shoulder to shoulder. "She heard about it before Davy went missing, but she hasn't seen it. It's not a reality with her, not yet. And, mate, she had more than a crush on you. I think the girl thought she was in love with you."

"Most humans have stupid idealistic fantasies. They live in a delusional world."

"Regardless, the lass was hurt. I wonder how the wolf is going to handle that. It can't be easy, knowing that your mate has feelings for someone else and a different species too."

"They're not real." Roane turned away and grabbed a bottle of bourbon.

"They're not real to you, but they're real to her."

"Shut up."

Gavin grinned. "Oh come on. You've never had your heart shattered by someone that you only fantasized about? Fantasized so hard that you tricked yourself into thinking she was real?"

"Maybe when I was human?"

"She *is* human. So is Davy." Gavin watched his mate and saw that Roane gave nothing away. He never did. Then Gavin clinked his glass with Roane's. "Here's to us. Breaking hearts and breaking blood. There's going to be a load spilled with this war coming on."

Roane didn't comment, but gripped his glass tighter. Gavin

was right, something that Roane tried not to think about every day, but he couldn't get Wren's voice out of his head. She told him that they'd need Davy and that they'd need her powers. He knew it was true. If they were going to survive the future, they'd need a miracle. They'd need the Immortal.

15

Saren was crouched in the corner of the room. I was on the opposite side and we stared at each other, waiting for the other to attack. My eyes were locked on her. I watched every breath she took, every twitch the hairs on her arm made, even how the iris in her eye widened a bit. When the skin at the corner of her mouth stretched out, I flung myself in the air and tucked my feet in to spring off the wall as I flew down to her.

She was ready. She ducked her head down and rolled over till she was on her back. Then her hand came up and zapped me, just as I was about to tackle her.

"Ouch!" I glared as I thrust my body through the air and back to my corner. I rubbed my stomach. "That one hurt."

"You were trying to hurt me."

"I wanted to tackle you."

"You wanted to overtake me." She stood, her body fluid, gliding upwards till she walked towards me. The fire in her eyes had vanished, but two small embers had been ignited. I watched, always amazed, as it built slowly at first until it was a rolling fire. Then she blinked and shook her head. "You can't think about how you're going to sneak up on me. It won't work with me. It won't work with Jacith."

"Why do I have to be the one who fights him? You're better than me. You should do it." I stood and brushed off my pants. The room we had been training in hadn't been cleaned from the animals that had been in there before. Piles of straw were everywhere and they clung to my pants. Not Saren's. Her pants were spotless. "Are you sure there isn't poop in here from before? You said animals were kept in here."

She rolled her eyes and led the way out the door and through a tunnel. "I already told you that it had been cleaned a long time ago. The straw was put in there for the same reason we use that room, training. It's an old castle. There's a lot of history. Knights used to go in there. And no, you're the Immortal. I am not. You are supposed to be better than me."

Just then we passed another hallway where a display of armor was hung on the wall. I could never stop the shivers when I went past it and I felt them again. The place was old. Saren was right, the history hung in the air. It suffocated me at times, but I missed my own history. I missed my old life. "When can I go back?"

Saren pushed open a wooden door with her back and glared at me. "I told you, when you can hide from the Alpha. He came earlier than we anticipated and you were supposed to be further along in your powers."

Sireenia looked up from a counter as she stirred something in a bowl. A bright smile lit her face and she tucked a long braid behind her ear. She left a trail of flour on her cheek. "How's she doing?"

"She's blocking me. She's blocking herself. It's like she doesn't want to progress," Saren grumbled as she hopped on a stool at the counter. "What are you making?"

"Chocolate chip cookies. Davy, you like these, don't you?"

My finger had been raised in the air, ready to swipe some of the batter when I was caught by the look in Sireenia's eyes. The uncertainty and eagerness shook me for a moment. Those were human emotions and I'd grown used to not seeing Saren or Sireenia as human. Magic oozed from them in every word, emotion, or look. They told me that they were once human and it surprised me when I saw moments such as this one that showed their humanity.

I smiled back. "I love these cookies. Kates used to buy the premade batter and that's all we would eat sometimes."

"The batter?" Sireenia paled. "You mean you didn't bake them? I thought you were supposed to bake them?"

Saren swore under her breath. "Don't worry about it, Sire. You're fine. You're being more amicable than she is."

"Hey!" I stole some batter and turned as I tasted it to glare at my trainer. It seemed that was all I did with Saren now. "What's that supposed to mean?" It felt like an insult.

"You know what that means. Why won't you transition? It's like you don't want to be the Immortal. Why don't you want to be the Immortal?" She shot to her feet and rounded the counter. Her body had stiffened, ready for a fight.

I stared at her. "Wha—huh? I don't want to be the Immortal? Why do you say that?"

"Because you don't! You hold back on every training exercise I've put you through. The only thing that you don't hold back is protecting yourself. I've sent missiles at you and you evade them. You've acclimated inside. Your power is complete, but you don't want to admit it. Are you blocking yourself? You must be. I don't understand you. This is why the Immortal should never have ascended into a human being."

"I don't agree with that." Sireenia put down the bowl and spoon. "Saren, please watch what you're saying."

"Why? It's true. We've done so much for her, fought so much, sacrificed, bled for her. And this is the end result? A human who doesn't want it? I lost my humanity for the thread, but—" Saren threw her hands in the air and bolts of fire slammed against the walls. A mural caught fire, but Sireenia waved her hand in the air and it was extinguished immediately.

"The Immortal chose her. Davy is the one who will stop Jacith. She can make everything correct. She *will* change it all."

With narrowed eyes, I watched as Sireenia held Saren's arms and tried to calm her, but Saren shook her head and broke free. As she walked to the door, I realized something that I had never even considered. "You guys had the thread before, didn't you?"

They weren't witches, but they came from witchcraft. Saren had told me before. And they weren't vampires or werewolves or anything else. She said that Roane wouldn't know who they were, but the way they talked about the Immortal, as if they had first-hand knowledge. That meant only one thing. They had been the humans who had held the thread before me.

I gulped.

That meant that I could meet Talia at any moment. And the idea sent my heart racing.

Both stopped and looked at me. It was like a blanket had been pulled off and I saw the relief in both of their eyes. Sireenia was the first one to respond. "It changes you, when you've had the thread in you for so long. I had it in the beginning of time. Saren had it in the 1800s. You go through a vortex when it leaves you."

"It feels like you're getting your heart pulled out of you through your throat when the thread jumps out of you."

"Or when it's forced out of you." Sireenia grew quiet as she looked down at her hands.

I saw the pain in her and wondered who had taken the thread from her, but Saren distracted me. "How did you know that? About us?"

How could I not, but then I realized that I wasn't sure how I knew it. "I don't know. It was just a feeling. You both talk about the Immortal as if you've had first-hand experience."

Before I finished talking, Saren zapped me. The bolt of power hurdled through the air, but I looked up and everything slowed in that instant. I saw it coming, but at a snail's pace. I deflected it and sent it into a wall. Then I looked up again and saw Saren in the air, soaring at me. Her hands were outstretched and ready to let loose two more bolts of power at me. I sidestepped her too. When she landed on the floor, her bolts shattered the floor beneath her, and I grabbed her collar. The floor crumbled underneath her while I lifted her in the air and kicked off the ground. I sent us both through the air to land in the opposite corner.

Sireenia watched where we had been. Her mouth hung open and her hands had lifted to her cheeks. Then it all stopped. Everything snapped back in place. They were no longer in slow motion and Saren stumbled backwards as she fell to the ground.

"Oh my goddess." Sireenia rushed to Saren's side. Both of them looked at me.

I grimaced as I saw the questions and shock in their eyes. Then I saw their mysticism and knew they had never thought I would transition, not completely. I swallowed that back. Their lack of faith in me shouldn't have been surprising.

"You *have* transitioned!" Saren shot to her feet. "When? How? Have you been like this the whole time? Has this been a waste of our time?"

Sireenia grew quiet.

"Are you kidding me?" How could she even think those things? "I didn't know until now. I had no idea when whatever happened. I just knew that something clicked in me and I knew both of you had been thread-holders. That was it and then you're throwing yourself at me. What am I supposed to do? I thought you wanted me to defend myself."

"Can you control it?" Saren stood with her hands ready at her side.

Sireenia stood beside her and tightened her robe. She glanced from Saren to me. Then she stepped forward. "Davy, it is very important to tell us, can you control your powers?"

"You mean: can I do this stuff at will? Not really, but sometimes. Sometimes I can do it and sometimes I can't." I shrugged. "When I really want something to happen, it happens. I wouldn't bank on it, though."

"Why could you stop me now and you couldn't before? I've been training you for three months. I've been hitting you with my powers for that long and you've been taking it?"

"They didn't really hurt." Even though they had and my body had been swollen the entire time. "I don't know, maybe I was just tired of it. Maybe I was distracted by something else. I have no idea."

"What were you thinking before Saren tried to attack you? I saw a look on your face. What was it?" Sireenia stepped forward. Her gaze was intent on me.

"I have no idea. I thought about you guys, what you were, and then I looked up and Saren's coming at me. That's all I remember."

"No, you had a different look. When you thought about us, you were surprised. When Saren attacked you, you were annoyed. She distracted you from a thought. What was it? What were you thinking between those two things? Think, Davy."

"I wasn't. Really. You guys were talking about vortexes and the thread being taken out of you. Then," I shrugged. "I have no idea."

"I felt pain from you." Sireenia tilted her head to the side. "I can feel emotions, not as well as you, but I felt sadness from you. Then panic. What were you scared of?"

"Or who."

"Who are you scared of?"

Both of them watched me. I wondered if they could hear thoughts too.

I shrugged again. "I have no idea. I just know that I haven't felt normal for a while." Not since the last time I had seen Roane when we had talked in the library and he left me.

"There! What are you thinking right now?" Sireenia surged towards me and her hands grabbed my arms.

The moment her hands touched me, a surge of memories rushed through me. The first time I saw Roane in the library, when I saw him in my dorm. Then he stood behind me when Sheila asked if he was my date. A rush of adrenalin went through me as I remembered our first kiss, when I slammed my mouth against his. And then I remembered when we made love. I'd never felt such a desperate fever before him.

"Oh dear." Sireenia wrapped me in her arms before she turned towards Saren. "It's him. It's the vampire."

I tensed and expected a biting comment from her, but it never came. Instead, I heard the door close a second later and felt Saren's absence more than I'd ever felt her presence. I pulled away from Sireenia. "What was it? Is she upset?"

"No, she's not. She's feeling her own memories." She moved to hold my face in both of her hands and then she closed her eyes.

Warmth started to pulsate through me. It spread from her fingertips into my skin, down my neck, arms, waist, and all the way to my toes. She was taking away my pain and giving me a different emotion, one of fondness. It felt good and I closed my eyes before I pulled away. "No. That's not real. It's not right that I take that from you."

"You do it all the time. You take away others' pain so I'm taking yours."

"You can't have my pain. You have enough of your own."

"I don't take it into me. Watch."

As I did, Sireenia moved back and held out her arms. She smiled and then closed her eyes. A moment later a coat transformed over her skin. It was a second layer of skin, but white. As soon as it was done growing over her it cemented to her skin and she opened her eyes with that same smile. Then she shook her body. The white skin fell away and left behind her normal skin with a rosy glow over it.

"See?" she asked. "I have some tricks up my sleeve too."

"I don't even know what I would look like if I could do that. I'd be like a quilt or something."

"I was empathic when I was human. My ability has progressed since I held the thread in me and since I lost the thread."

"What happened to you when the thread left you? Roane told me that every person dies once the thread leaves them."

"I did die, but I didn't. The human soul died, as it should, but we passed on to a different realm. There's a part in us, all of us, that connected with the Immortal and the essence of it gave us a different life. This is where we all go. This is where you will go too, I suppose."

"How many are there of you?"

"The older threads, what I call myself, have developed themselves into these bodies. I chose this body to look like this, the way Saren also looks how she wants to. We don't have real bodies. You can touch us and see us, but no one else can; only someone who is connected to the Immortal thread can. The magic is unparalleled. It is unimaginable, but we do know certain rules and one of them is that the Alpha werewolf cannot know who you are. You must be able to hide yourself to him."

So I needed to fight an ultimate sorcerer-vampire. I was being trained by some type of witch spirits and I needed to hide from an amped-up werewolf. And they still wondered why I wasn't sold on embracing the Immortal inside of me.

"My life sucks."

Sireenia patted my shoulder. "Everything will be fine. I can feel that inside of you too. You already know what you have to do." When she reached the door, she looked back. "She hasn't let go of the human world yet so you won't meet Talia as one of us. She still holds on there."

I closed my eyes when pain sliced through me, like I'd been gutted.

"And Davy?" Sireenia smiled, an ethereal look came over her as she stood with her white hair in a braid over one shoulder and dressed in a white hanging robe. "You mustn't assume the obvious all the time except one thing."

Dread filled me. "And what's that?"

"You're strongest when you're with him. You showed us that now. Go to him. I think you're ready."

"What about the werewolf?"

The door closed behind her, but I heard her answer, "I think you're ready for that too."

My mouth dropped. I hadn't been ready ten minutes ago and now everything changed? And how was I even going to get back?

I gulped. "Saren?"

16

S aren and I left the castle, walked down a wooded pathway, and then she clasped my arm. "Take us back."

"What? You do it."

"You do it. Sire thinks you're ready so you need to be able to do this. Take us back."

"I have no idea where we are."

"It doesn't matter. You know where you want to go. Take us there."

"But—" My mouth hung open. How was I supposed to do that? Then I heard a voice in my head. It was a whisper and it felt strangely familiar, too familiar. *'Think of where you want to go, where you want to be, then wish it and it will be.'*

"What?!" I snapped, spinning in a circle. The voice was in my head, but it sounded so real. "I thought I was done hearing voices in my head and now someone's back."

Saren grabbed my other arm. "What are you talking about?"

"Someone just told me to wish and it will be. It's annoying. You're all annoying. You want to know why I don't want to be the Immortal, it's because of this! I have voices in my head. I have

freaky witch spirits telling me that I can teleport myself somewhere and I have no idea how to do it." But as I spoke, everything
started to move around us. We were in the eye of a tornado and
time was being sucked around us, whipping, snarling.

Then the voice whispered again, *She can't hear me, she should
not. I am here for you, Davina. I always will be. You are never alone.*

Okay—creepy. And before I could reflect on that thought,
something snapped us away. It was like a hand reached into our
vortex and shook us into a different vortex. Before I could shriek
from surprise, we'd fallen to the ground and I hissed from the
pain.

"What was that?" I turned for Saren, but she wasn't there.
"Saren? Where are you? This is not funny. Did you do that?"
Scrambling to my feet, I couldn't see or feel her. She wasn't close
to me at all. I didn't feel her presence. It was like she was dead,
but she was a witch spirit so I wasn't that surprised. Well, a witch
spirit with some extra oomph to her.

"We're close."

A gruff voice spoke behind me and I whirled around to see a
blonde vampire sitting in front of a fire. She was hunched over
with her elbows braced on her knees. A bag was placed behind
her. It was slightly open. Some pictures poked out from the bag
along with a yellow cardigan and a beaded necklace.

"Fine," she sighed and stood lithely in one motion. When she
turned around, I found myself staring into Talia's face, but it
wasn't. This was a vampire, not the thread holder. She was older,
maybe five years older, but the same hazel eyes stared through me,
hardened. Instead of Talia's red hair flying around her, this girl
had blonde hair pulled back in a tight bun tucked behind at the
base of her head. She bent down and pulled a long sleeve armor
shirt over her. The front of it had a black wolf painted over it with
green eyes that seemed to see right through me. As I moved to the
left, they watched and then followed when I went to the right.

Freaky.

Suddenly, she walked right through me. I gasped, braced for the contact, but nothing happened. The girl walked straight through me as if I was air. Then I realized I was air. I wasn't there in body, but in mind. I had no idea why I would want to be there, but I turned with the intention of following the girl when a shadow jerked away from the fire.

The movement caught my eye and I whirled back around, but I didn't see anything except the flames that waved back and forth in a smooth rhythm. I started to turn again, but there it was. The shadow jerked forward and this time I was able to catch where it went. I focused all my attention on it.

"Who are you?" I asked. Was this an actual shadow or a ghost or a witch spirit?

It didn't say anything. It didn't move. It glimmered there above the bag. Some embers in the fire moved in that moment and flames exploded, the sky was illuminated for a second. I saw a face in the shadow and they looked downwards. It was focused on the bag, so much that I drifted closer so I could look at the bag too. Glancing back up, I could no longer make out the shadow, but I could still feel it. The presence was strong, so strong, and I closed my eyes. I let myself feel what this shadow wanted me to feel.

Urgency. Desperation. And such clear concentration that I was jerked out of my trance-like state. The thing wanted me to look in the bag and if it could've told me in person, it would've been screaming at me.

"Tracey, where are you going?"

I jerked around. She was coming back. Talia's sister was almost to the bag, reaching down.

'Oh god.' I sucked in my breath and snatched the bag before she could. Everything whirled around me again and I knew I'd broken through the vortex. She couldn't see me before, but she did now and she was pissed. Her eyes went from shock to a murderous rage.

"Hi! Sorry!" I squeaked and then closed my eyes again. *'Vacuum away. Vacuum away. Roane. Go to Roane! Go to Roane!'* I tried to command my Immortal insides and as Tracey's rough hands scraped my skin, the wind picked me up again and I was back in the same tornado.

When I landed this time, it took me a minute before I realized where I was. It was quiet, too quiet in the room, but there was loud music below me. It sounded like a bass booming underneath my feet and when I looked around, I saw a couple of leather couches, a bar, a desk, and three walls made from glass. Then I realized that it was the sound of bass under me. I was in Roane's office at the Shoilster. Then I gulped, oh goodness.

Just then the door opened, the bass sounded clearer, and I looked up.

Wren took two steps inside and froze. The papers in her hand ripped apart. She couldn't hide the terror in her eyes before I saw it. And then it was gone. She stood at her highest height and her leather corset creaked from the movement. The papers were forgotten when she moved her hand behind her back.

"What is that?" I lurched forward.

"What are you doing here?" She looked around, but no one was there. The door was closed. There was no escape.

"It's just you and me and whatever you're hiding from me."

"I'm not hiding anything from you."

I narrowed my eyes and studied her. I studied the vein that had started to pop in her neck. "Yes, you are. What's in those papers?"

"Nothing. They're for Roane, not you. And what are you doing here? I should be yelling for him right now."

I swallowed and looked back to her eyes. They were frosty now, but I narrowed mine and went inside of her. It was an old

empathic trick. I sensed the disarray inside. Wren was relieved I
was back, pissed that she was relieved, and another part was in
chaos because she smelled something familiar, too familiar for
her to handle.

I pulled out and then sniffed the air. Nothing.

"What do you have?" Her eyes looked frantic.

I lifted the bag. "This? This is what you smelled?"

"Wha—get out of my head!" She grabbed the bag from me.
Her long curls whipped against my head as she moved back. "Do
you know whose this is?"

"I'm the one who took it. Do you?"

Wren blanched and jerked backwards, stumbling to the door.
I watched as she went through it, but gaped as the door shut
behind her. The almighty hoity-toity vampiress had just ran from
me—me! She was scared of me for some reason. My gaze shifted
to the bag. I doubted she was terrified of a bag so that left only
one possibility. She knew the owner of the bag. Wren was scared
of Tracey, not me. Who was Tracey to Wren? How did they know
each other?

"Davy?" Roane was frozen in the doorway. His gaze was
riveted to me.

Oh god, he looked good. His hair had been buzzed again, but
it was how he was dressed that had my knees buckling. He had
on black dress slacks matched with a black soft cotton buttoned
shirt tucked inside. Roane looked like a business owner, one that
oozed sex appeal from extreme confidence. And he didn't care,
which made him even hotter. He looked so different from the
college student he'd been in the beginning.

I swallowed, my throat was tight. "Hey," I choked out with a
small wave. When I saw that my hand was trembling, I stuffed it
behind me.

I didn't know what to say. He didn't move. He didn't speak.
And my feet were glued to the floor. Maybe I shouldn't have

come. Maybe Sireenia had gotten it wrong and I wasn't my strongest around him. "I shouldn't have come. I'm sorry."

"No!" Roane jerked forward, but stopped. His hand was in the air. He reached out to me, but he didn't move or say anything more. A myriad of emotions flashed over his face before his hand moved back to his side. "Where were you?"

My eyebrows shot up. That was what he settled with? No hug? No kiss? No 'I missed you and was so worried about you?' My blood started to boil. "Are you serious? That's all you have to say to me?" Maybe I hadn't been gone that long? And maybe Roane hadn't missed me as much as I hoped he would.

"I—" He opened his mouth, but shut it without saying anything, again.

The door burst open behind him and Gavin came inside. He flashed me a smile. "Well, well, well. The prodigal superpower is back again. Where've you been, darling?" Then he opened his arms wide to lift me in the air.

Finally. Someone was happy to see me.

He twirled me in a circle.

I laughed and glared at the same time. "Put me down." But it was nice to know someone missed me.

Gavin set me back down and glanced over his shoulder. "Aren't you going to give your girl a kiss? You've been worrying enough to give your immortal body an ulcer. And a splendid body he has, Davy. He really does, but then again, I think you already know this."

I felt him patting my shoulder and knew he was trying to reassure me, but it wasn't helping. Roane still hadn't moved. He seemed normal now, no shock residing. His eyes were clear and focused on me, but I didn't see what I had hoped I would. Gavin was wrong, Roane hadn't missed me. If he was worried, it was about the Immortal being gone. It was all about the Immortal, not me.

"Gavin, can you give us a moment?"

"Sure." Gavin flashed another smile and winked at me before he left.

I remembered being annoyed with him the last time I saw him but now I didn't want him to go. He wore a white track suit that still gave him the athletic look, but somehow he made it look natural. All vampires should dress like that. When the door closed behind him, I wondered what color his track suit would be the next time I saw him. Then Roane cleared his throat and I no longer cared.

"You've been gone for three months." He moved around me to his desk.

We brushed shoulders as he moved past, but it wasn't close enough. I sucked in a breath and felt my body yearn for his touch. When it didn't happen, I felt cheated, but I turned and regarded him. "Has it been that long?"

Roane turned his back to me and looked out over the dance floor. "What happened that day? Gavin was there. He said you were fine. You were with your roommate and a witch. I've spoken to Emily and I've read the police reports from the witch and wolf. None of them know what happened and there's no video of you leaving."

Wow, the police had been called. "Emily's mate has Immortal essence in him. He was made with magic and I had to leave. He would've sensed the Immortal in me and tried to drain me. I might not have been able to control myself and I was scared of what could've happened. I could've killed everybody. So I left."

"Left where?" He turned now with his eyes narrowed.

I tried to sense inside of him, but was blocked. I could've pushed through, but it didn't take away the fact that Roane didn't want me in his head. He was guarded against me and I realized that he didn't trust me. Pain flooded me at that thought. I felt a knife to my gut.

"Where did you go, Davy?"

I sucked in my breath and blinked back tears. It shouldn't hurt that much, but it did.

"Where did you go? You said you left, but there's no footage of you leaving. Did you disappear into thin air? Can you do that now?"

He was so cold. I shivered in his office and wrapped my arms around myself. "It's an Immortal thing that I didn't know I could do. I came back once I figured out how to control it, not that I really can, but I think I'm figuring it out."

"You came back? You came back here?" Roane still stood in front of the glass wall, as far away from me as possible.

"I came here. I wanted to see you. I know that I'm stronger when I'm with you. I can control my powers better." I stopped because he didn't look convinced. He looked alarmed, but what was wrong about that? I hadn't expected any of this from him. He should've been happy I was back. He shouldn't be cautious.

"But where did you go?"

"I don't know, not really. I was in some castle somewhere."

"Alone?"

"I—yes." I had no idea why I kept Saren and Sireenia a secret, but if he was being cautious then I would too.

"And you decided to come back now?"

"No." Why wouldn't he understand? "I couldn't come back because I didn't know how. I couldn't control my powers and I don't know what to do about Emily's mate. He can't know I'm the Immortal. I don't know why he can't know, but I just know that he can't. It wouldn't be good if he did." And I was rambling like an idiot. *'Smooth move, Davy. Just remind him that you're still a dork and he really won't see what he liked about you before.'*

Roane cracked a grin.

My eyes popped out. "You can hear my thoughts, but you won't let me hear yours?"

Everything about him relaxed in that moment and he came around the desk with a smile. "I had to make sure it was you and not someone else. Jacith is a powerful sorcerer. He could do this. I'm sorry that I hurt you."

"What?" I glared. "Not fun."

But then it didn't matter. Roane moved close and folded me against his chest. He hugged me tight. The fight, the tension, the hurt all rolled out of me in that moment. Everything slipped away and I was wrapped in warmth again. With my hands fisted in his shirt and my forehead pressed against his chest, I mumbled out, "What made up your mind?"

"Only you would worry about me seeing you as a dork. No imposter could be that good." He rested his cheek on the top of my head and held me tighter. "It's good to have you back."

I felt his relief then. He *had* been worried, enough to grow ulcers as Gavin had teased. And then I felt desire burst inside of me. Nothing else mattered. It started low, in the pit of my stomach and spread out. It spread fast, shooting through me and then I was wet between my legs. The need throbbed there. It was powerful, so powerful that I was blind to everything else. Without thinking, I lifted my head, arched my back, and climbed up his body.

Roane grabbed the back of my thighs and anchored them around his waist. His hand caught my neck and tilted my head back. His lips brushed mine and I groaned. I needed more. As he touched them again, it was agonizing. He was gentle when I wanted him to dominate.

"Yep, they're getting along just fine."

Gavin's voice interrupted us and Roane growled. "Out!" His voice was low, so low it sounded like an animal and I knew his vampire side had come to the forefront.

"I'm going to be sick."

Wren wasn't far behind Gavin. The two ignored the warning and came further into the room. Gavin perched on the couch while Wren went to the glass wall and peered out. The door opened one more time and Gregory came through. His shoulders almost didn't fit, but he stooped down and shifted sideways.

'They aren't going anywhere.'

I felt Roane's reluctance as he let me down, but he held my elbow and lifted me to the opposite couch from Gavin. My legs weren't able to stand so I was grateful for his help. As I collapsed on the couch, my heart was racing. I pressed my sweaty palms between my knees and felt them throbbing, pulsating from need. Gavin gave me a knowing look and I ducked my head. I couldn't control my body.

Roane shot me a dark, primal look underneath his eyelids, but turned to the group. "The Immortal took her away. I assume that Emily called out for her mate and he was approaching the room. Davy feared that he would've attacked her and she wouldn't have been able to control herself. She worried that the Immortal in her would've reacted and killed people she didn't want to kill."

"So where was she?" Wren clipped out.

"Davy doesn't know where she was, but she came back once she could figure out how to get back." Roane gazed at the vampiress steadily for a moment before she lowered her gaze. Then he glanced at the rest with authority. "That's all we need to know. I trust her and she's right. The Alpha would've known who she was so Davy did the right thing in disappearing. He still can't know who she is."

Gavin growled, "The wolves want to take over. They always have. It's why they created him and it's why he's here. They know something about the Immortal – otherwise he wouldn't be here. His pack comes from across the ocean."

"Their ancestors originate from where Talia grew up," Gregory said as he watched his master.

Roane didn't blink. "Talia came from a gypsy family. They had no set place."

"Where did her mother die?" I felt all the desire drain from

my body. Any talk about Talia would do that. I just felt
empty now.

"In Veneto. Talia's roots are the Sinti gypsies. They had settled
there when her mother was killed."

"And when the thread went to Talia," Gavin finished.

"Does it matter where he came from? He's here now and he's
a pain in the ass. It's all nice and not really lovely that Davy's
back, but I don't care about where Roane's ex's mother died or
where she became the thread holder or where the Alpha is from.
He's here and so is Davy. What's the next step? Hide her?"

"What? No." I couldn't leave my friends.

Roane watched me throughout the conversation and
measured me with his eyes. "You said that you could control your
powers, can you? What's going to happen when he meets you?"

I gulped as I felt all of their attention on me. The air was
heavy in the room. "I think I can. I know I can. It'll be fine when I
meet him. It will, I promise. He won't be able to detect anything
in me. I won't let him."

"Really?" Wren scoffed. "Because I can 'detect' it right now.
You're not the same. You came back weird and there's something
extra in your smell."

I wrinkled my nose up. There was? How did I smell now?
"What do you mean?"

"It's not lemons, if that's what you're asking." She rolled her
eyes. "You're different. That's all I can say."

"You're stronger." Gavin spoke for her. His eyes were grave
now and I was reminded of the first and last time I'd met him. He
was dangerous then and seemed more dangerous now.

"I am?"

Gregory shifted in the background and remained quiet.

"You were strong before, but you hid it. There's nothing more
for you to hide behind. You are just strong now. There's no weak-
ness in you anymore, none that I can see."

"He's right. They're all right." Roane sighed. "You *are* different,

Davy. It's why I didn't think you were you, but you said you could control your powers. You're going to have to. Or you will have to stay hidden. No one can know who you are. The Alpha *really* can't know who you are."

"So how are you going to do that?" Wren sat on the edge of Roane's desk.

I looked at her and had no idea how to answer that question.

17

"Are you sure about this?" Roane asked when he showed me to a guest bedroom at the Shoilster.

So many vampires had come to town to join him that his home was full and the extra rooms at the Alexander were all taken. Even though the Shoilster and Alexander were a nightclub and restaurant, Roane had rooms built into them and tunnels around them. They were perfect to hide the entire army, but he kept a few rooms for his closest allies. Since my room was right next to his, I knew it meant something. They were attached by a door in the wall.

Was I sure? Yes. Did I want to? No. I sighed and turned back. He looked good, so good, but there was so much distance between us. We'd been excited before and had jumped at each other, but I'd had time to remember something that would guarantee more distance between us. Talia.

So I nodded. "Yeah, I'm sure."

"Okay." He glanced at the door. "You know where I'll be if you want to talk."

Talk. Yes. We needed to do some of that too.

"Davy." He sounded hesitant. "I thought we were fine. Before, in the room."

"I know, but I have to wrap my head around things." Not to mention that I'd forgotten about the day I'd met Gavin when waves had hit me with the same urgency I'd felt by the fire and from the shadow. The shadow pulled me there. It wanted me to find Tracey's bag. It was the same voice that had assaulted me the day before I'd disappeared.

'Tell Roane of my daughter.'

I wasn't stupid. That shadow was connected to Tracey. It was connected to a child. And it was connected to Roane. Common factor? Talia. I'd forgotten about it amidst everything, but it came back to me. As I glanced at my bag, I knew that Roane smelled Tracey from it. Wren had bolted from the room because of it. Why was Roane ignoring it? What did that mean?

"Things?"

I looked back at him. There was sadness to him. I felt the history from it. Oh yes. He knew that I had connected with Tracey. He was aware her bag was in my possession and he knew I had something else to tell him. Did he know it was about Talia? Did he know it was her child?

Oh hell. Why postpone it?

I dumped the bag out on the bed.

"What are you doing?" Roane jerked behind me. There was panic in his voice.

I started to shift through her things.

"Stop." He caught my hand. "Please stop."

I yanked my hand away and kept looking. Clothes. Weapons. A journal. Little remnants here and there. And then my finger touched something small, thin, and I knew it was a picture. I felt it in my gut. This was what she wanted me to find. Intense pain flooded me, dread formed in my stomach, but I gritted my teeth and lifted the photograph.

It was of Talia holding an infant to her cheeks. She was

smiling to the camera. Love exuded from her. The baby's eyes were open a fraction, but it was enough. They had the same eyes. All eyes were blue at birth, but this one had hazel eyes. This one was the same as her mother's. That also told me that this child wasn't an ordinary child. There was magic in her.

"Oh my god," Roane said beside me. He took the picture from me and lifted it for closer inspection.

I couldn't watch. I didn't want to see tears in his eyes or feel whatever he was feeling. I just knew that his love for her would be renewed. I couldn't handle it so I turned away. I felt gutted when I spoke. "She came to me before I disappeared. She wanted me to tell you about her child. And she's the one that took me to that bag. It's Tracey's, but you knew that. Wren knew too."

He didn't respond and I felt an overwhelming sense of longing from him. It was too much so I left. Roane needed time alone. Who was I kidding? I knew I shouldn't have left, but I did. As I wiped a tear away and turned down a hallway, I knew that I was running away because I couldn't bear to see the man I loved remember that he loved someone else.

Talia would always be first. That was the truth and I needed to accept it.

I kept going down hallways. I didn't watch or try to remember which way I was headed, but then I found myself at the door to a deck built on the second floor. Some patio tables were set up beside a small garden with a small waterfall that over granite rocks that had been piled from above the over-hanging roof. As I stepped out and felt the moisture in the air, I breathed in deep. I hadn't smelled water since I'd been gone. The castle had been rock and gardens, but no water. I'd missed it.

"Why are you out here?"

I turned and gulped when I saw Gavin at one of the tables. A lit cigarette was between his fingers and a glass of alcohol sat in front of him. He was in the shadows. A sense of brooding clung to him.

I inched a step closer to him. "I needed to clear my head."

"From what?" He tapped his cigarette on the ashtray.

He looked like he wanted to be alone. That was evident, but I didn't know where else to go. I sat down. "From Roane."

"Because?" His eyes were too knowing.

"I just told him that Talia had a child."

"Oh. Wow. That's not something I saw coming." Gavin glanced at the door.

"Please don't leave. I—" I closed my mouth. What was I going to say? That I didn't want to be alone? This was Roane's best friend. He was the person that should be with him, not with me.

"You didn't want to stick around?"

I snorted. "For what?"

My hands were so clammy and I looked down. I wrung them together. That's when I saw I was trembling at the same time. My whole body was shaking. I knew Gavin saw it all.

"It's not his, if that's what you're worried about."

"Huh?"

"Roane can't reproduce. None of us can except for the Mori or humans. She got with one of them to have a kid. You don't need to worry that Roane will take off to find the child. Guaranteed. And if you're worried that he'll pine over her, it won't happen." His eyes were cold as he watched me. Then he lifted his hand and took a drag off the cigarette. "Want my advice?"

I clasped my eyes shut. I readied myself.

"Go back to him. You're the best friend, not me. Trust me on that." Ice clinked in his glass as he took another sip.

There was a haunted look in his brown eyes, a sadness that resonated deep within me. I didn't want it. It wasn't mine to carry and I wanted it gone, but I knew that the pain in him would lessen if I took it into me. After a moment, he lifted his glass. "I can see why my best mate loves you. Not get back there before I do something I'm going to regret."

I grinned. "If I can find my way back."

"You'll be fine, Davy. Trust your gut. It knows where to go."

As I left, something made me pause. Was there something more to his words or—I closed my eyes and told myself to stop. He was right. I knew before I left, but I needed to go back and face Roane no matter the end result. And so, with a deep breath, I smiled goodbye and then tried to trace my way back. It wasn't hard. Every time I took a wrong turn, I opened myself and felt Roane. He was around this corner, then the left in the hallway, and finally after a few more walkways, I found myself at his office.

He sat behind his desk and had turned to watch the club's chaos beneath his feet. The office was dark, but the dance floor's strobe lights flashed through. All sorts of colors illuminated his face.

I didn't know what he was thinking or feeling and I didn't feel into him. He wouldn't like that.

"You came back." His voice was quiet, too quiet.

"Yeah." My own was raspy. "A little birdie told me I should."

A snort escaped him. "I've never heard someone call Gavin a little birdie. Don't think he'd find that complimentary."

"Yeah, well. " And I had no idea what to say. Again.

Roane stood in a fluid motion. His body was tense. "Do you think that I'll never be over her?" As his head lifted up, his eyes caught mine. Piercing. "You think so little of me? That I'll never be able to move past Talia? Is that what you think of me?"

Oh hell. This was not what I expected. "I think that she was a big part of you." What did I think? "I think you still love her and that you always will."

"Talia was a part of my life. A big part of my life, but she wasn't my entire life. She wasn't the reason I woke up. I didn't think of ways every morning to protect her, ways to help her live a better life, ways to make sure that she never felt the pain that so many others would in our world. I didn't start a war to protect her. I didn't make myself ache every day because I missed her so much when I knew that she needed to live a normal life. I didn't

kill vampires or humans without a second thought for her. I
never did those things for Talia."

My eyes couldn't leave his.

Roane started to come to me. "The elders thought I was
growing too close to her so they sent me away. I went. I never
argued. I never considered it. I didn't fight for her and I was gone
for over a year before I felt her death. And when I felt it, Davy, it
didn't hurt. She was where she wanted to be. She was at peace. I
loved her, but not like I love you. I love you to the point of starting
a war for you. I love you to the point where I want you to be in
college. I want you to have as normal of a life as you possibly can.
Because one day I know that you'll have to leave all of that. You're
going to have to stop being a normal human and come by my side
to be the Immortal. I know that you don't want that. I know that
you want me, but you want to be normal more. And I'm trying to
help you. I am, but it's so goddamn hard when you disappear for
three months and I can't do one thing to bring you back to me.
And then, suddenly, you're here. You've come back to me and I
had nothing to do with it. You brought yourself back. You saved
yourself. You did it. Not me. It's a hard pill to swallow when I'm
able to protect anybody, but I can't protect you, the one person
that I would do anything to save. I can't. And then you tell me
about Talia's daughter. I'm reminded that it's another thing I can't
give you. I can't have a child with you. And I want to. I want so
much to do that. I want to have a normal life with you, but I can't.
We can't, but you can have parts that are normal. You can still
have a child. I didn't think Immortals could, but she did so you
can—"

I stopped him and placed a finger over his lips. They were so
tender. And then I replaced my finger with my lips.

It felt right to kiss him again.

Roane picked me up and kicked his door shut at the same
time. He sat me down on his desk and his mouth opened. He
took control and his tongue swept inside. He demanded entrance

and I let him. I felt him rub against me, teasing, capturing. I grabbed onto the back of his head and held myself against him. He groaned as he sucked on my bottom lip.

A knock sounded at the door and Roane growled, "Leave!"

They didn't. They knocked again.

"No." I held him tighter.

"Who is it?"

"It's Gregory." We could hear his hesitation. "There's a guest asking for you. She wishes to enter the premises."

"A guest?" Roane pulled away now.

"No," I whimpered. Our time was here. I wasn't going to let someone stop us.

"I'm sorry." He kissed my forehead and stood back. "I should go. Gregory wouldn't interrupt unless it was important."

"But—" My mouth fell open and I watched him walk towards the door. "This is important!"

Roane flashed me a grin. "Don't worry. I'll be coming right back, quicker than you think and you'd better be naked."

I perked up at that thought.

He was gone then, but it wasn't long before he was back. When he came through the door, a pained look was on his face. I had a brief second to ponder why before the guest poked her head around Roane.

"Kates." My mouth hung open. I knew I should've said something more welcoming, but holy moly.

With a squeal and a skip, she threw her arms around me and hugged me tight. "Davy! It's so good to see you again."

I patted her back. "You left to find someone? Who was it?"

Not to mention, what was with the happy note? When she left, she'd been morose and depressed. She'd gone to search for someone. Now she was back. With a simple white tee shirt and jeans, her hair gleamed bright blonde instead of the dirty locks she'd had before. She looked nothing like the mischievous bad girl from before.

She laughed and pulled away from me. "I lied to you."

Shock. Not.

Kates added, "I made it sound like I needed to deal with my daddy issues and Blue suggested that I should go and find him. I'm not stupid. I knew that she wanted me out of your life. She can't brainwash you when I'm around."

I narrowed my eyes, frowning as I heard more evidence against my old sponsor.

Kates continued, "You're wondering what I was up to, but the truth is that I went on a mission for your boyfriend." She clasped a hand on Roane's shoulder, or she tried to. He moved away at the last moment and Kates' hand fell back to her side. She laughed. "He wanted me to find Lucan and I did!"

Silence met the last bomb she dropped.

I waited a beat. "You what?"

"I found Lucan."

My eyes shot to Roane. "She what?"

He'd been studying me with narrowed eyes and now he moved forward. "Kates, go with Gregory. He'll take you to a room. You can settle down for the night. I'm sure you're tired."

"Not really. I'm amped up. Mind if I hit the club instead?"

"There are vampires down there."

Kates gave me an incredulous look. "You know they're my forte."

"No killing and no screwing," Roane warned. "They've pledged their allegiance to me. I don't want any of them upset that a slayer is in their midst."

"You know I can't kill. I've followed the decree." Kates didn't seem to mind that she was being hurried out of the room. Just as she disappeared through the door, she looked back and winked at me. I relaxed as I saw the same Kates from before.

When the door shut, the mood wasn't the same. I wanted to smash his bones now, not jump them. "You sent her to find your brother?"

"I did."

"And when were you going to tell me this?"

"I wasn't." He didn't seem guilt-ridden by that answer.

I wanted to hurt him. Bad. "What else should you tell me? Anything else that you had my best friend do for you?"

He hesitated, but then answered emotionless, "Blue. I knew your sponsor wasn't being honest with you and I knew she was only trying to get close to Kates to try and control you. I told Kates about Blue, that she's working for Jacith and was sent by him. Her job was to report back to him when you became the Immortal. Kates was supposed to try and get information from Blue, not the other way around. When it wasn't working and when I knew Lucan had gone to the Mori for protection, I sent her to him. I can't get to him there. They're too strong for me, but she could. She's human and he loves her."

I sucked in my breath. "I thought no one knew I was the Immortal. I didn't think Jacith knew about me."

"There was a prophecy about an empath who would become the Immortal. Jacith doesn't believe in it. He doesn't think the thread-holder can become something more, but he sent her anyways. You know this. You know that Blue worked for him and that she had been picked for you."

I did, but I hadn't realized the extent of her betrayal. Or that Jacith knew about me.

"Davy, you knew when Kates had kidnapped Blue that time. She knew about you then. She knew you were the Immortal. You were in her head. You heard her talk about Jacith. He sent her to you."

"Stop." I held my hands over my ears. I didn't want to hear about another person who had lied to me and betrayed me.

"I'm sorry that I never told you. I didn't want you to get mixed up in all that deceit. I hoped not to involve you and then when I found out Lucan went to the Mori, it seemed like the perfect timing. Kates said that she couldn't get any information from

Blue without raising more suspicion. She worried that Blue would start to piece everything together. Blue still thinks you're merely a thread-holder. I want her to keep thinking that. I don't want her to raise Jacith's concerns. He thinks he's only sending an army to find the thread-holder. He doesn't think you're an actual threat. That time will come. It's coming soon. I didn't want to fight Lucan and Jacith at the same time so I moved first. I needed someone to get close to my brother. Kates fit the bill. I knew he'd let her get close."

Jacith, Jacith, Jacith. Everything was about this guy and I was starting to hate him. I gritted my teeth.

"I needed to know what Lucan is planning. He didn't just go away. He went somewhere to wait for his next attempt at you. I'm not stupid. I know my brother and I know he has every intention of getting your power. I needed to know what to expect from him so that I could bring the fight to him. I have to take him out first, at least before Jacith comes to us. You understand, right? Tell me you understand."

Did I? Well, I had to. It made sense. That was the problem. So many lies. So much deception. And Roane acted like none of it was personal. It was all business to him, but it wasn't to me. Kates was my best friend. She had lied to me. Roane had lied to me. Blue had lied to me. And this Jacith person had been manipulating me since I'd been born. Everything about this war was personal to me.

"Davy?"

"Stop!" He reached for my arm, but I backed away. "Just stop. I can't. She's my best friend and you sent her away to a lunatic. She's my best friend, Roane! She could've been killed. Lucan could've killed her."

"She's a slayer."

"She's human. She can die."

"Everyone dies."

"I don't. This is about me. Everyone wants something from

me. They want me dead or they want to take what's in me. Blue was like a mother to me. I thought of her like that. She was my mother. My own mom died. Did someone do that? Did Blue do that? Did she really die in a car accident? Is Kates really my best friend? Maybe Lucan sent her to me too. And you? Are you who you say you are? Do you actually love me? Or is this all a strategy too?"

A part of me cringed as I heard the hysteria in my voice, but another part of me shut down. I felt myself growing numb. I couldn't handle any more deception, any more lies. Where was the truth? I couldn't find it anymore. I couldn't feel it.

18

"**S** hut up."

"What?" I turned.

Roane had an annoyed look in his eyes and he shook his head. "Shut up."

Excuse me?"

"You're not that girl anymore. You're not naïve. You're not being sheltered. And you're in no way being fooled by anyone. Yes, I kept some things from you, but did you really want to know any of that? You knew I had to do things to protect you. You knew Lucan got away. What did you think I was going to do? What did you think about Blue? You knew she's been lying to you and you did nothing."

My mouth fell open.

Roane poured himself a drink, his shoulders tense. "You wanted a hiatus away from this world. I gave that to you. I dealt with the things you didn't want to think about. And your best friend signed up for this gig. She wanted to spy on Blue. She wanted to find Lucan. Unlike you, Kates won't sit back and let things happen to you. She wants to help stop it. Your best friend was looking out for you."

I was about to argue when someone knocked on the door. Both of us turned, but when Gregory looked inside the concern was evident on his face. Roane set aside his glass. "What is it?"

The Viking vampire's eyes darted between us. "We've encountered a scout."

The air in the room shifted. Roane was no longer annoyed. Gregory seemed apologetic and I was stupefied. Roane was out the door before I could think anything else. "I need to deal with this. We'll talk tonight."

The door closed on the last of his message. Okay, it slammed. And I was the irritated one now. Always keeping stuff from me. Before there had been an incoming of Roane warriors, now there was a scout. It all meant the same thing, something that I hadn't had the time to share. The Roane army was close. When I'd zapped in and out from Tracey, my senses knew that they were close. I'd heard the university's tower bell chime in the distance, but I'd been distracted by Talia's ghost and the bag.

A part of me wanted to zap myself to follow Roane, but he would've sensed me. It didn't matter. Lucas didn't want me there and I couldn't do anything to raise further suspicion. So I perused my bedroom once again, but alone this time. The bed was enormous. That wasn't surprising. Roane kept the best for those closest to him and a goliath-sized bed didn't shock me anymore. The silk sheets, the chiffon curtains. All of it set the mood. The image of me with Roane entangled together on those sheets popped in my head. It was so vivid, I had to take a breath and cool down.

"Whatcha thinking, best friend?" Kates drawled. She was propped against the doorframe.

I rolled my eyes and looked for the bathroom. "I'm thinking that it's going to get ugly real soon."

Kates narrowed her eyes and straightened. "You're different. Why are you different?"

Because I was sick and tired of the lies. And because Roane

was right. I had no one else to blame. I'd wanted to turn a blind eye. I hadn't wanted to deal with a lot of things. My best friend was one of them and I knew her better than anyone.

"So." I took a deep breath and sat on the bed. When I raised my eyes, I went inside of her. Kates could feel me, but I didn't care. I wanted her to be uncomfortable. "Are you on his side?"

Her green eyes went wide. "What are you talking about?"

"You know."

"I don't."

I knew she was trying to shake me out. It didn't work. "You went to Lucan. You're back. Whose side are you on?"

"Are you kidding me?"

"I think you might be kidding us. You still love Lucan. It's why you went to him. I know it. You know it. I'm not sure if Lucas remembers it. Did you come back to work for him now?"

We stared at each other. Neither of us blinked.

And then Kates threw her arms in the air. "Are you kidding me? You're my best friend. I betrayed the man I loved for you. What do you think? That I'd double cross you this time?"

"Yes."

She drew back. "You think I would betray you?"

"Knowing that I can't die? Yes. Knowing that whatever he has planned probably won't work. Yes. I think you would promise him the moon to get him to take you back."

"I can't believe you." She shook her head. "You think that I'd hand you over?"

"Is that why he sent you back?" My eyes narrowed and I felt how calm her heart was. The beat was steady, on rhythm. There was no erratic pulse. It didn't speed up or panic. And I wasn't sure what that told me, but I knew Kates. I knew what she was capable of. "Or why he allowed you to come back?"

She froze and I had my answer. The guilt was there. It felt like my question had been a key and it slid into the lock. A perfect fit.

Kates knew it too. The fight left her the next moment. "I never had any intentions of actually going against you. If I had to choose between you two, I would choose you. I always have."

"You didn't before."

She closed her eyes and pressed her fingers to her forehead. "You were never, it was never you or him. I thought you were on the sidelines. But then I realized who you were and that it was you Lucan wanted. I made my choice. I made the same choice when I walked back in here."

"But Lucan thinks—"

"Yes." The admission ripped out of her. "He thinks that you trust me and I can convince you to go back with me."

"Were you intending to tell Roane this?"

Kates shuddered and shook her head. "Do you know what he would do to me? If he thought that there was a chance I'd turn on you? You and I both know he'd slaughter me. And he'd do it with a grin on his smug face."

"You love that same smug face."

"As do you!" She surged to her feet.

I gritted my teeth. "Lucas doesn't want to kill me. He's not some psycho who tried to start a civil war to overthrow some decree."

She laughed and threw her arms wide in the air. "Are you listening to yourself? Have you looked around? I've been here five minutes and it already feels like old times."

"What do you mean?"

"Another war's been declared. It's just not from the smug face I like to kiss." Then she quieted. "Lucas might have different intentions, but he's doing the same thing Lucan did. They're brothers, Davy. They're not that different."

My eyes bulged out and my heart started to race. I felt the anger rise in me. "Lucas is nothing like Lucan."

Kates laughed to herself. "Look at us. 'My boyfriend's better than yours.' Really? That's what we've been reduced to?"

I closed my eyes and forced myself to calm down. No matter

what she did, I always knew Kates wouldn't want me hurt. She'd
push the limits and betray me, but not if it meant that I'd get
hurt. That was the final straw with her and I knew it. I still didn't
trust her when it came to Lucan. If she could find a way to do
what he wanted and be with him where I wouldn't get hurt then
she'd do that first. My saving grace was that Lucan did want to
kill me, or at least take the thread from me and that would
kill me.

Would it? Sireenia had the thread forced out of her. It had
killed her, but I was the Immortal. What would happen if
someone tried that with me?

"Who are you?"

I pulled away from my thoughts and saw Gavin in the doorway. A mask of contempt was on his face, mixed with hostility.
My heart sank. He had heard every word we said.

Gavin narrowed his eyes. I felt the disgust in his voice. "Roane
called. He wanted you to know that he won't be back till morning." He raked his eyes over Kates with a sneer on his face.
"Something came up."

My best friend smirked and stretched. Her arms stretched
wide and lifted her chest up. The entire movement was provoca-
tive. "You're new. Whose bed are you staying in tonight?"

"Kates!"

She snorted. "Like he didn't expect some slutty remark from
me. From the first word he overheard, he labeled me a whore.
Right, whoever you are?"

"This is Roane's best friend."

"I'm Gavin." There was nothing on his face. It was void of
emotion now.

"Well la di da." Kates sounded bored. Her eyes flashed at him.
"You can go back to your best buddy and report my lie to him. I'm
sure he'll be even more indebted to you."

With a growl, Gavin was across the room in a flash. I blinked
once and saw him holding Kates against the wall with a hand to

her throat. She stared at him in a heated challenge, but no snippy comments passed her lips. They continued to glare at the other.

I cleared my throat. "Put her down?"

My best friend smirked. "He would, but he's enjoying it. Aren't you? You didn't expect to be turned on? And by a vampire slayer too?" Then she grunted and slammed an elbow into his face. The positions were reversed in the next second, but Gavin didn't fight back. He wasn't lifted in the air as she had been, but he stood there. His eyes never left hers.

I felt Kates' surprise as she let go and stepped back.

Then Gavin looked at me. "If you need anything, lift the receiver and speak into it. They'll get whatever you need. Roane wanted you to be comfortable."

As Gavin left, I glanced at Kates and saw a look that I'd never seen on her face. Perplexion.

I grinned as I sat on the bed. "That was fun to watch."

"What?" She rolled her shoulders back, but her eyes were lost.

"Maybe Lucan's not the one for you after all?"

Kates crossed to the bar and poured herself a drink. She downed it in one swallow. "Don't go all fairytale romantic on me. That vampire is definitely not 'the one' for me. He's not 'the one' for anyone. Don't you feel it from him?"

"Feel what?"

She poured another drink. "He's cold to the bone, Davy. He might look pretty on the outside and seem flashy, but he's dark. If I were to choose between him and Lucan, I'll always go Lucan. He's not as dangerous as that one."

I'd never seen Kates this rattled so I slipped inside of her and felt her confusion. She was frozen to the bone and I retreated out of her. It gave me the chills.

"I'm going to go." Kates moved to the door.

"Where are you going?"

She lifted haunted eyes to me. "I'll be back. He's right or

Roane's right. Sleep. He'll draw the army away. That's what he's doing right now. You and I go back to Benshire University tomorrow." She flashed me a wolfish grin. "I wonder how Emily's going to welcome me back?"

The joke fell flat. "Where are you going?"

"Don't worry about me. I'll be fine."

"Kates, where are you going? I know that you're going to do something not-good right now. What is it?"

With a hand already on the doorknob, she smiled at me. An odd ray of honesty shone bright from her. I blinked back tears from the power of it.

Her smile turned down at the ends. "I know that I'm not a great person, but I will always be a good friend to you. I will never let you get hurt. Ever. But right now, I have to go do my own thing. I'll be back in the morning. I'm your cover story, Davy. You were gone to help me. I'm sure Roane will have everything in place by tomorrow morning so our story will check out."

She left before I could respond and I was left to sit by myself. I felt more alone at that moment than I'd ever felt my whole life.

WREN EMERGED from the forest behind him and scanned the horizon before them. They were ten miles from town. Lights glimmered behind them and a vast darkness spread out before them. A sneer formed at her lips when she drew beside him. "Tracey's two miles away. I can smell her."

Roane already knew where they were. He couldn't smell a past lover, but he felt them. Their army was intense, built on fury and lies. Some of them were confused. Those vampires followed their leader because they'd been told to, but a majority believed in finding the Immortal and destroying her. He could smell their fear, though many of them weren't aware how deep their terror lay inside of them.

"Jacith is behind this. He's not with them, but his influence is strong over them."

Wren glanced at him. "You think he knows?"

"No." Roane was void of any emotion. "He doesn't know what she is, but he fears it anyways. He knows something has happened. He's stirred something in them, made them fear for their lives if she lives. I don't know if it's from words or magic, but I can feel him among them."

"He's powerful. Maybe he's seen into her already?"

The sword felt heavy slung across his back, but it was where Roane wanted it. Close at hand and ready for when it would be used to kill. He just wasn't ready to kill thousands of what used to be his army.

"Lucas."

Wren surprised him when she spoke his first name. He felt into her, an ability that he'd developed from being intimate with Davy. The vampiress was also scared, but she was in longing. "Go to Tracey. I want her on my side."

"I don't think she'll be converted."

"She will. Tell her that Talia is trying to communicate with the new thread-holder. Tracey will come then."

He felt her shock.

He added, "If she knows that her sister is with us, she'll know that she fights for the wrong side. She can help us."

"And if she doesn't? If she turns on me?"

"She won't with you. If she chooses the Roane Family, she'll send you away, but she'll make sure you're safe."

Wren nodded and left. She moved with a grace that made her invisible and one of the best warriors he had trained. There'd been a moment when he had thought she would've chosen to be at Tracey's side, not his, but now as he watched her vanish into the forest, he was grateful for her loyalty. She was one of his best warriors.

She hadn't been gone long before he felt another's approach. Before Gavin spoke, Roane knew he'd seen Kates.

Gavin spoke in a rough voice. "You could've warned me. I didn't know Davy's best friend was a slayer."

Roane grinned, but the night hid it. "Why would that be important to you?"

"Don't be an ass."

"I thought you were over Isabella."

Gavin let out a ragged breath. "I thought I was too."

Roane waited and knew he'd need a few moments. Gavin would either talk about her or forget the mention of her. He had his answer in the next second.

"Their army is close. What are you planning?"

"I don't want to fight them now. I've sent Wren ahead to convert Tracey to our side."

"But what about the army? They're too close and our numbers aren't enough. We need more vampires." Gavin shifted on his feet. He wanted to fight, purge the memories. Killing would do that.

"Release their scout. He will lead them in the opposite direction."

"And how'd you get him to do that?"

"Jacith isn't the only one who can use magic."

Gavin grinned with a hard look in his eyes. "So you changed his memories."

"It's nice to have a few friendly witches on our side."

"So we wait and make sure they leave?"

Roane stretched his legs out before him. They both sat on the darkened hill. Then Gavin murmured, "What are you going to do about the Bright witch?"

He hesitated for a moment. Roane had felt her when he came to town. He followed Davy to Benshire, but the young witch's presence had been overpowering. She was strong, even with her magic still locked inside of her. The determination he'd seen in her when he had checked on Davy at the library had surprised him. She would unlock her magic and Roane knew Davy, as her friend, would help the witch. It was in her nature. Davy didn't like anything locked away or kept hidden. He just hoped the witch would stand on their side. If she chose their allegiance, she would be more powerful than either she or Davy knew.

He was resigned. "I'm letting that one sort itself out."

19

When I woke up, the room was dark. It was just me and the darkness. The club had shut down hours ago. A sense of emptiness swept through me, but then a different feeling came and took its place. I knew what had woken me so I sat up and hugged my knees. I pulled the sheets close to my chest. "You're here, aren't you?"

No one else was in the room.

But I felt her and I wanted to see her. I wanted to speak to her, hear her answer back. A sudden intensity took hold of me, starting in my feet and sweeping up. A vacuum had formed and it sucked everything up in me. Then I was inside of it. I squinted as my eyes adjusted. What was dark was light now and I knew the Immortal had answered my wish.

Talia stared back at me, perched on the end of my bed. A woeful look was with her, but when I focused on her, she screamed and jumped back. She vanished from the room, but was back in the next instant. I knew I had caught her so I reeled her back. An invisible hand lurched out of me towards her. She appeared again and was more fearful.

Her red hair floated around her as did the white dress she

wore. It was the same outfit she'd worn the night she had
jumped. She looked the same as a spirit as she did as a human.

"Can we talk?" I spoke out loud, but when she frowned I
thought it instead. *'Can we talk?'*

*Her eyes widened again and I felt the panic in her. 'This isn't right.
How are you doing this? You're not supposed to be able to do this.'*

'I don't think I'll be able to do this again.' I felt her start to calm
down and she settled more on the bed. Could a ghost feel
comfort?

'Lucan has my child. You've told Lucas?'

'Yes. Well, not about Lucan. I didn't know.'

She nodded. *'What does he plan to do?'*

'I have no idea.' Did she know about us?

*'Lucan was the one chasing me that night. He and his men. They
killed everyone that was there. They were all trying to protect me, but
none of them were Lucas. Only he could've fought them off. Lucan took
my daughter. He took her and then he wanted to kill me so the thread
would jump to her. I couldn't have that. I couldn't condemn her life. But
then the thread took over my body and I went to you. I have no idea
how I got there, but all of a sudden you were there and I felt it leave
me. I knew they didn't see it leave me so you'd be safe. I wanted to warn
you about Lucan, about my daughter, but I couldn't. I couldn't say
anything.'*

She closed her eyes and flinched. Both of us replayed that
night as she jumped off the building. The peace had been evident
on her face.

That same peace was with her again, but she lifted still-
stricken eyes to my face. Sireenia had said Talia hadn't let go of
the human world and that something still held her there. It was
her daughter.

'I will find your daughter. I will make sure she is safe.'

Her eyes clung to mine. She wanted to believe me. The
desperation was evident, but she held back. I knew she didn't
trust me so I shifted forward and reached for her hand. I held my

breath, but then my fingers touched hers and I let it go in a rush. I could touch a ghost. I could feel her. It was mind-blowing. As I blinked back tears, I couldn't believe it. And then her fingers grasped mine. She tightened the hold and smiled as tears of her own fell too.

'I cannot believe this. You are the true Immortal. You're the one all the prophecies speak of.' Her relief washed over me. 'My daughter's name is Lily. I named her after my mother, but I don't know if they've changed it. Her growth will speed up with the Mori. She could be older than seven months, but she will answer to Lily. It's engraved in her and even Lucan can't take that from her. Please find my daughter. Please make sure she's safe.'

I nodded, feeling overwhelmed. I'd grown accustomed to the weirdness that came with being the Immortal. I could do so much, some of it at my control and most of it not, but this time I was taken aback at the intensity I felt from her and how much my body reacted. My heart pounded stronger with each second I held her hand. I had to find Lily. The child was important, more than me, but before I could ask, something changed and Talia was gone.

"No!" I reached for her, but only felt air. She was gone. Not even her spirit lingered and I knew she wouldn't be coming back.

Lily. I had to find her. I had to protect her.

"Hey."

I shrieked, but calmed when Roane put a hand on my shoulder. "I thought—nevermind what I thought." I brushed away my tears and looked at him. Some light shone into the room from the hall and it cast a shadow over his face. His eyes were hooded and the light reflected off his cheekbones. Two plump lips were visible and my heart skipped a beat at the sight of him. I'd forgotten how good he looked.

Anything I was going to say was forgotten. He opened his mouth to speak, but then I licked my lips. His mouth closed. The air changed in that moment. It pulled us both in and things were forgotten. The world was forgotten or maybe I wanted to forget it for a moment. I didn't care; I just knew what I wanted at that moment. Him.

His hand cupped the side of my face. "What's wrong?"

My heart started to pound, but I shook my head. We should talk. There was so much to tell, but I didn't want to. There was always something wrong.

We'd been apart for too long and now that I knew he loved me, that it was me and not her. I reached for him and pulled him close. His thigh brushed against mine. I closed my eyes and hoped it wouldn't go away. Then his thumb started to caress my cheek and his other hand rested on my chest. He felt my heart pick up speed.

I wanted this. I needed this.

His lips touched mine, but held there. No pressure was applied and then he retreated to close the door. And then with one swift movement, he climbed above me. His thighs cradled mine, but his upper body hovered over me. His lips hadn't moved and I felt my body jerk upwards, starving for his touch. When he held back, I bucked against him. He was torturing me. I felt him between my legs and groaned. It'd been so long.

His thumb still caressed my cheek and then he slammed his lips onto mine. Finally. He took control.

I couldn't think anymore. He slid a hand up my stomach, underneath my shirt. It teased the sides of my breasts and went between up to my neck. As his hand splayed out and grasped my throat, he held my head captive. His tongue swept inside. He went deep, so deep that I could only hold on and let him. My arms wound around his shoulders and my legs wrapped around his waist.

He licked. I nipped. I panted. He claimed. My hands found his shoulders and his went between my legs. One finger slipped inside and I screamed into his throat. Two fingers pumped and my entire body convulsed against him. We blended together. And then what seemed like hours later, I felt him push into me. He filled me and pushed further than I thought my body could handle. I panted and fell onto the bed as Roane stretched me. My arms were pinned down. My legs were under his and he started thrusting.

'You're mine.'

Through a haze, my eyes found his. Dark with desire, a predatory look was in his eyes and I answered to it. I needed it. And then my mind went blank again as he continued to thrust. He built the fever, thrusting harder and harder until both of us panted. Our hands intertwined as he climaxed. We hurdled over the edge, but before I fell back to sleep, Roane started again. The night was spent savoring each other's body. We explored and rediscovered.

He nuzzled my shoulder hours later. "You should sleep."

I heard the exhaustion in his voice and smiled. My own was raspy. "You should too."

He tightened his arms around me. His mouth lingered on my cheek and I closed my eyes when I heard his voice. "I can't. I came back to check on you. I was supposed to relieve Gavin."

I flipped my body over and pushed against him.

Roane groaned as he closed his eyes. He skimmed a hand down my arm, tracing my leg and then brought it back up to rest underneath my breast. It teased me as he rested it there. I felt him push against me and he slipped inside once again. He held himself still instead of thrusting farther inside. We felt each other. My eyes closed and I rested my forehead against his.

'I should go.' Roane kept his eyes closed as he kissed me.

'I don't want this to end.' It'd been too long.

'I'm planning more nights like this.' His eyes opened again.

In that moment, I felt the world come back. It slammed down as it settled over us. When he pulled out and started dressing, I sat back up with the sheet pulled over me. It wasn't to cover up my body, but to hold off the chill. I'd grown cold again.

Roane pulled on a dark shirt over black pants.

"Where are you going?"

He paused while reaching for a vest that housed enough weapons to make my mouth go dry. Why would he need all those? And then I remembered. I clasped my eyes shut. I didn't want to wonder if he was leaving to kill or just to hunt them. That was what he was best at.

"Davy." Roane sat back down on the bed.

"What?"

He searched my face. "Something happened before I came in. What was it?"

My heart picked up its pace. Dare I tell him about her now? So soon after we'd been together? A vision of us in bed flashed in my mind and my heart clenched. I could still feel him in me. I wanted that again. I didn't want him to leave.

"Where are you going? Can you tell me?"

Roane hesitated. He saw my need, though the need was for something else. "We're watching the Roane Army. A scout should've told them they were headed in the wrong direction. I need to make sure they believe the scout and leave."

"Will they be back?" My throat hurt.

"Yes." He tried to smile at me, but it fell short. "They'll be back. I bought us some more time. I need more men to fight on my side."

"What do I do?"

Now he frowned and pulled away. "Where did Kates go? She's to go back to the university with you. Didn't she tell you?"

"She did." It felt so strange now. We talked of business, as if we hadn't loved each other moments ago. "She said that she was my alibi and that you had stuff set in place to back up the story."

"She was supposed to fill you in."

I jerked a shoulder up. "Her and Gavin had a weird reaction to each other. She took off. She's coming back, but I think she had to go and do—" *'What we just did.'*

A grin peeked out from the corner of his mouth. It felt genuine and I relaxed when I saw it. Roane pulled me close and tucked his head into the crook of my shoulder. *'I know you can feel me pulling away. I'm sorry for that.'*

'Why are you doing it? Why won't you let me inside?'

'Because it distracts me too much. I don't want to do what I need to do. I want to be with you and only you. I'm sorry.'

I knew he was apologizing for something more, but I didn't want to know. Not really. And then I couldn't hold it off any longer. He was going back to war and for once, for the first time, I wondered if everything would be okay. A prick of doubt settled inside of me. I didn't want it there. I didn't want to think of what was to come. Not yet.

"I can go back? Everything will be alright?"

"Yeah." He pulled back. He seemed resigned now. "You can go back."

'For now.'

It wasn't permanent. When he stood and went to the door, a part of me died as he left. I felt it curl up and fall down to the pit of my stomach.

I nodded and closed my eyes as he left. The door shut again, but this time the light shone in from the window. Even though the curtains were closed, the day had started and it had invaded my room. I lay down and could've stayed there in bed for the entire day. A part of me wanted to go back to my old life. I could be normal once again, but it wouldn't last. It was a lie. It was only until I'd have to leave again.

The war was real to me now.

A knock at the door woke me. When I looked at my phone, I saw that I'd been asleep for three hours.

"Yeah?" I croaked.

"It's Kates. Your door is locked." She pounded on it again.

I looked underneath the sheet and saw I was still naked. Thankful that Roane had locked the door; I jumped out and threw on the nearest clothes. When I unlocked the door, I tried to smooth my hair down.

She stepped in, took a breath, and then choked back laughter.

"What?"

"I can smell sex all over you." She rolled her eyes.

I wrinkled my nose up and cringed. "And what'd you do the whole night?" I sniffed and then tried to block her aroma. "It's not just booze I smell on you."

"Yeah, well." Kates shrugged. "Can you blame me?"

As she crossed the room and sat in a chair, I heard the swoosh of her clothes. That's when I looked closer. "Are you serious? You're wearing leather?"

A look of pure delight crossed her face. "Are you kidding me? We're going to be seeing Emily again. Nothing else is appropriate. She hates me, Davy. Don't take that away from me. You know I love her hatred."

I rolled my eyes and pushed back my hair. It blocked my sight and I needed to see. I needed to think too. "She's dating a were-wolf now, you know."

Clothes. I needed clothes. Wait, I had clothes. Did I need new ones?

Kates grunted and kicked a bag to me. "I got these for you."

I picked up the bag and looked at it with caution. "I'm not wearing leather."

"It's not, but that look would be hot. Bet you'd get Roane back here in a flash for round two." She gave me a seductive smile. "Don't even act all virtuous right now. I know you want nothing more than to wrap those legs around him and let him dominate you."

I snorted. "Maybe, but we need to talk about Emily. She's not as dumb as you think and she's not as ignorant anymore. She knows witches and werewolves exist. Her mate is one of the strongest there is."

She threw a leg over the side of her chair and struck a sultry pose. "Why do you think I didn't shower? The sex is going to drive him crazy."

Before she had left, I would've made her shower. I would've lectured her on being good and keeping the peace, even though I knew she wouldn't. I didn't say a word now. Instead, I grabbed a towel and walked into the connected bathroom. Then I turned the shower on and stepped underneath the spray.

I needed a shower. I needed to rid myself of the past because I knew that Emily wasn't the only one with questions. Brown. Pippa. Even Blue. They'd all want to know and I'd have to be the best actress in the world. When I moved back into the room, I was dressed and ready to go. Kates narrowed her eyes. I waited for her to say something, but she didn't. She stood at the door and waited in silence.

"We're ready."

20

Kates cast a worried look to me when we were in the backseat of another black car. Roane always sent the same car for my transportation. I'd grown accustomed to them by now, but I wasn't used to my childhood mate being the one worried about me. It was usually the other way around.

"What?"

"Are you okay?" She reached for my hand resting in the middle of the seat between us and hooked her pinkie finger around mine.

I took a deep breath. "I'll be fine."

"You're different."

She should've noticed the night before. I'd been different since I got back, but I kept my mouth shut and shrugged instead. "I just want to be with Roane."

My answer appeased her and she patted my hand. "I'm sure he'll find time to sneak in a quickie. He'll be calling for you by the end of the night."

The war was coming. It was at our doorstep. It might not have rung the bell, but it would. Our time away from it was short lived and Kates had no idea. She was usually the one who knew what was going on. I had been the one in the dark, blinded by my own denial. But this time, everything had changed.

I felt like I was just biding my time. Waiting.

Then we were at the police station and I took a deep breath. Roane said we should head there first since an official investigation had been opened. When I walked in, the clerk hadn't recognized me, but when I told her my name, the pen in her hand dropped. After a moment, she hurried away and I was shown inside. I was stuck in an interrogation room for over an hour. The detective had sat me down at her desk, but too many people were around. They all wanted to hear and some even asked their own questions so she sat me in a private room. Then Kates was brought in too. She took over most of the questions since she was the reason I'd been gone. My acting skills weren't as honed as hers. She was animated and believable while I didn't give a crap.

When everything checked out, that she had called me to help with her mother who had died and then stayed to help with the funeral planning, the detectives let us go. My case was closed, but I knew the detective still had questions. I heard them. She didn't believe me, but why would someone lie about helping out a friend? Or taking care of a funeral? Or that my phone was broken and I didn't think about replacing it. When she ran my name, nothing had come up. Then she ran Kates and a lot came up, but none of it was substantial. The detective had nothing to keep us and I looked fine. So we walked out and I knew I had part one of the subterfuge down. Part two was Emily and she was going to be the hardest one.

When we arrived at the dorm, Kates cast another look at me and bit her lip. "Maybe I should do the talking."

I snorted and then grabbed my bag. "Come on. She'll never believe us. Let me handle it."

When we went inside, the desk clerk had a similar reaction as to the one in the police station. Instead of her pen dropping, her textbook fell to the floor. A few girls were in the lounge and their conversation halted as they stared. I ignored it all. They'd hear the story soon enough. Gossip was good for some things.

And then I felt it. Or I felt him. His power was overwhelming. It came over me in waves and I staggered back from it.

"Davy?"

I saw Kates' lips move, but I didn't hear her. I couldn't. His power blanketed everything else. I couldn't smell. I couldn't hear. I couldn't feel. I could barely think. It was a dense fog that formed a cement box around me. And I was alone in it. No one else felt it and no one else was aware of it.

How could they not know?

I shook my head and tried to push some of it away, but it didn't matter. His power was too much and I started to panic. I reached out blindly. My hand hit something. I felt movement beside me, but I couldn't discern what had happened.

My heart rate picked up. It pounded in my ears. It was so loud. I wished I couldn't hear in that moment, just for a moment. I couldn't handle any of this.

I tried to scream, but nothing came out. And then the power grew. I felt it coming closer. The walls doubled. I fell to my knees and cradled my head. How was I going to do this? I couldn't move past the front desk in my dorm.

A loud thunder blared in my ears. Then another and another. I turned for the door and strained to see through it, but I couldn't see a storm. It wasn't raining.

"Davy!" Kates' cried out. Her voice was so quiet.

I reached out to her and then gasped. I couldn't find her, but then as my heart picked up its pace. More thunder sounded. It was coming closer. It was now one big crackle in the sky. The boom shook me.

'*Suppress your power, Davina,*' Saren's voice snapped in my head. '*Suppress it now. He can feel you too. He knows there's something coming and he's hungry for your power. Suppress it all! Wrap it up and lock it in a box. Push that box deep inside of you.*'

Another boom jerked my body aside.

She screamed this time, *'Do it now!'*

And then it happened. I gasped as my own power swirled in a vacuum. A tornado formed inside of me and everything went around and around. I swallowed thickly, my hands were shaking from the effort, but I imagined a blanket. I saw it happening in my mind. The immortal was snarling, but I kept it in the swirl and the blanket wrapped around it. Then it was forced down, down, further down into a box. As it got there, the lid shook. It couldn't contain it, but I gritted my teeth and I snapped the lid in place. It shut with a violent force, but then I pushed it all the way deep in me, further than I could reach.

Then my eyes opened again and I was trembling in place.

"Davy!" Kates screamed at me. She twisted her hand free from my hold and hissed as she examined it. "I'm bleeding! Holy cow!"

"What?" I couldn't stop shaking. "What happened?"

"You went crazy. That's what happened." She shook her hand as she watched me with weary eyes. "What happened to you?"

And then a guy rounded the corner.

He was tall, built lean, and soft in the face. He had the face of a little boy who'd grown into a pretty boy, but his eyes made me pause. They were old, had seen too much for being so young. Then he stopped altogether, his nostrils flared and I felt him sniffing around me. He started low, around my feet, but his eyes held mine. I slipped into him without realizing it. Images of him as a young wolf came back at me. His fur was a golden bronze with white eyes. He was running and playing with Pippa when she had been a pup. The two nipped at each other, licking each others' toes at the end. And then an image of a woman flew at me. Her hand was outstretched to me, her red hair streamed behind her. She wore a similar dress to what I'd seen on Talia. When her eyes found mine, I sucked in a breath. I was horrified. She was Talia's mother, or the essence of her. There was no soul within her. This was only her residue, left in him. This was Emily's boyfriend. This was the Alpha.

I shut it down. I shut the last bit of power down and got out of him before he knew I was there. He wanted to know why I smelled familiar to him, but Kates' scent distracted him. The booze and sex pulled at him like a drug.

When she winked at me, I knew she'd done it on purpose. Then she drawled, "Got a good enough whiff? Are you a horny puppy now? Gonna go hump something?"

He snapped back and bared his teeth.

Kates rolled her eyes. "Please. Unlike vampires, I can kill your kind. There's no decree saying I can't."

He composed himself and stood at his fullest height. Then he smirked." You couldn't handle me, slayer."

"Maybe not alone, but I've got a few friends. You can't hurt me and I've got no such rule. If an animal's attacking me, I have every right to protect myself."

His lip curled upwards in a heated snarl.

I felt his anger start. It was low, but strong. As it rose in him, it grew even more powerful. Then it got to his eyes. The dark brown color had grown black with a silver haze that clouded over the white in his eyes. His eyes had been white as a pup. I was waiting for the full change now. He was within seconds of transforming in the hallway, but then his mate called him.

"Pete?" Emily was walking towards us.

He turned back and held out a hand. "I'm fine. No worries, hon."

Her eyes skimmed past him and fell on me. Her mouth fell open and she paled. "Oh my god."

My eyes widened too. "Don't faint!"

"Davy?" Her voice had grown weak. She wavered on her feet and then leaned against the wall. "What are you? Are you real? Oh my god."

"You already said that." Kates brushed past them to walk into our room.

My feet were still frozen, but I felt Pete's curiosity double.

"Davy? Is that really you?" Emily seemed to be on the brink of tears, but then Pete took her hand and she pushed them down. He steadied her. I saw the connection between them and it was remarkable. Before, she'd been more neurotic and almost hysterical at times. Now she was strong and calm. He did that for her. I could see his strength flow into her. It tripled when their hands touched.

I wasn't the only one who had changed.

"It's me."

"Davy?" A squeal came from behind me before two arms wound themselves around me. Her voice was muffled into my back. "Thank god you're home. I was so worried."

Only one person would react like that. I laughed. "It's nice to see you too, Brown."

She squeezed harder. "I did magic. I created spells. I begged for my sister's help. Nothing. I couldn't find you. And now you're back. My prayer must've worked. I finally had to go to God, though I hope the goddesses don't condemn me. I was at a loss, but it doesn't matter." She let go and then skipped in front of me as she beamed. Brown threw her arms in the air. "You're home! Welcome back."

"Davy?"

I looked back up and saw Pippa in her doorway. She tugged on her two braids in shock. "Are you—is that you?"

Pete turned to her, but she looked away.

I waved a helpless hand in the air. "Hey everyone. I'm back."

Kates stood in my doorway and lifted up the phone. "Can I order pizza? I'm starving."

Pippa looked taken aback. Brown frowned. "Who are you?"

Emily seethed, "Out! Get out! She was gone because of you, wasn't she? Of course, you would do something like this. I bet you wouldn't even let her call home. I bet you said that you did, that you took care of it all. And Davy, being the good friend she is, believed you. It's all your fault."

Everyone was taken aback, even me. Kates looked annoyed, but I caught the amusement in her eyes. When her lips curled up in a malicious smirk, I darted forward and stood between the two. "It's not her fault. Yes, I left because of her. Her mom died, Em. Be nice. And since Kathryn was like a mother to me, I didn't really think to call. I'm really sorry. The funeral took planning. Then her family and my family were there. When it was time to come back, I didn't want to come back. I didn't know how to deal." I lifted both my shoulders up in a helpless shrug. "I'm sorry. I really am."

"Good one on the guilt," Kates murmured under her breath.

"Shut up," I hissed through my teeth.

Emily frowned. "You were gone because of a death?"

Pippa remained quiet and then Brown exclaimed, "We didn't even think about that! We're so stupid. What else would make someone leave so quickly? I wouldn't call if my mum died. Well, I might call Davy now, but I wouldn't call anybody else. No one would care."

I watched my roommate and waited. Did she buy it? Kates was right, I'd added some guilt in the hopes that it would push Emily into accepting the story. I couldn't have her asking any questions. I kept an uneasy eye on her boyfriend. He didn't buy the story, but I hoped he wouldn't say anything. It wasn't his place. He didn't know me or my relationship with Emily.

"I'm sorry, Davy," Pippa spoke in a soft voice. "We didn't even think to call your home."

"We didn't have a number *to* call."

I heard the anguish in my roommate's voice and relaxed. I was a horrible friend. "Maybe we should go to a hotel? I don't want to be a bother. I know that you're probably used to having a single room."

"No," Emily spoke up. "No, please. Stay. I'm sorry." She looked past me. "I'm sorry, Kates."

She sniffed as she opened a bag of chips. "It's no problem." Then she glared at Pete. "I don't want the wolf here. He makes me uncomfortable."

Emily sucked in her breath.

Pippa held a hand to her mouth. Brown opened her mouth and then closed it. Then she repeated the motion.

"I don't believe you—" He surged forward, but Emily caught his arm.

"Honey, stop. Please."

"You're going to let her get away with that?" His hands were fisted at his side. "And I don't buy their story. It sounds fishy to me."

Brown closed her mouth with a snap.

"It doesn't matter." Emily moved close to him. "Even if it isn't true, my roommate's back. I need to be here for her. If Davy went somewhere, it was for a good reason. I know it was."

'She didn't trust me enough to tell me. I can't push her. I care about Davy. I want her to trust me. Please, Pete. Please go.'

'There's something that doesn't smell right about her.'

Emily drew upright. "You can go. Thank you. I'll see you tomorrow for lunch."

The dismissal was swift and harsh, but effective. Pete went, but not without glaring at us. Even Pippa melted away.

Brown bounced past us and into the room. She plucked the bag of chips from Kates' hands and settled on our couch.

"Your boyfriend doesn't like me. Is that going to be a problem?" Kates smirked as Emily followed everyone else inside. She lounged back on our couch.

"What. Huh? No. I don't even like you."

Kates quirked an eyebrow up and winked at me. *'That was easier than I thought. Your holy roommate barely put up a fight.'*

I looked away and stood there. What do I do next?

'Don't pretend you can't hear me. I know you can. I can't hear you, only human and all, but seriously. Emmykins folded like a rag. What's up with that? Where'd her backbone go?'

She had a backbone, but I'd snapped it in two. Manipulation and guilt could confuse almost anyone. When Kates started sending her thoughts to me again, I closed my eyes and blocked her. I already felt bad about lying to Emily and I'd only been back for five minutes. How had I kept up the lie before?

"Davy?" Brown had stopped her chattering. "Are you okay? Your aura looks green."

21

The afternoon was strained in my room. Emily wanted to murder Kates. Kates enjoyed fueling that fire and Brown was confused by everything. Her eyes were wide as she studied me at moments, and then studied the tension between my roommate and best friend. After awhile, she threw her hands up in surrender and announced we should go drinking.

To my surprise, the other two jumped on board.

Kates suggested a vampire bar, but since I still didn't know if Emily knew they were real, I vetoed that suggestion. Then Emily suggested a werewolf bar and Kates shot that down. The truce was Brown's idea.

"What's the name of it?" Kates narrowed her eyes.

"Bosom's."

Emily's eyebrows shot up and I asked, "Like boobs?"

"No, like, well. Yeah. It's all about sisterly love and stuff." The more we stared at her, the more uncertain Brown became. She was staring at her shoes by the end of that statement.

"It sounds like a witch bar," Kates said in a flat voice.

"It's not a witch bar." But Brown was busy inspecting anything around us. No eye contact.

"Wait!" Emily held up a hand and skirted from the room. She was back within minutes with a full grin on her face. "I asked the girl across the hall and she recommended a place called Barbwire?"

"Sold," Kates sighed.

I surged to my feet. "I'm good with that one."

Brown frowned. "Where is that place?"

"It doesn't matter. That's where we're going." Kates raked her up and down. "You need a wardrobe change."

She looked down. "What are you talking about? I think I look good."

"For a witch." Kates bent into her own bag and started rummaging around.

"I *am* a witch."

I couldn't help but watch Emily through their exchange. She had seemed uneasy about the witch stuff before I disappeared, but now she didn't blink an eye. I started to wonder if she knew more about the supernatural than she was letting on.

"Not tonight you aren't. If you hang out with me, you gotta look good. None of this stuff." She waved a hand up and down Brown's figure.

Brown looked down at herself. "What do you mean?"

"Nothing." Kates threw an arm around her shoulder and drew her close. "Trust me. I'm going to make you hot. The witch look isn't attractive. You're going to send the guys running away. You want them to come to you."

And make her hot she did. Brown emerged from our room with skintight jeans and a flashy white camisole. Kates wanted her to wear a black bra underneath, but it was vetoed by everyone else. She matched Kates, who wore skintight white pants and a black camisole. When my roommate disappeared with clothes, I was a little scared she would return with her Target outfit from the last time she had gone out with Kates and me. I was wrong and impressed when she came back in loose-fitting white pants and a conservative black tank. She had a classy look to her now. I frowned at my own closet. Kates would want me to look like a slut. Brown wouldn't care and Emily would vote for something similar to her outfit. I ended up with basic jeans and a pink top that ran around my neck, wrapped around the opposite side and looped together in the back.

Kates whistled when I stepped out of the room. "If only Roane could see you now."

I grinned and then stiffened as I sent a furtive look towards my roommate. Emily went rigid for a moment and then relaxed. Brown started to bounce up and down. "Girls' night out. Girls' night out."

She stopped when Kates grabbed her arm. "Chill, girl."

"Oh, okay." But the stupid smile wasn't wiped clean.

Emily fell in step beside me as the other two led the way. She remained quiet all the way until we got to the bar. We followed the directions the girl from across the hall gave us. After we parked five blocks away and crossed over a park, I caught a glimpse of Barbwire. The entire building looked like an old warehouse with a simple red door in the front. A line of people wrapped around the building. There was nothing glamorous about the place, but as we drew closer, I saw someone in line and groaned.

"What?" Emily looked ahead. "Is that Holly from the hotline?"

My joy for the night was gone.

Holly looked the same. Oval face. Pasty skin. Brown eyes that reminded me of an owl. She looked like a librarian intent on getting drunk. She wore a gray skirt and a low-cut white top underneath a matching grey lace vest. When she reached behind and grabbed the arm of a guy, I felt the desire inside of her. Oh yes. The girl was on a mission. Then she looked my way.

And I froze. Adam was with her.

She gasped and a wide smile spread over her face. "Davy?! Is that you?"

Kates asked underneath her breath, "Who's that?"

"She works at the hotline," Emily murmured back.

"Wasn't he the guy that got killed from there too?"

"What?" Brown gasped.

Holly darted our way. Her hand was still attached to Adam's arm and he looked like he had seen a ghost.

Holly clapped her hands together. "How are you, Davy? You never showed up again to cover Adam's shifts. Adam, aren't you going to say hello?"

"Hi, Davy." His eyes darted behind my shoulder.

When he tensed, I knew he had recognized Kates. Then she jostled forward and threw out an arm. "How's it going? I'm Kates, Davy's best friend. Hi, Adam. Remember me?"

He froze. Even his eyes didn't blink.

Holly's bright smile dimmed a bit and she glanced to her date. "Hi, I'm Holly. You know Davy?"

"Best friends. Childhood." Kates threw an arm around my shoulder. Her smile was easy, but her eyes were pinned on Adam.

"Oh. That's great."

Then Brown burst forward. "I'm Sarah, but you can call me Brown. I'm a witch. What are you?"

Holly's eyes threatened to burst out. "What did you say?"

"I'm a witch. I'm not very powerful. Or, well, I barely have any power, but I will. Someday."

Kates muttered under her breath, "You really need to stop telling people that."

Emily moved forward. "I agree. You need to learn some boundaries."

"Boundaries? But she's a friend of Davy's."

"There are different types of friends."

Emily nodded.

"Wait, what?" Holly kept glancing between all of us. Her hand tightened on Adam. "What's going on? Davy?"

Adam looked everywhere and anywhere, just not as us.

"Oh look. It's almost time for you to go in." Kates pointed behind them. When Holly saw the bouncer motioning towards them, she swallowed and then came to a decision. "You can come in with us."

"What? No. That's okay." I shook my head.

"I mean it. The line's really long and they have a limit. Come on. Come in with us."

"What the hell." Kates broke free and led us forward. Holly seemed uncertain, but then nodded before jumping forward. She motioned to the big guy in black. "They're with us."

When the bouncer's cold eyes passed over us, he paused on me and then nodded. "Sure."

A shiver went down my spine. I felt like he had looked inside of me. As I passed through, I looked back over my shoulder. He was still watching me, but Kates grasped my hand and dragged me the rest of the way. When the door closed she whispered in my ear, "He's one of Lucan's. Don't draw any more attention. He knows me, not you. Let's keep it that way."

I nodded and then was distracted when Adam stopped beside me. When I looked into his eyes, I was shocked. The Adam I knew had been happy and carefree. He had liked me before, but now he feared me.

The old Adam was gone. I had been a part of that.

I didn't say anything. He didn't say anything either, but his eyes went to Kates again. No matter what he'd told the police before, he knew what she had done. I went inside of him and felt how he blamed her for Shelly's death. That's when I knew that no matter how much time he took off, he'd never be over the past.

"Let's get something to drink." Kates gestured towards the bar and then grabbed Brown and Emily. She pulled them around groups and weaved through until they were on the other side of the club. I followed at a more sedate pace, but I couldn't shake the look from Adam's eyes. He watched us go as Holly stood silent beside him. She had a hand over her mouth, but she didn't stop us. When we found an empty table, I saw the relief in Kates' eyes. I wondered why, but then she plopped her purse on the table and took out her clutch. "I'll buy. Save my seat."

Emily scooted onto a high-top stool. "Is this going to be a repeat of the last time all three of us went out? I still don't quite remember what happened that night."

I gritted my teeth and realized that no one had explained she'd been love-bitten by Bennett. But that had been when she hadn't known about vampires and werewolves. Now she knew about werewolves, which reminded me. "How'd you handle it when Pete told you he was a werewolf?"

Emily blinked. She didn't look surprised at the question. "I thought he was nuts at first. And I ran away from him, but then he changed in front of me. I had to believe it after that."

"He changed in front of you? He could control the werewolf?"

She nodded. "It's a part of him. He can change whenever he wants. It's very exciting at times."

"You're okay dating a werewolf?"

"You're okay dating Lucas?" Emily shot back with a hard look in her eyes.

It made me pause. Did she know what he was?

She added, "We never talked about him before you disappeared."

We hadn't. "This is awkward."

Brown scooted off her stool. "I'm going to the bathroom."

Now it was just me and Ems, and there are so many lies I had told her.

I cleared my throat. Emily had a guarded look in her eyes, but she stared right back. So I started, "I met Roane—"

"You call him Roane."

"That's his last name."

"How long?"

"What?"

"How long have you two been together?"

"A few months, I guess. We started a few months ago, but I guess we didn't get together 'together' until yesterday?"

"Yesterday?" Emily gulped and reared back. "I thought you didn't come back until today. You went to see him first?"

"I—" I had no idea what to say now.

Kates appeared with a tray of drinks in hand. She pushed her purse onto my lap and shoved the tray on the table at the same moment. Then she scooted next to me on a stool. "I forgot how grabby guys can be. I've been spending too much time with stiffs. One guy had his hand down my pants before I could knee him in the balls."

A look of hurt flared in Emily's eyes before she grinned and looked down. As she did, I met Kates' knowing look and knew she had come back at the right time.

I no longer wanted to be there.

"I would recommend no one going to the bathroom without me." Brown returned and pulled up a stool on the other side of Emily. "I have sanitizer with me and you'll want it. I think people were having sex in the stall beside me. And I think a girl was puking in the *other* stall."

Kates choked back a laugh. "Something tells me you're a magnet for fun."

"Fun for you maybe, but not me." Brown reached for a drink and downed it in two swallows. Then she reached for another.

Kates laughed and pulled the tray out of reach before she pointed at Emily. "This girl was wasted the last time we went out. Davy took care of her and so that means it's my turn to take care of the drunk. I don't want to have to take care of you."

"Oh, that's okay. It takes a lot for me to get drunk." Brown tipped her head back and finished the second drink.

"There are seven shots in each of these."

The glass fell to the table from Brown's hand, but Kates' caught it. Her grab was lightning fast and Brown's eyes went wide.

As Kates placed the glass on the table, Emily let out a ragged breath. "Oh wow. That was, that was fast."

Brown had new emotion in her eyes as she watched Kates. "You're really fast, like crazy fast. Oh my—"

Emily grabbed the witch's hand and dragged her off the stool. "I'm going to take her to the dance floor before she goes into too much shock."

"Did you see how fast she was?" We heard Brown ask Emily before they were out of earshot.

Kates turned to me. "So what'd the roommate have to say?"

I shook my head and reached for a glass. "I don't want to go over it."

"It was about Roane?"

"Yeah." Then I took a sip and wrinkled my nose. "This is awful, Kates."

"I know." Kates shook her head. "And that says a lot about the witch. The girl isn't normal. What are you doing hanging out with her?"

I tried another sip, but it tasted too horrible. "I thought you liked her?"

"I do, but she's off. I can't get a good read on her and that makes me nervous. What read do you have on her?"

What read did I have on her? That she was going to be a very powerful witch and sooner than I had thought. But I wasn't going to tell Kates that so I smiled. "She's a good person. I trust her."

"Okay." She lifted her glass and saluted me. "Here's to you and who you pick to surround yourself. I shouldn't complain. You're still talking to me."

"Very true."

As I reached forward to clink my glass with Kates, tingles shot up and down my spine. Someone was watching me. I scanned the club and then backpedaled when I saw a lone female in a narrow hallway. She watched me back and then I realized it was Pippa. When she saw that I'd seen her, she motioned to me.

"I'll be right back." I slid off my stool before Kates could ask me any other questions. As I drew closer, I asked, "Pippa?"

She looked scared. Pale.

"What are you doing here?"

Her eyes glanced over my shoulder. "You're in danger."

"Come again?" When she looked behind me again, I turned as well. Emily and Brown had returned to the table with Kates. All of them were smiling and laughing. "Do you want to go over there?"

Her eyes went wide. "No. I can't. And you shouldn't either. You have to get out of here, Davy."

"Why?"

"Um." She bit her lip and her hands were twisted into the ends of her shirt.

"Pippa, what's going on?" I couldn't look away from her hands. They kept twisting around each other. Something was wrong, horribly wrong. And then I slipped inside of her.

'She has no idea. I don't know how to tell her. Oh god. Why couldn't he leave it alone? He had to go and tell Mother Wolf. What's Emily going to think?'

I grabbed her shoulders. "Pippa! What is wrong? What's happened?"

"It's Pete," she wrung out. "I've been shielding you from Mother Wolf, but he didn't. He went straight to her. I could tell he didn't like you. He knows that you're different. He doesn't know what it is, but neither do I. He went straight to her."

"To who?"

"To Mother Wolf." She took a deep breath. "She sent a small army for you. They're coming here. Now."

I gulped. "How big is a 'small army'?"

"Twenty wolves. Her best fighters."

"And Pete? Is he one of them?" I had no idea what to do if the

Alpha was going to attack. Saren helped me evade him once. And after my first encounter with him, I didn't think I could suppress the Immortal again so quickly.

"No, but he'll be watching. They aren't supposed to hurt Emily, but it's hard to control that in a fight. Especially when it includes vampires." As she finished speaking, her eyes went over my shoulder again.

I turned, but I already knew who she meant. Roane stood a few feet from the doorway. Gregory trickled in behind him, followed by Gavin, Wren, and Tracey. Another vampire stood behind her, but all of them stood as one force.

22

R oane saw me in the next second and jerked his head towards the door. As I grabbed Pippa's hand and pulled her with me, Gavin hurried across the club to grab Kates' arm too. She yanked it back, but when he whispered something in her ear, she relaxed and looked for me. I gestured towards the rest of the group and watched as she switched from best friend to vampire slayer. It was shocking, but also not. Before Gavin found her, Kates had been laughing. A different look now slithered over her face and her eyes sparked in anticipation. She was born to hunt, much like Roane. It was what she loved.

As she met me at the door, chills went down my spine. She was once again the stranger that had kidnapped my friends not long ago. Emily stood behind her with frightened eyes and I knew she recalled the same event. Brown was beside her. She stared in befuddlement at Gregory. Her eyes trailed up his giant form and back down, and then repeated. As the group started outside, Brown scurried to follow him.

Gregory looked at her and his eyes narrowed. The rest of his face was emotionless, but he glanced at me as we followed Roane into a back alley. I shrugged.

Wren and Tracey fanned out to stand at one end of the alley. They both passed me, but Tracey met my gaze for a brief moment. She was taller than I had realized and wore darkened red armor with her long blonde hair pulled into a braid to fall at her waistline. When she passed Gavin, I saw they were built the same. Tall and muscular. Gavin was lean for a guy, but she was sturdy for a female.

'The wolf told you?'

I looked at Roane, who stared at me with hard eyes. He was brimming in fury, but it was suppressed. He asked again, *'She told you? A pack of wolves are coming. We need to move. I don't want to fight them in town.'*

'The Alpha went to the Mother Wolf and told her about me. I don't know what he said, but he knows I'm different. He doesn't like me. Pippa came to warn me about them. How did you know?'

'Some wolves are loyal to me.' Then Roane barked at Gavin, "We'll cross the park. Kates, you'll drive their car back to the dorm. We'll follow and transport everyone somewhere safe."

Gavin nodded and walked to the front of the alley. Gregory took position next to me and Brown followed behind him. The other vampire trotted back in, past Wren and Tracey towards the group. He swept cold eyes over me and spoke to Roane, "They're coming in fast. If we hurry, we can meet them in the park."

Roane's jaw clenched together, but he gave a brisk nod. As soon as he did, Wren and Tracey rushed past us. Gavin ran with them and they went in three different directions.

"My orders?"

Roane glanced at me and then said to the vampire, "I'm staying with Davy. Gregory, you—"

He jerked his head behind him and everyone looked at Brown, who was nearly pressing into his side. She scurried back a couple steps and gave everyone a sheepish grin. "He's like the jolly green giant, but not green."

"—can stay with the witch," Roane finished with a frown.

Brown perked up. "Gee, thanks. You know I'm a witch."

"Lucas?" The other vampire stood to the side.

"Gregory, keep Emily with you too."

"And the wolf?" Gregory glanced at Pippa, who stood behind the group. She looked unsure.

Roane's eyes hardened. "I'm sure they won't hurt their own."

"Lucas?"

He jerked his head in a nod. "Bastion, circle behind us. Wren, Tracey, and Gavin will set up a perimeter. Anyone who gets through them, Gregory and I can handle. You'll scout around and sweep back. I don't want anyone trying to get us from behind."

"And me?" Kates asked in a firm voice. "I can fight too."

With a smug look, Roane told her, "There's no decree against them."

A bright smile filled her face. The anticipation in her eyes doubled. It sent a shiver down my back as she purred, "That's what I thought."

'Lucas, they're here!' Wren's thought warned the vampires.

As one person, Roane, Gregory, and Bastion jerked around. Emily squeaked. Brown grabbed hold of Gregory's shirt and flew with him. Her body picked up in the air as if she were a balloon. Kates jerked forward, but stopped at the sight. As the vampires disappeared down the alley, she held back.

Kates looked at me. "Your friend is crazy."

I had enough time to shrug before she shot after them. Pippa, Emily, and I were the only ones left in the alley.

"What's going on?" Emily hugged herself tightly.

Pippa stood next to her, but didn't say anything. She looked at me instead. They both looked at me. "What?"

"They're here for you. What's going on?" Emily gave me a 'duh' look. "Are we under attack?"

"Oh my god!" Pippa burst out. "You're not stupid, Emily. You know what's going on. That's why you're not that scared. I can tell when you're scared and you're not."

"What are you talking about?" Emily's lip trembled.

"He just said 'what about the wolf?' and the other guy said 'I doubt they'll hurt their own.' You know we're under attack. They're all acting like they're going to war. What does that mean? That they're going to war! Figure it out, or at least stop acting like you haven't because I know you have. You're just acting like this so that people will take care of you. God forbid that you'd have to fend for yourself."

Pippa started to walk away when Emily cried out, "What do you mean by all of that?"

"Davy!" We turned at the fierce command. Roane stood a few feet away and he gestured to me. "Let's go!"

I looked back. What would happen to Emily and Pippa?

Pippa waved me to go. "I'll take care of Emily. We'll be fine. Be safe."

I opened my mouth to ask if she was sure, but there wasn't enough time.

Roane grabbed me around my waist and flew out of the alley. We were in the park within moments. When he stopped, I was plastered against him and a wolf was in the air. He had leapt in the air with his mouth opened, fangs extended, but Roane reached up, grabbed his hair and flung him across the park. The wolf bounced against a tree. As it snapped in two the wolf threw his head back up and snarled at us. He took off again. Bounding towards us, he tried to go around us this time. Roane bent down and sped towards him. He met him halfway and caught the wolf unaware. With another throw at the same tree, the wolf was impaled on the broken stump. The body twitched and jerked to get free, and a high pitched whimper came from its mouth as it did. Two more wolves snapped to attention. They had been stalking Wren, but whirled around. As one went to its mate the other flew at us.

Roane tucked me behind him. *Under any circumstance, no powers. You are human and only human. Got it?*

I gave him a mental salute, but the wolf was on us. Roane ducked underneath the massive jaws, caught him around the neck and twisted. It snapped in two and the giant body fell limp at his feet.

Five wolves froze in place. As one body, they turned and regarded Roane. Wren plunged a dagger into one of their necks. Gavin took hold of another and threw him, but the other three bounded towards us.

"Gregory!" Roane called out.

The Viking vampire looked up, saw the situation, snapped his wolf in two and took three long-legged strides towards us. He jumped and grabbed me from his leader's arms in mid-air, just as the three wolves ascended on Lucas. Brown smiled at me from underneath Gregory's long arm. She held onto one of his belt loops with a knife in hand.

"Hi, Davy. Isn't this exciting?"

"Brown." I shook my head at her. "You are crazy."

"I tried doing spells, but they didn't work. So then I tried to twist their tails when I caught them. I distracted a few, but one of them just swished me away." She showed me a red welt on her cheek. "It got me good so now I just hold onto Green's belt."

"Green?" I said faintly, but was distracted when Gregory deposited us both of the ground. We were away from the fight now and I expected him to return. He didn't move. I knew his job was now to guard us.

"It's my nickname for him. I think the leader called him Greg, but I like Green." Brown spoke as if we were shopping for a couch.

"Not much fazes you, does it?"

She let out a puff of air. A strand of her hair flew back in place. "Not much, no. You fight. You either live or die. It's easy to know what to do. Other stuff's harder to figure out."

Gregory glanced back and we quieted.

From there we watched the fight unfold. Roane was quicker

than the others. He reacted faster and with more strength than the wolves expected. The body count grew around him, but the fight continued. Wren and Tracey had their own system. Wren would distract the wolf and lure it in while Tracey would come behind with the fatal stab. After the first one they killed, I saw that Tracey knew where to hit their heart. The wolves fell instantly. Gavin and the other vampire, the one who Roane had called Bastion, didn't fight with weapons. They threw the wolves around or were thrown by the wolves. Eventually, each of them would have enough of a hold on the necks to snap them. They just weren't as quick at it as Roane.

Kates fought her own way. She punched, twisted, rolled underneath them. I realized that she used her smaller size against them and moved around until they couldn't keep up. That was when she'd bring her gun up and shoot them in the head. Her arm was steady, her feet planted apart. She knew what she was doing and she had no qualms about it.

For some reason, the other vampires didn't bother me when they killed the wolves, but watching Kates brought chills down my back. She was human, but she wasn't at the same time. Was that how I was going to be? Was I going to become like her? I shuddered at the thought, but I knew I couldn't hide much longer.

When only seven remained, the wolves began to disperse. A few tried to drag their fallen comrades with them, but then Roane announced, "We will allow you to take them with you as long as you do not come back. This is my territory. No wolf will come in and take what is mine. Take that message to your Mother Wolf. Tell her that she's mine."

All of them stopped in their tracks and then turned to one in the back with a fur coat of sleek black. He padded forward and lifted piercing blue eyes.

Roane waited and held his gaze.

The wolf lowered his head in submission. The fight was done, simple as that.

I looked to my far right. Pete stood in an alley with his fists bunched at his side. He wanted to go out and fight with them. I felt the immense control it took to keep him where he stood, away from the fight. It was costing him. Sweat poured down his body to puddle around his feet.

His eyes caught mine and he jerked back in surprise.

As I held his gaze, I let him see inside of me. I wanted him to see inside of me. I was strong. I wasn't afraid. And I knew, without a doubt, that I'd have to deal with him at some point. Pete felt all this from me. I didn't let him go too far, not far enough to sense the Immortal, but I wanted him to know that I wasn't scared of him. The vampires had defended me this time, but there was going to be a time for my fight. I was starting to look forward to that now.

Then Roane stood in front of me and blocked my view. He snarled at Pete, "Leave."

I grabbed Lucas' arm. "No. This is my fight."

"It's not!" He turned on me and grabbed my arms. "It's really not, Davy."

"Yes." I took his fingers and lifted them off my arm. "It really is." But when I moved around him, Pete was already gone.

I was conscious of Brown's gaze. She watched every interaction between Roane and me, but I didn't feel judgment from her gaze. Then she took my hand and I felt her calm slip into me. Immediately, my heart slowed down. Rational thought returned and then I was able to remember Emily and Pippa.

"Where's Emily?"

Kates had come over. She pointed down a hill. "They're safe. The Werewolf Wonder didn't stick around for his mate. I wonder why."

"Because she's not his, not yet." I held Roane's gaze as I spoke, "She's still my friend more than she's his girlfriend."

I moved forward, but Kates stopped me. "She's going to have to pick sides, Davy. Or you're going to have to let her go."

"She's not a part of this. She's not supposed to be a part of it. She shouldn't have even been here."

But then Roane pulled me closer. "Enough." He turned towards Gregory. "Take them to the estate."

"All of them?"

"Wren, Tracey, grab the other two. Yes, all of them."

"Roane," I started.

He turned and walked away. Gavin gave me a soft grin before he followed behind him. Bastion went next and then Gregory spoke up, "Davy?"

Brown patted my arm.

"Yeah," I sighed.

Kates laughed, "Road trip."

"Shut up," I snarled at her before I followed the jolly green giant. Brown was already going after him. Pippa and Emily got into a car with Wren and Tracey while the rest of us climbed into the back of Gregory's car.

"Where are they going?"

Gregory didn't answer.

Kates did. "They're following the werewolves, making sure they leave town."

Why wouldn't they? I should've thought of that in the first place. I rolled my eyes at my own sarcasm. What was my problem? Roane had come to protect me. He did it for me. If he hadn't, I would've used my power and the truth would've been out. Everyone would know it was me. My friends would know too and maybe that was my problem. Maybe I was sick of hiding? Maybe I was tired of being protected like I was some helpless weakling? I wasn't one, not any longer.

I sighed and then settled back in my seat. As I turned to look outside, I bolted back up. Saren stood on a hill. She was watching our car and I knew she'd been watching me the whole time.

When our gazes met, she grinned and lifted two fingers in a salute. Then she disappeared and something in me went with her.

It was over. I knew at that moment that my normal life was gone. Werewolves had attacked. Vampires had defended. And one of my guides had stood back because she knew I could handle it on my own.

I couldn't stay out of the war any longer. I was the entire reason for the war.

A tear slipped down my cheek and I felt someone take my hand. Brown gave me a smile and then squeezed my hand. *'I might be going out on a limb here, but I'm pretty sure you can hear thoughts. Maybe you can't. If that's the case, then I'm just thinking to myself which is normal. I do that a lot, but I know something's different about you. Maybe this is it or maybe this is a part of it. I don't know. All I know is that whole fight was about you. And the other thing I know is that when I'm not around you, I don't feel the magic in me. Okay. I feel it a little, but I always thought I was just fooling myself. But when I met you, I felt the magic in me. It was the first time I knew it was really there. I always feel it when you're around and that means something. So whatever's going on, I'm always going to be grateful to you. You made me not believe everybody when they said I was crazy.'*

Another tear fell down my cheek.

'Thank you, Davy.' She squeezed my hand once more.

23

Everyone was quiet when we arrived an hour later. Even Wren seemed withdrawn as she showed the rooms to everyone. Tracey stayed in the foyer, which was big enough for a tennis court, but I felt her eyes. They hadn't left me since we'd arrived and despite the private room I was shown, I still knew she could see me. When someone knocked on my door, I wasn't sure if I should answer. I didn't know if I wanted to talk to Talia's sister or not, but then Kates burst through the door.

"That was a welcoming invite." She flung herself on my bed and flashed me a smirk. "What's your problem? Your honey came to your rescue and now you get to sit back and wait for him to come to bed tonight. I don't know about you, but that would give me the shivers, the *good* shivers."

"I was just attacked by werewolves. Unlike you, I don't find that thrilling."

"You should." Kates sat up. "What's your problem?"

"Have you seen what's going on?" My voice went shrill.

"Have you?" My childhood best friend shook her head and got off the bed. "Davy, this is what happens. We fight. We deal. Then we wait for the next fight. Why are you acting all shocked and bothered by it? Wait. I should've thought of it before, but I didn't." Then she sighed. "You can't deal, can you?"

"Shut up."

"You can't." She stood behind me. "I can't believe it, but you were the one that lit Craig on fire. It's not like this is the first time you've had to deal with something bad."

"Craig wasn't bad. Craig was a nuisance. He didn't mean that my entire life would change. I did what I did so that my life wouldn't change."

Her voice gentled. "You lit him on fire. You burned him alive, Davy. I was there and don't act like you were doing it to save yourself. You were doing it to hurt him. You wanted him dead."

"I didn't kill him. Those hunters—" My voice trembled.

"Those hunters ripped him apart, but he was dying anyway. He was already on fire when they got him. You killed him; they just made it go faster. You're going to have to do worse. You know that, right?"

Could I deal with what I'd done in the past? Craig had been obsessed and a vampire stalking me had made me go crazy. I won't ever deny that, but to acknowledge that I'd made the decision to kill him, I wanted to hide from that reality. I knew it was there. I'd made the decision, but what sort of a human was I if I could do that and then pretend I was still normal? What did that say about me?

"Davy, this is just the beginning." Kates sounded shaken. "I thought you were ready. I thought Roane had been prepping you this whole time, but he hasn't. You aren't ready for anything."

"I'm ready for what I need to be!" I shouted at her, but stopped when someone else knocked on my door.

Emily poked her head inside. "Can we come in?"

"We?" Kates laughed under her breath.

Pippa and Brown followed behind. All three of them looked around the room.

"You have a better room than me," Brown exclaimed. "You could have two bedrooms in this room."

"Three." Pippa gave me a shy smile.

Emily was quiet, but she glared at Kates before she sat in a far corner.

Kates' eyebrows went up. "Could you find a seat farther? In the next room maybe?"

"Kates."

"What?" She looked at me. "The girl's got a problem with me. I'm just pointing out the nonverbals."

"Nonverbals?" Brown's eyes danced between us.

"She glared at me and then sat as far away as possible. You know what that's called? Passive aggressive. I've heard that's not good."

"Leave her alone." I felt a headache coming on.

"Tell her not to glare at me."

"She didn't say anything."

"That's the point. Passive aggressive. She's being passively aggressive with me and it worked. She's got you doing her dirty work."

"That makes sense," Brown murmured as she sat beside me on the bed.

"Thank you."

"I don't like you. You know that." Emily glared again.

"It's like you're blaming me for this. I had nothing to do with it. If you want to blame someone, blame your wolverine, not me."

"What are you talking about?" My roommate stood. "Not all werewolves are connected to each other. They don't all know each other."

"No, but when your honey runs to the Mother after meeting Davy for two seconds and she sends a pack after her, I'd say he had something to do with it."

"Pete had nothing to do with that. And what does this have to do with Davy?"

"Please. Everybody knows it. Even the witch knows."

Brown gave Emily a tentative smile. "He was there."

"Pete would never hurt anybody. He's not like that."

Pippa's eyes went wide and Kates snorted in disbelief.

"What?" Emily looked around. "He wouldn't."

"Do you know that he changes into a werewolf?"

"That doesn't mean he hurts people."

Kates laughed. "I just want to make sure you're not denying that too."

My roommate's face twisted into an angry scowl.

"Ask her." Kates gestured to Pippa. "Weren't they friends since the cradle or something? She's the one who warned Davy."

Emily gasped. "Pippa? Is that true?"

The wolf squirmed. "I think there are things about Pete you may not know about right now."

"Did you warn Davy about the attack?"

Pippa nodded.

"Pete was behind it?"

"I really shouldn't say anything. Pete wants to be the one to explain things. It's not my place."

Kates snorted again. "Way to take the pussy way out. You're not running for office."

Pippa snapped her mouth shut and her cheeks flamed.

"I agree." Emily's eyes were accusatory.

"Hell's frozen over," Kates muttered under her breath with an evil grin on her face. "I think you two should clear the air. It's obvious something's going on between you two."

Both girls grew quiet and glanced at each other, but the door burst open and they shrieked in the next moment.

Kates groaned, "We were just getting to the good stuff."

Wren strode inside. "I could care less. You and you." She pointed to Emily and Pippa. "Come with me."

"Davy?" Emily looked at me in fear.

"It'll be fine. You haven't been kidnapped this time. You're just here for our safety."

My reassurance fell on deaf ears as Emily went pale when Wren and Tracey both grabbed an arm on each girl. They were lifted into the air and carried out the door. The two looked like dolls from the ease each vampire moved them.

When the door closed again, Kates spoke, "I wonder if we'll see them alive again?"

"Kates, shut up!" I pushed her off the bed. "Get out."

She laughed and shook her head. "Come on, Davy. That's a little funny."

"Out." I pointed to the door.

After she gave me a sarcastic eye-roll, she grabbed Brown's arm. "Come on, witch. Let's go find Gregory and see if we can get the Jolly Green Giant to find us some food. I checked the kitchen and it's bare."

Brown followed and I heard her say before the door shut, "Vampires don't eat food."

My headache had gotten worse. I had no idea where Roane was or when he would come to the estate, *if* he would come to this place, but I knew I couldn't do anything at this time. When I closed my eyes, I wasn't sure if I could fall asleep. Maybe I'd rest. So much had happened today.

ROANE DROPPED to the ground after the last werewolf bounded across the field. When Gavin dropped beside him, he turned and held his best friend's gaze for a moment. Neither spoke. Then Bastion sidled up to his other side and threw a cigarette on the ground. His heel ground it out and he spoke, "It's been ten miles. They're gone for good."

Gavin grunted. "Let's hope."

Roane watched over the field. They'd gone, but he knew

they'd be back. The Mother Wolf knew about Davy. He wasn't sure what she knew, but she knew she was connected to the Immortal. The Alpha's alarm would've piqued her interest. Even he had felt it as they had fought. The Alpha had hid in an alley, there to make sure his mate went unharmed, but his fear of Davy was strong underneath his fury and concern for Emily.

Roane knew the wolf had been given strict instructions not to join the fight. If the Alpha had fought, then the truce between the Benshire wolves and Roane would've been destroyed. But he hadn't and the Mother Wolf knew sending her own wolves from a different pack wouldn't violate the truce. She had only agreed that Benshire wolves wouldn't claim his territory. The truce had been mediated years ago and Roane hadn't given it much thought since. He'd been too concerned with the impending vampire army, but the number of wolves had been increasing. Their pack still didn't match the vampires' numbers, but it was a two to one ratio now. If they succeeded in getting Davy's powers it could've been a five to one ratio and it wouldn't have mattered. Her power mixed with the Alpha's magic would've made the werewolves unstoppable. The Roane army with Jacith wouldn't have been enough.

"What are you going to do about the Alpha?" Bastion asked. His eyes were cold. "He'll figure out who she is."

"We need to strike first."

Roane knew they were both correct. It was why he had Wren take the roommate and the wolf with Davy and the rest. He wanted them away, far away. If the Alpha came for his mate, the more secluded the better. He wouldn't travel with his pack, he wouldn't dare. Roane wanted to choose when the Alpha would find out Davy was the Immortal and not a thread-holder.

"We will," Roane spoke with an icy calm in his veins.

"He's going to come for his mate. That's the plan."

Gavin didn't blink, but he looked at his best mate in surprise. "That's what you want, isn't it?"

Bastion grinned. "Seems like a good plan to me. He'll come for her—"

"And he'll come alone," Gavin added.

"Then we'll kill him. Even the Alpha can't be a match for the six of us. We're too strong together."

Gavin glanced at Roane. The mask he wore to the world had classic handsome features. Gavin had watched many times as vampires and humans alike had fallen prey to the mask Lucas showed to the world. Noble. Honor. Determination. Those were some of the traits that Roane's conquests had loved about him, but it wasn't often when they glimpsed the darker side of the hunter. He saw it now and knew their own speculations weren't at all close to what Roane had in store for the werewolf. Gavin also knew he'd be wasting his time if he tried to guess more. Roane always surprised him, but this time he worried what the price would be.

"She cares about her roommate." Roane looked at him. His gaze was emotionless, but Gavin still felt fear tug in his gut. Even so, he kept talking, "She's still a human."

Bastion's eyes skirted between the two.

Roane narrowed his. "And your point is?"

"She cares as a human. She won't understand about casualties."

"Anyone who is mated to the Alpha is a casualty. She has to die." Bastion moved back a step.

"Davy's not just a human."

"She hasn't been for awhile, but there's a part of her that still feels like she is. She's going to hold onto those friends tightly because they preserve that side of her. She feels like a human when she's with them."

Roane shook his head. He knew what Gavin warned wasn't to be taken lightly, but he didn't know Davy. He didn't see how she had faced the Alpha in the park. She wanted to fight him and she wanted him to know that she wasn't scared. That confrontation was inevitable, but he hadn't wanted it to happen then. If it had been his choice, the Alpha would've been kept in the dark for another month, maybe more, but Davy had ended those chances. No one stood up to the Alpha unless they had power inside of themselves. No human would *consider* staring down the werewolf and since Davy had, the Alpha would know there was power in her. She let him look inside of her. She wanted him to see that power, but she hadn't shut him off quick enough. The werewolf had sensed more than she realized, but Roane knew. A flare of shock in the Alpha's eyes had been enough for Roane to know. The Alpha already knew she was the thread-holder.

"When he comes, he's not coming just for his mate. He's coming for Davy too."

"The truce," Gavin reminded him.

Roane faced him. His eyes were fierce. "The truce means nothing. We killed too many of her fighters. They'll rise up now. They were going to anyway. It was just a matter of time."

"But the Roane Army—"

"—is the perfect timing for their revolution. They want this land and they want the thread-holder. Now they know who she is. We'll be divided against the army and the wolves. It's perfect timing on her side."

"They'll have to fight the Roane Army then," Bastion spoke.

Roane shook his head. "No, they won't. The army doesn't want this territory. They'll search for the thread-holder. When they won't be able to find her, they'll leave. We'll be destroyed by then and the wolves will stake their claim."

"Why won't they wait it out? Let the Army destroy us and come in afterwards?" Bastion itched for another smoke. He gritted his teeth against the craving. No vampire should be dependent upon something men invented.

"They'll move soon. They know where she is now. And they won't want me to move her where they can't find her."

Gavin knew how Roane cared for Davy, but he wondered if he

cared more about keeping the Immortal from his enemies. When the Roane elders hadn't listened to Roane and instead had sent a hunter after him, he knew his best friend had been shattered by the betrayal. Roane had always been loyal to his Family. He had lived and breathed by what the Family wanted. His post as the hunter and then protector of the Family had been the creed that he lived by. When they didn't listen to him and decided to try and destroy the thread-holder, Roane had taken it as a personal attack. Gavin wondered how much his best friend's ego was mixed with protecting Davy.

Then a different enemy popped into his mind and Gavin asked, "And your brother? I know you haven't forgotten about him."

Roane turned cold eyes on him. "I haven't forgotten."

Bastion remained quiet, but he was aware of their tension.

Gavin kept quiet and Lucas instructed, "We'll go back to the estate. Keep on patrol when we're there. I expect Davy's roommate will call her mate soon. I want to be there when he arrives."

Then the three turned as one and sped away. In the night sky, they blended with the ground and were only shadows among the darkness.

———

I WOKE TO DARKNESS. When I sat up, I knew someone else was in the room with me and I could hear him undressing.

"Roane?"

"Yeah?" He pulled back the covers and slipped underneath. I felt him slide in next to me and then his arms wrapped around me. He tucked me close. I relished the feel of his body against mine. It calmed me.

"Why were you angry with me before?" I yawned as I asked him.

"Because you showed yourself to the Alpha. He knows too much now."

My mouth was pressed against his shoulder as I mumbled, "I'm sorry. I was so angry."

He tightened his arms around me. "I know."

"Did I mess up?"

"A little, but we'll be fine. We can handle it."

"Did they go away? Those wolves?" I tried to keep my eyes open. I wanted to see him, but it was a struggle. They were becoming too heavy.

He kissed my forehead and smoothed my hair back. In a gentle voice, he soothed me. "You can go to sleep. The wolves are long gone by now."

I reached for his hand and entwined our fingers. "What about you? You don't need to sleep that much."

"I'll stay with you for awhile. Go to sleep, Davy. You need it." He pressed another kiss to my forehead and then my shoulder. His arms turned me and he shifted so he spooned me from behind. I felt protected and sheltered in his arms.

"G'night, Davy."

I tried to return it, but I couldn't. My mind had already ventured into dreamland.

24

When I woke again, Roane was on the edge of the bed. He sat with his elbows on his knees and his hands cradling his head. I scooted beside him and looked at his back. Not long ago, I would've itched to caress it. This day, I felt nothing.

"I'm numb."

He looked at me. "I know."

I lifted haunted eyes to him. "I should feel something. I've tried to fight this. I try to feel something and sometimes I do. I feel guilty. I look at my friends and a part of me doesn't feel like I'm friends with them anymore. What's wrong with me?"

As his hand reached for mine, I heard him sigh. "I feel it too."

"I don't like feeling like this."

"Your mind is preparing you for what's going to happen. Bad things are going to happen."

I didn't want to hear him, but he was right. My body had started to shut down. Emotions weren't going to help me anymore. "I don't like being this way. I'm becoming a robot. I don't even care what's going on anymore. When Kates kidnapped Emily, I was so irate. I was hurt by her betrayal, but now she could betray me again and I wouldn't blink. What does that say about me?"

Roane pulled me to his side and pressed a kiss to my shoulder. He murmured against my skin, "I think it means that we're going to survive. Whatever happens, we're going to survive."

"I should feel. I don't feel anymore."

He kissed my forehead with a sense of desperation. "We'll get there. I promise."

"What about Emily?" I felt him tense beside me, but I had to ask. "I know Pete is my enemy, but she's in love with him. I saw their connection. It's deep, really deep. And she's my roommate. She was a good friend to me."

He pulled away and stood to cross the room. His voice was distant. "If she's with him, she's with him."

"What about Kates? She still loves Lucan, you know."

Roane's eyes pierced mine. I could feel the struggle in him, but he shoved me out. "I'm sorry. I can't lie to you. You're going to lose friends. What do you want me to say?"

His words whipped me. They stung.

He added, "I am sorry, Davy, but this is what war is. And we're in one. It started with Lucan and then it began again with the wolves. They'll be coming back. I moved us off my territory so that he would come."

"What are you saying?"

"I want the Alpha to come. Then the Roane army will be coming too, and then my brother. We can't survive all of them. Not all of us are even going to survive this first round."

Something in his voice made me cold. I heard everything he said. He said it before, but it was how he did it now. He was trying to tell me something else. He wanted to prepare me for something. I could feel his regret. It went deep, down to his bones, but he wouldn't let me in. He used to let me in. We wouldn't even have to speak out loud, but now he was a stranger again. It seemed so long ago that we had shared a bed.

My gut twisted inside. "What aren't you saying to me?"

Pain flared in his coal eyes, but it was gone quickly. Regret replaced it and then a steel wall slammed over it. He stood upright. "I'm saying to you that you're going to lose some of your friends. I've tried to shelter you from this, but I can't anymore. You're not just a human anymore. You're the reason for all of this and you've been taking a backseat. This is when you stop crying about the war and start becoming a part of it."

"You haven't wanted me to be a part of it." I couldn't believe him.

Roane hissed back, "Because you haven't wanted to step up. You've had this 'poor me' attitude the whole time, even before I met you. I felt it in the library that day and I hated it. You act like a victim. That is what's going to make you a victim."

My mouth fell open; I couldn't form a single thought. How dare he—how dare—He was right. I couldn't fight it anymore because he was right about everything. I had been feeling sorry for myself this whole time.

"You stopped transitioning awhile ago." Roane brought me back. His voice was soft now. "Since you came back from wherever you were, you've been ready. You came back ready. You just didn't want to admit it. That's why you've shut down. That's why you can't feel anything and I know that you've been forcing yourself to ignore it. I could feel that from you too. You don't trust your friends anymore. You want to, but you don't. Stop lying to yourself."

My mouth snapped shut. Each word hurt more than the last. "It's a hard pill to swallow. I hate when things change, especially when I have no control over any of it."

"That's life." His eyes were hard. "Deal with it."

It was then that I really looked at him. He snapped me out of my reverie and brought me back to our reality, to the two of us in that room. I was highly aware of how close he stood to me. And that he only had on a pair of unbuttoned slacks. They had fallen low on his hips. His stomach and groin muscles were defined. Each ridge and line stuck out against his body.

"You've lost weight." My eyes were hungry. I was hungry.

He sighed and ran a hand through his hair. "The last few months haven't been easy on me."

"Do you need to feed?"

Molten heat flared in his eyes. "And become human? I think not, Davy."

I knew that. Of course, I knew that, but I didn't like it.

"What?"

I shook my head. "What if there's a way you could feed from me and not become human? I wanted your brother to become human. Maybe I can control it. You could get power from me."

"I did get power from when you bit me. I got a lot of it. I still have it in me."

"You do?"

He nodded and watched me with a knowing look. I flushed under his perusal. "Sometimes I think you know me better than I know myself."

"Because I do. I love you, Davy." He crossed the room and cupped the side of my face. "How are you feeling now?"

"More normal."

His lips were so close. "You feel better?"

I nodded. My throat was thick. The need for him flared inside of me. I was becoming blind to everything else. "I need you. When we're not on the same page, I can't handle it. I feel disjointed. I'm strongest when I'm with you."

He grinned and dipped down. His lips met mine, but stayed still. I closed my eyes. I waited as my heart pounded loudly in my eardrums. Then his lips brushed against me. "I can help you with that."

Before I had time to respond, he picked me up and threw me on the bed. I shrieked in laughter, but his mouth quickly silenced me. Everything in me hummed in pleasure. His arms went around me. His mouth explored mine. His body demanded everything from me and I gave it to him. As he lifted me higher on the bed and slid inside me, I was blind to anything but him. The world ceased to exist. It was only the two of us.

And then an hour later I rolled over as Roane lay beside me.

"Now I feel really connected to you," I drawled and panted for a minute in silence.

Roane grinned and then groaned as he pressed a quick kiss to my shoulder. He sat up in the next moment. "I'm sorry, but I should go. I have things to do. So do you."

"I do?" I enjoyed watching him getting ready to protect me.

He spoke as he began to dress, "I can't take on three enemies without help."

"You said no powers. They'll know then."

"They already know. They might not know you're the Immortal, but they know you're the thread holder. Maybe it's time they find out the rest." Roane flashed me a grin before he left.

Whatever I'd been feeling before was gone. As I dressed and went in search of the kitchen, I couldn't keep myself from grinning. He did that to me and when I finally found it, Kates looked up and laughed. "You've got the Roane Glow again. Lucky."

Brown smiled and gestured to the table. "They have doughnuts, Davy."

Indeed they did. The kitchen table was filled with cartons of the frosted pastries along with bowls of fruit. Some bread sat beside boxes of cereal and a dish of pancakes was placed in the middle.

Pippa gave me a tentative grin. "They have a chef. He made me an omelet."

Emily was quiet as she sat on a stool by the counter. Kates caught my look and rolled her eyes.

"Davy?" Gavin brandished a metal spatula in the air. "Give me an order. I'm here to please."

"You're the chef?"

He smirked. "I have many skills."

"Okay," I replied as I scooted onto a stool beside Emily. She stiffened and bowed her head. "Surprise me. Whatever you want."

"Anything?" His eyes lit up.

"She just said anything." Kates scowled.

A heated look passed between the two before he jerked away. I heard the control in his voice as he forced a light tone. "You said anything, Davy. Be warned."

I watched Kates, but said to him, "It'll be fine. I'm sure."

She rolled her eyes at me this time, popped a strawberry in her mouth and left the room. Brown watched her go and I saw the same nonjudgmental curiosity from when she'd studied me with Roane before fill her eyes.

"This is a really nice place, Davy. This is your—" Pippa frowned.

"Boyfriend's?" Emily supplied. She looked up again.

My roommate was in love with a werewolf, but she was acting jealous. I thought she was over her crush. "I guess. I've never been here before."

"Lucas seems to own a lot of places."

Though Gavin didn't act any differently, I could feel his interest in the conversation. His hands slowed as he opened an egg.

"Davy."

"Yeah?" I looked back over. Emily had been studying me. "What?"

"So you and Lucas are serious?"

Pippa moved away from the counter, but Brown inched closer. The witch stepped away from the table to round the counter so she was behind me. It was a slow movement, but I knew that Gavin had noticed it. His eyes jerked up once, but went right back to the skillet.

"Why are you asking me about him?"

Emily drew back. "I can't ask you some questions? You lied to me about him, remember?"

"We've gone over this."

Annoyance flashed over her face, but she cleared it quickly. "I thought you were in love with Adam before. I'm just wondering how serious this is. I don't want you hurt again."

She was lying. I knew that much, but this sudden loathing shook me. "I thought you cared about me."

"I do." Emily smiled. "Why do you say that?"

What could I say without making it worse?

"A bitch." Pippa jumped as she spoke.

All eyes turned to her.

"What did you say?"

Pippa jerked to the side. She met Emily's gaze. "A bitch. You're being a bitch."

"Excuse me?"

The wolf crossed her arms and leaned back on her heels. "You heard me."

Kates chuckled behind me and Gavin was all eyes. He didn't hide his attention now.

"I can't believe you. You have some nerve, Pippa! You're the reason we're all here."

"No, I'm not!" she shouted back. "We're here because of Pete. He didn't like Davy and he could tell there was something different about her. He's the one who went to the Mother Wolf. I've been trying to shield Davy from her. I've been trying to protect her. I wanted to protect all of us."

"Why? And what's so special about her? I don't understand any of this." The hysteria in Emily's voice was evident.

Pippa opened her mouth and then clamped it shut. She grabbed the ends of her braids and held on.

"Well?"

She pulled harder on her braids. "I don't know what Davy is, but she's something. I could tell right away. But Pete didn't care.

He got mad. He didn't see that she's a person and a good one. And she's your roommate. And she cares about you. He didn't stop to think about any of that."

Emily turned heated eyes to me, but looked back at Pippa. "What are you talking about?!"

A plate was placed beside me gently and I saw that Gavin had a resigned look in his eyes. Then I saw behind him that Wren and Tracey had filed into the room. They stood in the background waiting for an opening. Something had happened.

Roane and Bastion came in next. He jerked his head to the side and motioned for me to come. Before I left, I looked back once more. Brown and Kates both saw where I was going, but neither said a word. When I followed Roane out into the hallway, I heard Pippa explode, "Because it's not right! They want to hurt Davy and I know it's never right when someone is going to get hurt."

Roane reached for my hand and led me into a different room. When the door closed, he didn't say anything for a moment. "The Alpha's coming. He's on his way right now. They're waiting for me to talk to you and then when we go back in, they're going to grab your friends."

"How do you know he's coming right now?"

"Gregory called it in. He was on sentry duty last night. We don't have long. They're coming fast."

"They?"

Roane nodded. "I wanted him to come alone, but he's not. It's going to be a full fight. Your roommate's boyfriend is bringing twice the number. Forty wolves, plus the Alpha. I'm not going to lie to you. Some of your friends won't make it out alive, especially the female wolf."

"Pippa?"

"They see her as a traitor. He's been talking to Emily. He's brainwashed her into thinking you're the enemy and so is the other girl. Emily's no longer Emily anymore."

"That's not true. She still has feelings for you."

He sighed again and leaned back on a desk. He braced against the edge, his arm muscles bulging. "Maybe. Maybe not. She feels lied to. She saw us last night. I'm sure she could see how we feel about each other. You've been lying to her since the beginning and she doesn't understand our side. No one's been talking to her to explain it."

"She should've talked to me."

"She came to your room last night. I think she heard us talking. I knew she was there, but she left. I should've given it more thought."

It didn't matter anymore. What was done was done. I swallowed back the pain and asked, "What do I do?"

"You do what you can." Roane held my face in his hands. He tilted it up so his eyes held mine captive. He'd been guarded before, but now he let me in. The wall lifted and I saw his love. It was clear as day and I had to choke back tears. "I love you, but stay close to me. Okay?"

My throat was thick with emotion. He wiped some tears from my face. Then he pressed a kiss to my forehead and dipped to meet my lips. I pressed against him.

Someone rapped on the door with their knuckles. Bastion poked his head inside. "Gregory's here. We've got five minutes."

Roane straightened and the hunter took over him. He was cold. Ruthless. "Let's go."

"And her?" Bastion nodded to me.

"You don't have to protect me. I'll be fine. I promise."

"Let's go!" Wren shouted from the hallway and then all the vampires sprinted away.

The kitchen had grown quiet when I went back. Kates straightened from the wall. "What's going on?"

"The Alpha is here. He brought forty wolves with him."

Pippa paled. "They're going to kill me."

Emily looked at her sharply. "Don't be stupid. You'll be fine."

"She's right, Emily." My voice was strong. "They're going to kill her. They think she's a traitor."

She flushed. "They're not going to kill her. That's insane, Davy."

"Yes, they will. She chose to protect me against them. Kates, protect Pippa. She's one of ours. Brown, stay with Gregory."

She perked up. "I don't know where he is."

"He came back. We've got three minutes."

"Davy." Emily looked shaken.

"Wake up," Kates barked. "Nothing's the same anymore." She was serious, more serious than I'd ever seen her. "The numbers are unmatched. We're not going to keep a unified front. That means it's going to be every person for herself."

"I'll be fine."

Kates snorted and then turned to me. "Will you?"

She was asking a different question and I nodded. "I'm ready. I'll be fine."

The Immortal stirred inside of me.

25

W e started to scatter, but Roane spoke in my head, *'Davy, stop them.'*

"Wait!"

Everyone froze. Brown tripped.

"Davy?" Kates frowned. "What's going on?"

"Roane said to stop."

"Huh?" Brown looked around. "I can't hear him. Am I defective?"

Kates snorted. "No, girl. Oh my god. They have a mind thing. They can talk to each other in their heads."

Emily scowled and Pippa gave me a dreamy smile.

"I was right!" Brown snapped her fingers in the air. "You heard me in the car, didn't you?"

'Tell them to shut up,' Roane snapped.

I held up a hand and everyone quieted.

'Change of plans. Tracey and Wren are going to cover the south corner. Bastion and Gregory are on the west side. Gavin and I will take the north edge. I need you and your friends to watch the east side of the house. It's a cliff, Davy. Make sure no wolves can climb up from the rocks below.'

'How are we supposed to stop them?'

'I don't know. Use your Immortal power. Figure it out. You'll be fine. There's a slayer with you.'

Use my Immortal stuff. Easier said than done, but he was right. It was time I fought beside them.

"What'd he say?" Kates moved forward a step.

I skimmed the group. Brown looked scared and excited at the same time. Pippa was wary. Emily looked like it was beneath her to be with us and Kates gave nothing away. She was ready to fight. In that moment, I knew everything was going to be okay. It had to be. I'd just gotten this group of friends, even my brainwashed roommate.

Before I replied, I caught a mischievous glimmer in my room-mate's eyes. It was masked quickly, but it was there. Then I caught Kates' gaze and nodded in Emily's direction. She understood immediately, shuffled one step to the side, and backhanded the girl. Emily went down hard.

"Ah! What'd you do that for?" Brown slapped her two hands to her cheeks.

Kates snorted. "Like she was really going to help us."

Pippa bit her lip. "She's right. Emily can communicate with Pete. She would've told him everything that was going on with us."

"So what did your lover say?"

"Right." On to business. "We're supposed to guard the east side. He doesn't want any wolves to climb up the cliff."

Pippa's eyes went wide, but Kates smirked. "Have you seen that cliff? A bird wouldn't come that way."

"What do you mean?"

Kates led the way to the east side. When we stepped outside, the entire east side of the house was a stone patio. It extended outwards and around the back of the house. A basketball court could've fit on it. We went to the edge and looked over the cliff. Brown gasped and reeled back. I didn't blame her. My own stomach jumped into my throat at the sight beneath us. Water crashed onto boulders below. The fall would've been two miles down. Huge boulders littered the floor of the ocean. Wind rushed against us at a violent speed.

I could see why a bird wouldn't fly upwards.

"It's a vacuum effect," Kates explained. "Nothing could climb up those walls. They're made completely of rock so it's going to be hard for any werewolf to scale it. If they come up in their human forms, the wind's going to just knock 'em down. Anyone climbing that thing is suicidal."

"He wants to make sure."

She rolled her eyes. "Roane doesn't want you near the action. Forget that. I'm going."

"Me too." Pippa jumped next to Kates. "I'm going to fight too. You guys are protecting me, but my family's bloodline is old."

We all stared at her.

She blushed. "That means I'm stronger than the normal werewolf."

"Ah."

"Gotcha."

"That makes sense now."

"Let's go." Kates started to turn.

"Wait. What about us if werewolves come up?" Then I looked at Emily, who groaned from the lounger that Kates had placed her on. "And what if she wakes up?"

"Really?" She quirked an eyebrow at me. "Put her back to sleep, Miss Almighty."

With a curt gesture to Pippa, they were both gone within an instant.

Brown mused, "Why'd she call you Miss Almighty? Was that metaphorical or rhetorical? Is there a difference? I should look them up when I get home." And then it didn't matter. Brown circled around me with her hands in the air. "I was thinking that I could try some spells. When I'm around you, I feel my magic more. Maybe if I'm connected to you, I might be useful."

"Connected? What do you mean connected?" I moved back a step.

"Our minds. Like meditation. We can chant together."

Suddenly a howl split through the air. Brown grew silent. And the air grew heavy. A somber feeling came over me. I felt him in that howl, the Alpha called to his pack. A second later a unified chorus howled back.

Brown jumped back. Her eyes went wide and her golden skin went white. She grabbed my arm, but I couldn't reassure her. My own heart was pounding.

The essence of Talia's mother was in him. He wasn't holding anything back. That deep magic sparked into me. He could feel me and even as I shook to the core, I couldn't dwell on it. I felt him searching for me. Something shifted and a channel opened to me. I heard him talking to Emily.

"*Ems. Emily, are you there?*"

When she didn't answer, his anger kicked up a notch.

"*That bitch. What'd she do to you?*" I heard his growl. "*Wake up!*"

Emily stirred behind us. She rolled over on the lounger, but her eyes stayed shut.

"Davy, this is not fun."

"Was it ever?" I asked through gritted teeth.

"What if I can't do magic? I don't know how else to help."

They howled again. The sound echoed all around. It ricocheted off the rocks. They zapped around us. Brown gasped again and whirled in a tight circle. Her fear was so strong. She was rattled to the bone.

"Brown," I started.

"What?" She glanced everywhere, but at me. She kept jumping in place. The shadows were terrifying her.

It grew dark in the next instant. The light sailed away and the night sky rolled in its place. Only one person had the magic to do that.

"What just happened? This isn't right." Brown clung to me. Her nails dug into my arm.

"It's Pete," I seethed. "It's easier for wolves to hunt at night. Vampires don't see as well as they do."

"I'm really starting to get scared now," she whimpered.

I grew tired of the wolves' antics with their howling. I felt the Immortal kick inside of me and closed my eyes. It was only a matter of time before she burst free. When that happened, there was no going back.

I said again, "Brown."

"What?"

"Look at me."

She grew still and turned. When she did, her eyes widened. "Aren't you scared?"

"No."

"I wet my pants, not in the good way." She shuddered.

"I'm not scared because—" How could I say it?

"Because?"

He howled again. This one was long and drawn out. It was meant for intimidation, but it had the opposite effect on me. The Immortal rattled inside of me now. I could barely hold her back. She wanted out. She wanted his blood. She wanted to reclaim Talia's essence into the rightful body. Mine.

I opened my mouth, but my body shook.

Brown's eyes grew into saucers. She stepped back and her hand let go of my arm.

The Immortal burst free in me. I couldn't hold her in and my eyes switched like a light had been turned on. It now looked like daylight to me. Brown's ashen face was stretched from her fear. I saw the veins in her neck and the blood that pumped into her heart. Everything in her was a colorful three dimensional x-ray.

Pete's howl was cut off. He'd sensed my transition and now he sat back, waiting for the next move. It was mine and I shot off from the patio. I was everywhere at once. I could see all the wolves, how they hunched down behind their hiding spots. Some overlooked the vampires, but most of them still hadn't found where Roane's small army waited. The element of surprise was everything among these two supernatural beings.

Bastion stood behind a tree. His form was camouflaged. I wouldn't have known he was there except for the blood pumping in him. His eyes were closed and he waited. He sensed where they were and they hadn't moved close enough for an attack. Gregory had taken a position behind a boulder. The giant blonde Viking had a bow and arrow in hand, notched and ready to fly. He waited for Bastion's signal.

Then I saw Wren and Tracey. Both knelt down behind a small wall. Each looked graceful, content with their heads bent between their knees. They, like all the others, were waiting. Roane and Gavin stood on separate ends of their area. Unlike the others, they didn't hide. They stood at the tip of their hill. They wanted the attention. They wanted the wolves to come to them.

Roane's head bent and his nostrils flared. He had sensed me. When his head turned towards me, I knew he wanted to see me so I stepped forward.

"What are you doing?"

Gavin tilted his head to the side. "You look good with the white eyes."

I'd forgotten how I looked as the Immortal. I smirked at him. "He wants to be invisible." My anger sparked and magic exploded inside me. "So you will be instead."

Gavin's mouth started to open, but he was gone in the next second. So was Roane. And I knew all the others were too. They were now the invisible ones among the night. Only the wolves remained in true form. I felt Pete's shock when the magic exploded. He knew the thread holder was present, but the new power in the air was a surprise.

Then I bent backwards and my body swooshed to Brown. When I landed behind her, she didn't react. She had no idea I was there so I reached inside of her. My hand found the box where her magic was locked. It was stretched at the seams, ready to explode. My thumb brushed against the lock and the door opened an inch. Magic slipped through and Brown gasped. Her back arched upwards. Her arms shot out. I could see the blood rushing through her. The ends of her fingers tingled and sparks shot out.

The box's lid remained in place. Even as I watched, I saw how it was trying to close again. Magic older than me had put it there. It fought against the Immortal. Something moved in me and I knew it was a response to Brown's box. The magic surrounding it was angered by my interference, but the Immortal's magic was too powerful. I reached back in and lifted it once more. It went open all the way, but when my finger moved away, the lid started to close once again.

"Oh my god," she shrieked and squealed at the same time. In the next moment, she had her eyes closed and was chanting. If I'd been nervous she couldn't control her magic, it would've been for nothing. Brown had complete control over herself. The magic filled her and the paleness of her skin grew into a rosy tan. The fear was gone. She glowed.

"Thank you, Davy," she spoke in the next breath.

A wolf howled in pain. The sound split through the night air.

It had begun.

I lifted my head and was there in the next moment. Wren pulled her sword back and stood over the wolf. Its body quivered in pain underneath her feet. It lifted his head and looked at her, but the fight quickly left its body, its neck slumping back down.

The first kill went to the vampires. Pete's anger exploded into full force. He leapt through the air, right behind Wren and Tracey. Both vampires jumped out of the way, but his mouth was opened. One of his fangs nicked Tracey's leg and she screamed.

Her body twisted and convulsed. Poison from him shot through the vampire. Wren screamed and lunged in the air. Her sword was poised above her head, ready to strike, but he turned his head. He waited, ready to open his powerful mouth.

I appeared in that moment. He turned to see me and sniffed into me. His eyes widened. He wasn't ready for what he saw, but it didn't matter. Wren's sword pierced his eye in that moment. Instead of reeling back from pain, he snapped his jaw at her. I threw myself forward and opened my arms. A light from me blinded him and he recoiled.

"What the—" Wren gasped, but he was gone. She ran to Tracey.

I knelt on the other side of her and reached inside. The poison was flowing throughout her entire body. There was a glazed look in her eye and her body began convulsing in a seizure. Her head was thrown back and her body lifted off the ground. When her eyes met mine, I knew she saw me. Wren had no idea I was there. I was invisible to her, but it didn't matter. Tracey's blood saw the thread in me, the same one that had been in her sister and mother before that. I felt her mother's essence battling to get back into me. It wanted to rejoin the Immortal, but it couldn't. It was still locked inside of Pete, but Tracey saw that too.

"Mom?" Her eyes were white around them.

"Tracey, honey, don't go. Stay with me." Wren patted her cheeks.

"You," she gasped. Her tongue got stuck and she repeated the word over and over. Her throat was convulsing at the same time. Her eyes locked onto mine. I couldn't look away.

Wren lifted her head and looked around. Sounds of battle filled the air now. Wolves growled. They whelped. They screamed.

My eyes couldn't leave Tracey's in that moment, so I went into her. My empathic nature shifted and separated from the Immor-

tal. I felt her fear, but I also felt her yearning. She wanted her
family back. She loved Wren, but she had returned because of
me. I was connected to her sister and she wanted her back. The
love she had for her sister and mother was blinding. It brought
tears to my eyes. Before I left her, I took some of the fear from her.
She calmed and her body lay back down on the ground.

Wren's fear subsided then.

My empathic side connected with the Immortal again and I
reached inside of Tracey. I sucked the poison into my hand.
Unlike the vampire, the poison bonded with me. It was from the
essence of the Immortal and it wanted to be back with its master.
When I stood back, Tracey was already healing. I watched as her
strength sparked and built. Wren sat back and gaped in relief.
Before long, both of them were looking at the other. No words
were shared, but they turned as one and jumped at a passing
werewolf.

I returned to Brown the next moment and found her bent
over the deck's edge. She cast spell after spell below her. Werewolves had braved the treacherous terrain. They were slowly
inching their way up. It wouldn't be long before they overcame
us.

Brown groaned as she gritted her teeth. Magic sparked from
her fingertips. One by one, werewolves fell, but then they got
back on the cliff. It was as if she had never hit them. I snapped
back to my human form and could feel their magic in the air. The
Alpha was keeping them from falling to their deaths.

"Brown," I said.

She gasped. "They won't die. Why won't they die?"

Each spell she sent to them was powerful, but the Alpha's was
even more so. My eyes shifted into the Immortal's and then I was
able to see through the darkness below. A net had been strung up
below them, made of magic. When the wolves were hit by Brown,
they fell, but bounced back up. They bounced to a higher place.
She was helping them.

I laid a hand on her arm. "Stop."

"I can't. They keep coming."

"His magic is stronger than yours. He put up a net below them. They can't fall through it."

"How do we break it?" Brown wanted to help. I felt the need in her. It was strong. Tears filled her eyes. "I need this, Davy. I need to help. I need to be useful for once. All my life, everyone's laughed at me. I'm tired of it."

I nodded. "Instead of hitting the wolves, shoot below them. I think your magic can undo the net. The wolves will fall then."

She clamped her mouth shut and turned. Her shoulders were squared. And she concentrated with everything she had. She drew up a spell stronger than she had ever imagined. It came out from the depths of her magic and built at a furious rate. I stood back, slightly awed at the gift Brown had. If this was what she could do now, I wondered what she could do when that box was broken in pieces.

"Tres all conte, break the binds he has made. Break the net to fall free. Tres all conte, tres all conte, tres all conte, break the binds he has made. Break the net to fall free. Tres all conte," she repeated. As the power built in her, she narrowed her eyes and the magic blasted from her. The net burst into flame the next moment. It singed the air and crackled. As it fell, the sounds faded. Then a smug look came over Brown's face.

I grinned and stood back. The wolves didn't stand a chance against her.

"*Davy!*" Gavin shouted at me. I whirled.

When I flashed to Roane and Gavin, I saw the Alpha in mid air. He was lunging with his massive jaw open and ready to tear into Roane, who stood with his back to him. He was facing Gavin, who had another wolf lunging at him.

"No!" I thrust my hands up. Everything stopped in that moment. Both wolves froze in mid-air. Only Roane turned to me.

I walked towards the wolf that was ready to pull Gavin's spine out. After a jerk to the fur underneath his neck, I knew the wolf would fall on the ground. Then I went to the Alpha and stood there.

"No—" Roane started.

I snapped my fingers and time started again. Pete's jaw closed around me instead of Roane.

"No!" I heard Gavin yell in the distance, but I closed my eyes. I felt Pete's surprise, but it didn't matter. He tried not to clamp his teeth together, but everything happened so quickly. He couldn't stop in time. I wanted all my Immortal power to burst within him. I wanted it to be like a bomb. And I wanted to take back Talia's mother's essence. She belonged to me. She wanted to be with me and I wanted to take her with me. As the Immortal's energy built up, I felt her beside me.

Pete struggled. He knew what had happened and was trying to take it all back. He was trying to open his jaw and unclench what he had accidentally swallowed. It didn't matter. He wasn't the Immortal, though he thought he was. I saw that now. The Mother Wolf had told him that he was the Immortal. He had the essence therefore he was the one all the prophecies foretold.

He had been wrong. He could feel it now.

For a split second, I looked up and saw Talia's mother. Her hair was red like her daughter's and flowed back. Her black dress billowed beneath her hair and blue eyes flashed at me. She smiled and I heard her thoughts, *'It is time for my energy to join the rest. He is not to blame. What was put in him was not his fault or his inspiration. He has been led astray in many ways.'*

It didn't matter. Pete meant to hurt someone I loved. Her pleads wouldn't save him. I pushed forward and let the Immortal explode within him. When it sparked, he reeled backwards and tried to spit me out of his mouth. It didn't matter. I wanted this to happen. It needed to happen. The Alpha's body twisted and convulsed round and round. He tried everything to get me out, but I held firm and then the explosion happened. When it did, his jaw snapped open and I was flung from it. Talia's mother and her essence went with me. She had joined the Immortal and was at peace. As we were thrown in the air, her eyes closed. She laid her hands on her chest and melted away. Then I felt her join the Immortal.

We landed on the ground a few feet away. Pete was flung across the hill. Roane and Gavin had fallen back too. I was beside them before they awakened.

A sudden tingling on my neck made me look over. Pippa stood above Pete's body. She watched him. Somehow she knew what had happened, though I didn't know how. I didn't care at that moment.

I stepped towards her. "Let him be."

"He loved her," she wrung out. Her eyes didn't leave his form as he lay on the ground, writhing in pain.

I watched as she knelt at his feet.

"He's not the same, Pippa," I warned her.

It didn't matter.

She shook her head and ran a finger over his forehead. "No matter what he's been told, he loved her. He's lost Emily as well as the trust he had in Mother Wolf. You don't understand the betrayal he's feeling." She looked up with tears in her eyes. "He was supposed to become my mate. She changed that. She changed everything."

Pippa closed her eyes. The wolf spirit within her went into him. I closed my eyes and followed. Where I went, I wasn't expecting what I saw. The two were pups again and they were playing in a field. Pippa tripped him with her large paws and Pete grinned crookedly, tongue hanging out as he bounded towards her. He stumbled over his own paws, but the two rolled over each other in the grass. Though in wolf form, their joy was evident. Both grinned and whimpered in excitement until the air cooled. They stopped in the next second and lifted their heads to gaze at the far corner of the woods.

An older woman in black garb floated out of the trees. She held a long arm with a finger pointed to them. As a spell started to spew from her mouth, I lunged at her. Black eyes widened and whirled to me before I fell on her. All her battles were won or lost through words and magic. I grinned in enjoyment as I wrapped both hands around her neck and lifted her head free. The fight was over. Her body slumped to the ground, both pups breathed in relief, and her head melted in my hands. It became a puddle of black gunk and I dropped it in disgust.

I felt Pippa's approval, but was back in my real form the next moment. She was still bent over his body. The air sizzled with relief instead of despair and I breathed more lightly.

Roane grasped my elbow and frowned. "What just happened?"

"I have no idea." I smiled at him. "But I think it was good."

He cast a concerned look at the two wolves. "Are you sure?"

"It's for the best. I promise."

Pippa looked up now. She brushed tears away. "Everything's better now. She can't touch him again."

"Mother Wolf?"

She jerked her head up in a nod. "That was her inside him. She was trying to come back in and fix him. She underestimated you." A laugh sputtered from her. "Who knew you could do that? You stopped her, Davy. Thank you."

Pete still lay on the ground unconscious. He had curled into a fetal position.

"Is he going to be okay?"

Pippa shook her head. "I have no idea, but I'll take him back with me."

"To school?" Alarms went off in my head. If Emily went back there too, how would that go?

"No." A grave look entered her eyes. "I'll take him back to my family. I won't be returning to Benshire again."

"Huh?"

"I come from the old wolves. We want to remain hidden. We don't want to war against the vampires. We'll never win. That was her agenda for the last hundred years, but now that the Alpha doesn't exist anymore, we'll make our stand. You shouldn't have to worry about us anymore."

When she turned to leave with a determined glint in her eyes, I was taken aback. There was fierceness in the female wolf that I'd never witnessed before. She was like a new person, but one that I already respected.

"How are you going to move him?" But as I asked, the words died in my throat. Wolves emerged from the shadows surrounding us. Their green eyes glowed in the night. I jerked forward, but Roane caught my arm. He pulled me back.

He murmured in my ear, "They're allies."

"How do you know?"

"She called them."

"Pippa?"

I whirled back to where she was greeting one of the larger wolves. He had shaggy grey fur. His old age was evident, but his eyes looked through me. In wolf form, he towered over Pippa. He would've stood a foot higher than even the Alpha's wolf form. As more wolves moved to the unconscious wolf, a sense of ancestry filled the air. I felt it surrounding us and knew it came from them. They were old, wise, and strong.

I was grateful that they had chosen the side they had. If we had gone against them, I wasn't sure who would've won.

Pippa turned back and approached with the older wolf beside her. Pete had been transported away. Fresh tears filled her eyes when she stopped before me and then she threw her arms around me. As she hugged me tight, she whispered, "Thank you so much, Davy. For everything. I don't know what we would've done if you hadn't helped us."

All this because of the essence in Pete? That was all they needed from me?

She smiled. "We didn't know it was possible to separate it from him. If we had and if I'd been more certain that you were the Immortal, I would've asked you right away."

"What?"

A carefree laugh broke from her and she wiped more tears away. "I came to Benshire for my family. We knew the Immortal was here. I was supposed to find you, but I didn't know it was you until now. I still can't quite believe it. I didn't even really like you."

"I know. You loved Emily. You guys were bosom buddies."

"I sensed her mate in her, but it wasn't Pete, at least not this

Pete. This Pete is supposed to be mine." Her face sobered at that thought.

I asked, "What about the mateline? Are you able to recover it so he'll be your mate again?"

She shook her head. "I have no idea. That's old magic. No one would dare interfere with something like that, but Mother Wolf has become impervious and foolish. This will anger the Elders greatly. Matelines are never to be manipulated and now that it's been done, we'll have to see what other damage she did."

"About her, is she dead now?"

"No. You just stopped her magic from getting to Pete again. You put up a block within him. I'm sure the Elder wolves will move on her soon. She's weak now." She smiled again. "Thank you, Davy. You have helped so much. I can't express our gratitude in words."

The elder wolf dropped his mouth to her neck. His eyes locked with hers and Pippa nodded a second later. "This is Christane. He's my Elder and he wants you to know that the Christane family is indebted to you. If you ever need us, we will come."

Elders. Christane family. All this ancestry among the wolves. It was getting overwhelming.

"Davy?" Pippa frowned.

"Sorry. Yes. That sounds nice." I lifted a shoulder up in an awkward shrug. "All this is new to me. I've never had a werewolf feel like they owed me something. I'm just used to him," I jerked a thumb beside me. "He's always telling me to lay low and be quiet."

Roane barked out a laugh, but moved forward. "Thank you, Christane. I am indebted to you as well."

The wolf lowered his massive head to the ground and then turned as one with Pippa. She melted into her white wolf form and soon they vanished from our eyes. It wasn't long before I felt all the wolves disappear and then I turned to Roane. "Why are you indebted to him?"

"They came to show their allegiance to me."

"They came because of Pippa."

"She called them, but they were here to fight on my behalf. If you hadn't stepped in and taken care of Pete, it would've been worse. If the Christane bloodline had fought with me, they would've showed their loyalty to a vampire. That would've meant declaring their own war on the Mother Wolf."

I shuddered at the thought of her. "She sounds like a bitch."

Roane put his arm around my shoulder and drew me close. "Well, she's their problem now."

Gavin approached and flashed a grin. "Is this the official victory walk?"

I felt Roane tense. "For now."

"One victory down, two more to go?" As we treaded down the hill and neared the estate, Kates darted to meet us. Her eyes were gleaming and her chest was heaving. A glow appeared over her skin.

She lifted a hand. "They've gone. All of them. What happened?"

"Davy took care of the Alpha," Gavin responded in a curt voice.

Annoyance flared in her eyes, but she didn't bite back.

"Wren and Tracey are waiting for us in the hall. Bastion and Gregory will follow and make sure the other wolves don't double back." Roane's hand slipped to my waist. His thumb started to rub the side of my hip.

When we entered the house, the two female vampires stood from their table. Brown panted from her seat. She gave me a loopy smile. "I can't stand. My legs have turned into goo. They're all melty. I did magic. Can you believe it?"

I couldn't contain a smile. "I knew you had it in you."

"Oh man." She slumped back. "I feel drunk. Is this normal?"

"Where's the traitor?" Kates looked around in contempt.

Brown tried to lift her arm, but dropped it on the table. "She's still out there, snoring away. They didn't take her with them and they could've. A few of the wolves got around me, but then they all ran away. I must be awesome."

"The wolf?" Wren spoke for the first time. She shifted in her stance and I saw pain flare in her body. She couldn't contain a grimace.

"She was a Christane wolf. She left with them." Roane narrowed his eyes. "You should rest, Wren. Heal. Tracey, take her to your room. Everyone should go to their rooms to clean up and rest."

"What?" Gavin lifted his head. "No party? We should be celebrating."

"We will." Roane's eyes glimmered in amusement. "But no one is fit for that right now." His hand spread out over the small of my back. "Let's enjoy our rest first."

Gavin and Kates shot a look at each other, but quickly looked away. I pursed my lips at that. It wasn't the first time there had been a spark between the two, but then Roane urged me in front of him and I didn't care. I wanted my bed. I wanted him. And I wanted a night away from the war.

H er eyes snapped open when she felt the defeat. The magic had been destroyed, banned from the Alpha. When she tried to go back in, a block was set in place. There was no way she could get past it, but then an explosion occurred and her magic was thrown back at her. It slammed into her and recoiled onto itself. She felt it quaking and knew the tremors were from fear. As she gritted her teeth, her anger rose swiftly. Something had not gone to plan and she was determined to figure out what it was, who it was. No one banished her.

The door burst open and a servant rushed inside. "Mother, what has happened?"

It was then she realized the room was shaking. She wasn't surprised. The rage in her was tightly controlled, but when she stood and turned, the appearance of Gailith made her pause. A bruise was forming on the top of his head; blood spilled from it and soaked his shirt. One of the lenses in the small glasses he always wore had a crack and his hair was matted from his blood.

"What happened to you?" She tried to keep the disgust from her voice. Servants wanted to be cared for. Everyone wanted to be cared for. They found it comforting. They were pathetic.

He hesitated and ran a hand through his hair. It caught on the blood and he withdrew it quickly to tuck behind his back. "Was there an earthquake?"

"What do you mean?"

"The whole house, Mother. It's been shaking for the last few minutes. Many of the servants died."

"Why?" Had her rage been so suppressed?

"They're human, Mother."

She couldn't hold back her disgust any longer and snapped, "What are you talking about? Why would my servants die from a small earthquake?"

"It wasn't small. This is the only room that's still standing."

Her eyes widened and she couldn't speak for a moment. Nothing and no one ever surprised her, but it had happened twice in the space of two minutes. She hated that. Someone was more powerful than her. The wolf inside her raged to get out. It needed to kill, but she took a deep breath and calmed herself. More deaths would not satisfy her. She needed to know what had become of the thread holder. That would satisfy her. She had gone to great lengths to get close, but if it had all been for nothing.

She clamped her eyes closed at the thought of the possible repercussions. "Are the wolves okay?"

He jerked his head in a nod. "Yes, ma'am."

"Ma'am?"

"Mother Wolf. Yes, the wolves were able to escape. I got away because one of them carried me out."

She narrowed her eyes and turned back to the window. Her home had been built during the Civil War. It had been made to survive anything, but she had not considered her own power. Never would she have imagined that she'd hurt something she had built and nurtured. But she had hurt it. Sheds that had surrounded the plantation were in pieces on the ground.

Someone made her do this and that someone needed to be dealt with.

"Gailith, I want you to go to someone."

"Who, Mother?"

Her eyes were flat when she looked back. "The vampires."

He paled and his hand jerked to clench around his shirt. Filth. Everything about him was filthy. "You're human. They'll love you."

He closed his eyes and bent his head.

She smirked. They were pathetic, all of them, which is why she knew the thread holder had been underestimated. She had underestimated the girl, so Jacith must've also.

"You will go to Durres to see the Romah Family."

His body started to shake.

"There is a powerful sorcerer there. His name is Jacith."

Her nostrils flared as she smelled his fear. It wasn't long before his bladder emptied itself. It trickled down his leg and pooled on the floor. His head hung in shame, but he couldn't stop himself.

She could barely keep herself from killing him. Worthless humans. They couldn't do anything, much less refrain from wetting themselves. If she asked this of him, how did she know he'd succeed? Maybe a wolf would be better? But no, as she watched him through narrowed eyes, she reconsidered. A human was a perfect messenger and gift. Jacith would see him as one and that he had been one of her servants would mean something to him. The sorcerer was stupid in that way, but he had his uses. And he was powerful. He would be angry to find out the existence of a thread holder who could use the Immortal's powers. It was his fault. He should clean this mess up himself.

"You need to go and tell him what happened to the Alpha. The thread holder destroyed his precious experiment. Tell him this and then return home, Gailith."

He jerked his head in another nod and bolted from the room.

As she sat back down in her chair, she took a deep breath. Everything would have to be rebuilt.

"You're sending a servant to Jacith? He won't be returning, you know that."

She turned and a smile spread over her face. "Hello, Christian. Did you come to make sure I was okay?"

He was tall and muscular with piercing black eyes. That wasn't what attracted her to him. It was the wolf inside of him. He was the inspiration behind the Alpha. Christian Christane was the reigning Alpha wolf for his family. He had many grandfathers still alive, but he was their leader. A union between her family and his would cement the werewolves' dominance over the vampires. No creature could stand against power such as theirs and Christian was raw power in himself. As she watched, she saw it thriving within his body.

She licked her lips.

"No, Caralie. I came to tell you that my family knows what you did. You took the mate that was supposed to be for my little sister and joined him to another. You should not manipulate magic like that. It's old, older than your family."

"Older than yours too."

"Yes," he clipped out. "Older than my family, this is why the Elders have called a meeting."

He wasn't there to flirt. He never was, but there was gravity in his voice. Her inner wolf stirred. It sensed something that she hadn't yet. She stood and gave him a sultry smile. "What are you saying?"

His disdain for her flared. "The Christane Family will be separating themselves from yours. We no longer have to sit back and let you do what you want. We're going to stop you, Caralie. Your fight is now against us."

Her smile vanished.

His nostrils flared once more. "Good luck."

GAVIN HELPED Emily to a bedroom close to ours. She snored when he picked her up and she was still snoring as Roane and I lay in bed. It was a few hours later and the sound kept me awake. When I rolled over, I saw that Roane was too. His eyes were open and he stared back at me with an arm on my hip.

We hadn't talked much when we got to the room. Both of us had showered and then crawled under the sheets. I had rolled to my side as he spooned me from behind. His arm hadn't moved the whole time.

"Why can't we sleep?" I asked now.

A ghost of a smile filtered over his face. "Because of the adrenaline."

"I bet no one can sleep."

"I wanted to be alone with you."

My heart skipped a beat. No matter how many times he said it, I knew I'd always love hearing statements like that from him. "You don't want to make love?"

"I wanted to hold you tonight."

I rolled over so I was facing him. His arm slipped behind me and he pulled me tighter against him. One of my legs slipped between his and my hand found his to hold. Our fingers interlaced and I closed my eyes. I wanted to savor the feeling of holding his hand.

But I knew it wouldn't last and I asked, "You're leaving tonight, aren't you?"

His arm tightened around me for a moment. I heard the regret in his voice. "I have to go. The Roane Family could've doubled back."

I bit back tears, but I couldn't fight the wave of sadness that washed over me. He was always leaving. "When?"

"In a few minutes." He hesitated a moment. "Bastion's been

waiting for me. Once I return and learn how things are, I will come back or I'll send for you."

"I can't go back to a normal life, Roane." My eyes searched his. He must know this. "I can't be the college student anymore. Too many people know about me. Pippa, the wolves." Who else?

He nodded and pressed a tender kiss to my forehead. "I know. Trust me, I know."

"I'm coming back. I'm going to be at your side. We're stronger together than we are apart."

He held my gaze for a moment, a long moment. The minute stretched into another and then a third. My heart pounded the whole time and I held my breath. Was he going to accept my plea? He couldn't protect me any longer. I had to start fighting on my own. It was time for everyone to learn who I was. I felt it in my bones and I felt the thirst within me. I wanted to fight.

"I know, Davy. You don't have to worry, I'm going back to check on everybody. If the Roane Family has returned, I won't risk my best warriors. I'll go alone. Don't worry. If I need you guys, you'll be the first to know. Gavin and the rest have strict instructions to never leave your side. Think of them as your personal entourage."

"Great," I groaned. "Wren is part of my entourage."

"She's not so bad," he teased. "She might act tough, but she's grown a little fond of you. I can tell."

No matter what he said, that vampire was still tough. She might be happy with Tracey among the group, but I knew if or when things went south between them, Wren would blame me. There was nothing logical about my speculation, just a gut feeling.

"Tracey asked if she could speak with you."

I took a breath. She wanted me to tell her about her mother and sister. Did Talia want me to tell her about the child?

"Roane, do you think I should tell her about Talia's daughter?"

There was silence for a moment and then he murmured, "I think Tracey would be indebted to you for the rest of your life if you did."

"So should I tell her?"

"If you were Talia and you had a child, would you want your sister to be told?"

I closed my eyes as a wave of sadness washed over me. "I would want her to be told."

"There's your answer. And Davy?"

"Hmmm?" I looked up.

He kissed me softly and whispered against my lips, "Can we not talk anymore?"

"Why?" But the sudden darkening in his eyes told me and I felt my own desire leap in response.

"I think you know why," he responded, his eyes half closed already. Then he reached for me and it wasn't long before both of us were groaning.

It was an hour later before we could even move from the bed. When I thought of going to the bathroom, my mind screamed in protest. My bladder didn't agree and I tore myself from the bed to dash for the bathroom. When I came back, Roane was sitting on the edge of the bed. The blankets pooled around his waist and the Roane tattoo was prominent on his arm.

I traced it as I sat beside him. "You're not a Roane anymore." It felt weird to say that.

He glanced at me and then lifted one of my legs onto his lap. As he caressed my thigh, he murmured, "I'll always be a Roane. I'm just not on their side with this one."

"You think you will be in the future? Can you go back to them?"

"They're wrong about you. I hope they figure that out, but history is filled with moments when leaders make wrong decisions. They rarely apologize."

I was about to say something about how they should apologize, but someone knocked on the door. Roane was across the room in a flash. He stuck his head out and then he looked back. "Gregory spotted a new army approaching. I have to go."

I stood and dressed as he did the same.

He stopped with his jeans in one hand. "What are you doing?"

"I'm going to walk you out." And then I thought, *'I love you, Lucas.'*

His head snapped up in shock and he was across the room the next instant. His mouth ground against mine and I felt myself being lifted up. My legs wound around his waist and I held on. We couldn't get enough of each other, but then we heard another knock at the door.

He groaned as he pulled back, but whispered against my lips, "I love you too."

Both of us dressed after that and walked down the hallway hand in hand. When we got to a small door, we stepped out and saw a car waiting there. Bastion and Gregory were conversing on the side, but both looked up. They stood at attention, ready for their orders. Roane jerked his head to the side. Bastion got into the vehicle as Gregory ducked his massive head and went into the estate. A moment later Gavin came back outside and waited next to us.

Roane pulled me against his chest for a hug.

After we kissed again, he thought, *'I will be back soon or I'll call for you. Stay with Gavin or Wren. They are to protect you from now on.'*

'Be safe.'

He nodded and kissed me one last time. His lips lingered over mine as I clung to him. Every instinct in my body told me not to let go. Something bad was going to happen. I knew it. I felt it, and so did Roane. His eyes darkened and I knew he had heard my thoughts, but it didn't matter. He needed to go and be the leader. We had another battle to fight.

As he stepped back, Roane shared a look with Gavin. They both nodded and then he was in the vehicle and it pulled away. The night air had a chill that I hadn't felt before. It wrapped around me and I hugged myself as a shiver wracked my body.

Gavin touched the back of my elbow. "We should go in."

I nodded, dazed. Roane had gone. I knew he had to, but it was different when I felt it. He urged me inside and the door shut behind us. It seemed to slam with extra force, but Gavin didn't react. I stumbled.

"He'll be fine."

I looked up. Gavin watched me with concern. He said again, "Roane's the toughest ass I know. If anyone is going to be fine, it's him. He's just gone for now. He'll be back within the week."

That didn't reassure me. It should've, but it didn't. Then we walked into the kitchen and found Gregory in the kitchen. Brown was slumped down at the table. She gave me a sloppy smile. "Heya, Davy. I still can't walk."

"Big man." Gavin slapped a hand on the Viking's back. "What are you making?"

"Pancakes and scrambled eggs." Both of the vampires grimaced in disgust, but Gregory shook his head. "Sarah insists this is appropriate food for humans. This is what she wanted."

Brown laughed. "It's the middle of the night and I feel like we just had a rave party. That food is what we need. Right, Davy?"

My eyes danced in delight. "What else would we want to eat?"

"Blood," Gavin and Gregory spoke at the same time.

I rolled my eyes. "We're not vampires. We're human."

"Speaking of vampires and humans," Brown spoke up. "What's going to happen with school?"

"What do you mean?"

"I was excited to go back to college, but then I was thinking about all the vampires coming to town. There's going to be a huge fight, right? I mean, there was already one with those werewolves in the park. How are the humans not going to know what's going on? Isn't it going to be too big to hide?"

Both vampires became still at her question and that was when I knew the answer. "It won't be hidden."

Gavin turned apologetic eyes to me.

I gulped. "Benshire is going to be destroyed, isn't it?"

No answer again, but that was my answer. A part of my heart fell. I had wanted to think a small part of normalcy wouldn't be wiped away, but that didn't seem to be the case. My life wasn't the only one that would change. Everyone's life was going to change.

Then Kates walked into the room. She moved in a stiff manner and had an odd expression on her face. Her eyes found mine, but she turned away quickly. When her jaw clenched and moved back and forth, I saw that her teeth were grinding against each other. She did that when something was wrong.

I sat up straight. "What is it?"

Gavin's head snapped up. Gregory paused in his cooking and Brown grew quiet.

Kates' eyes darted between all of us and she jerked her head. "What are you talking about? What are you guys doing?"

I narrowed my eyes. Something was wrong, very wrong. I stood up. "What did you do, Kates?"

Suddenly there was an explosion in the air, except there was no fire. Nothing blew up. No one was thrown backwards and no smoke filled the air, but I knew it was an explosion. I felt it and it staggered me. I fell backwards, but no one else did. They looked at me. In slow motion, I saw all of their different expressions. Gavin started to reach for me. Brown's mouth started to open and Gregory's eyes shifted over my shoulder. Kates never moved. She already knew. I turned my head slowly.

Roane walked into the room with a cocky swagger. His mouth was twisted in a smirk and his eyes held an evil glint. His hair was long. It reached below his ears and was tucked back. There was

no fear in his eyes. There was nothing in his eyes. Then everything clicked in my brain.

This wasn't Roane. This was Lucan.

My eyes whirled back to Kates' and she looked away. She bit
her lip and ducked her head down in shame. Then Lucan threw
his arms out wide. "Hello everyone! It's good to see you all."

"What?" Brown looked at Gregory for explanation, but he and
Gavin both couldn't move. They seemed frozen in place. As I
tried, I found that I couldn't move either. Whatever had exploded
in the air worked magic on all of us. Brown started to lift her
hand, but I shot her a pleading look.

'Brown, don't move.'

Her eyes went wide. *'Holy crap, I can hear you!'*

'Don't move.'

'Why? What's going on?'

'That's not Roane. It's his twin brother, his evil twin brother.'

'This is like a soap opera.'

'He used magic. None of us can do anything.'

'I can.'

'I think it's because you're human. So is Kates.'

'Davy, what should I do?'

'Nothing.' This was important for her to understand. *'He can't
know that you have magic.'*

'I don't have much. I think I used it all up.'

I closed my eyes in frustration for a moment. I couldn't tell
her that the box inside her had closed again. *'Brown, this is really
important.'*

'What's going to happen?'

Fear started to creep into her thoughts and I felt it in her
emotions. It began to choke her, but I couldn't think about that.
*'He's going to take me. I don't know what he'll do to Gavin or Gregory,
but I hope he'll let you go.'*

'Davy,' she whimpered. *'I'm getting scared.'*

'*You have to get to Roane. Tell him what happened and that Lucan used magic against us. Tell him that Kates knew about it.*'

Vampires came into the room behind Lucan. They swarmed everywhere, searching for something. A moment later, they returned with Wren and Tracey held captive. Both female vampires struggled against their captors, but it didn't make a difference. When they set foot in the kitchen, they were frozen like the rest of us.

Lucan clipped out, "Is that everyone?"

A vampire snapped to attention before him. "He's not here."

He let out a deep breath. "I don't know if I'm disappointed or relieved." Then he swung his dark gaze towards me. "Where'd your lover go?"

I narrowed my eyes at him and dared him to enter my mind. Whatever magic held my body immobile didn't affect my thoughts. As we stared each other down, I felt the Immortal rally in anger inside of me. She was angry and she wanted to hurt him. Rage filled me and I tasted revenge in my mouth. I didn't know what I could do, but I knew I could do something if he entered my mind.

Lucan came to a decision and jerked his head around. "Fine. They go with us then."

One of the vampires reached for Brown and lifted her in the air. She squealed and he asked, "The human?"

Lucan looked at Kates in question. She spoke in a bored voice, "Leave her. She's nothing."

The vampire dropped Brown and everyone swept out of the estate. All of us were placed in different vehicles. I was put in the backseat with Kates across from me and Lucan beside me. One other vampire sat beside Kates and we started off.

My best friend refused to meet my gaze. I swallowed hard and realized that she'd known the whole time. Had this been her intention since she came back? I had been handed to her lover on a silver platter. Did she choose to wait until Roane was gone? Or until we were all weakened from our battle against the Alpha?

When her eyes finally found mine, I saw sadness in them. I didn't care. I narrowed mine and opened a channel in her mind so she could hear my thoughts. *'You don't know what you've done, but you will. I will kill you myself.'*

Kates didn't look surprised, but she thought back, *'Not everything is how it seems, Davy.'*

'You better hope not.'

It was days later before I realized where we'd been taken, and my heart sank.

Continue in the conclusion, Davina!
www.tijansbooks.com

ALSO BY TIJAN

The Insiders (trilogy)

Sports Romance Standalones:

Enemies

Teardrop Shot

Hate To Love You

The Not-Outcast

Young Adult Standalones:

Ryan's Bed

A Whole New Crowd

Brady Remington Landed Me in Jail

College Standalones:

Antistepbrother

Kian

Contemporary Romances:

Bad Boy Brody

Home Tears

Fighter

Rockstar Romance Standalone:

Sustain

An MC short story:

Kess

More books to come!